Relative Risk

Nancy C. Baker

Relative Risk

Living with

a Family History

of Breast Cancer

FOREWORD BY SUSAN FORD BALES

VIKING

VIKING
Published by the Penguin Group
Viking Penguin, a division of Penguin Books USA Inc.,
375 Hudson Street, New York, New York 10014, U.S.A.
Penguin Books Ltd, 27 Wrights Lane, London W8 5TZ, England
Penguin Books Australia Ltd, Ringwood, Victoria, Australia
Penguin Books Canada Ltd, 2801 John Street,
Markham, Ontario, Canada L3R 1B4
Penguin Books (N.Z.) Ltd, 182–190 Wairau Road,
Auckland 10, New Zealand

Penguin Books Ltd, Registered Offices:
Harmondsworth, Middlesex, England

First published in 1991 by Viking Penguin,
a division of Penguin Books USA Inc.

1 2 3 4 5 6 7 8 9 10

A Note to the Reader
The ideas, procedures, and suggestions contained in this book
are not intended as a substitute for consulting with your physician.
All matters regarding your health require medical supervision.

A portion of this book first appeared in *Good Housekeeping*.

Illustrations for breast self-examination reproduced
by courtesy of the National Cancer Institute.

LIBRARY OF CONGRESS CATALOGING-IN-PUBLICATION DATA
Baker, Nancy C.
Relative risk: living with a family history of breast cancer /
Nancy C. Baker; foreword by Susan Ford Bales.
p. cm.
Includes bibliographical references.
ISBN 0-670-83700-8
1. Breast—Cancer—Risk factors. 2. Breast—Cancer—Popular
works. 3. Adjustment (Psychology). I. Title.
RC280.B8B35 1991
616.99'449—dc20   90-50538

Printed in the United States of America
Set in New Caledonia · Designed by Francesca Belanger

For my mother

Foreword

MY PERSONAL INVOLVEMENT in the battle against breast cancer began in 1974, when my mother, Betty Ford, had a mastectomy shortly after we entered the White House as the First Family. During the time of my mother's surgery and recovery, I experienced firsthand the impact of breast cancer on our family. My mother's courage inspired me to become involved in bringing the facts about breast cancer to all Americans.

For the past five years, I have served as national spokesperson for National Breast Cancer Awareness Month, which is sponsored by a number of leading organizations concerned about the early detection of breast cancer. My position as spokesperson takes me all over the United States, to tell my own story about the effects of breast cancer on both patient and family. As the daughter of a woman who has had breast cancer, I am at increased risk for developing the disease, as are my two young daughters. I feel strongly that sharing my experiences with this disease can help to focus public awareness on the importance of early detection and proper treatment.

When my father became president in 1974, it was the most exciting moment in our family's history. But before we could absorb the pleasure of this triumph, we were struck with our family's greatest tragedy. My father was trying to cope with the monumental day-to-day responsibilities of being president of the United States, but realized that this did not exempt him from his obligations to our family. My father said he cried in the Oval Office the day he learned that my mother had breast cancer, and that it was the "lowest and loneliest moment" of his entire presidency.

My mother's diagnosis of breast cancer was frightening for

our entire family, but especially for me as the only daughter. At seventeen years old, I not only had to face the fact that my mother might have a fatal disease, but was suddenly thrust into the national spotlight, standing in for the First Lady at formal presidential functions and social gatherings.

In the next few terrifying weeks, during my mother's surgery and recovery, I saw how my father's caring made a difference. I also realized how important it was for my mother to have the emotional support, devotion and love of her entire family while she was fighting the battle of her life.

When my mother had breast cancer, she had the courage not only to fight the disease but also to acknowledge publicly what had happened to her. In the days before AIDS, medical problems were not discussed so openly; even a mention of breast cancer in public was considered embarrassing. My mother was the first woman to speak openly about her own experience and to discuss the associated psychological and emotional trauma. She felt strongly that by talking about breast cancer she could educate women and their partners about the disease.

I will never forget how strong and brave my mother was at that time. She is more than my mother: she is truly my friend and I feel that I owe her something in return for her struggles. Today my mother continues to support a host of educational efforts, and her interest and experiences have enhanced my role as national spokesperson.

In more recent times, many others have joined us in the fight against breast cancer. The openness and bravery shown by Nancy Reagan, Ann Jillian, Jill Ireland, Jill Eikenberry, Kate Jackson and many others who are less well known have helped to increase public awareness that this life-threatening condition can happen to any woman. Today American women are better educated about breast cancer than ever before. Most know that early detection is important and that treatment options are available.

But we can't stop now. We need to keep educating the public. We need to convince all women to take charge of their own health. I urge all of you to become partners with women close to you, helping them to learn more about breast cancer, as it is a potential threat for every one of us.

While we should all be concerned about developing breast cancer, it is especially worrisome for those of us with a mother, sister, aunt or grandmother who has had the disease. However, as Nancy C. Baker explains in *Relative Risk*, many factors influence a woman's chance of getting breast cancer; it is *not* always hereditary.

Relative Risk is written for those of us at increased risk of developing breast cancer because of a family history of the disease. The book explains the simple, three-step early detection program and talks about the good health habits that might help to forestall the development of cancer. It also explores in depth the various emotional and psychological issues that frequently develop with breast cancer patients and their loved ones. It offers advice on how to cope, based on interviews with numerous health professionals; with the daughters, sisters and other close family members of women who have had breast cancer; and with breast cancer patients. Above all, this book offers support, encouragement and hope, which can be invaluable to all of us.

—SUSAN FORD BALES,
National Spokesperson,
National Breast Cancer Awareness Month

Acknowledgments

THE CONTRIBUTIONS OF EXPERTS from a variety of fields, including psychology, social work, medicine and genetics, were invaluable to me in researching and writing *Relative Risk*. Among those who generously shared their time, efforts and thoughts with me are Ronnie Kaye, Jimmie Holland, Wendy Schain, Shirley Devol VanLieu, David K. Wellisch, Margaret Stuber, Robin S. Cohen, Sandra Jacoby Klein, Patricia T. Kelly, Ruth Dworsky, Carolyn Russell, Cathy Coleman and Amy Langer.

I would also like to thank Martha Humphreys, Carol Kerner and my sister, Judith Moll, all of whom spent many hours discussing *Relative Risk* with me and helping me conceptualize the book.

The suggestions of my editor, Mindy Werner, helped shape the book in a number of positive ways, as did those of my literary agent, Vicky Bijur, whose efforts on behalf of this project have been exemplary.

The support of California State University, Northridge, which gave me a Meritorious Performance and Professional Promise Award to assist with the costs of researching this book is greatly appreciated.

Countless others have my gratitude as well, although their names do not appear here. They are the many mothers, daughters, sisters, grandmothers, aunts and nieces who told me about their experiences with breast cancer in the family. Many of their stories are included here; all of them helped me understand the powerful impact of this disease on women's lives.

Finally, as always, I am grateful to my husband, Jerry Jacobs, whose sage advice and unwavering support have been crucial to me in writing this book.

Contents

Part I

Calculating the Chances

CHAPTER 1

Mothers, Daughters, Sisters and Breast Cancer

A WEEK BEFORE THANKSGIVING IN 1983, my father called from St. Paul to tell me that my mother's physician had found a "tiny spot" on her routine mammogram. She was scheduled to enter the hospital in a few days for a biopsy "to rule out breast cancer." The results of the biopsy, which Dad felt certain would be negative, would determine whether he and Mother would be journeying the two thousand miles to my Santa Monica home for our long-planned holiday celebration.

My father's casual and confident tone did not reassure me. He'd used the same voice over the previous five years whenever he discussed his own failing health; he'd been battling an incurable bone marrow disease that his doctors had said could kill him without warning. If Mother was planning to travel ninety miles from their St. Paul home to Rochester, Minnesota, to have Mayo Clinic doctors do this biopsy, I knew there was good cause for concern.

When I spoke with her, Mother would say only that she too was certain the biopsy would turn out to be negative. She swore she was not a bit worried; this minor surgery was simply an ordeal to be gotten through before traveling to California for

3

Thanksgiving. As usual, she insisted that my father's precarious health represented far more reason for concern than her own. Since she would see me and my family the following week, she said I definitely should not come to Minnesota.

I knew a little about breast cancer in those days, although it never had struck in my own family. Some months earlier, I'd written an article for *Good Housekeeping* about one of the first mastectomy patients in the country to undergo a new kind of breast reconstruction surgery. The procedure used only this patient's own skin, muscle and fat from her abdominal area to create her new breast; essentially, the surgery combined a "tummy tuck" with breast reconstruction. My research for that article had introduced me to the various treatments available to women with the disease.

In addition, I was completing the manuscript of a book about the influence of physical appearance on women's lives, and in it I was including information about the effects of breast cancer surgery on body image.

I asked my mother whether she'd considered what she would do if the biopsy showed that she did indeed have breast cancer. She said she would do whatever the doctors recommended; she did not feel competent to challenge them.

With my usual penchant for research, I quickly made copies of my breast cancer files—including an article about an Italian study showing that women with early breast cancer did just as well when treated with lumpectomy and radiation as they did with modified radical mastectomy—and mailed them to my mother. My sister, Judy, who lived in Boston, added her own research to the deluge of information being sent to Minnesota. She and I, like our parents, wanted to believe that the spot on that mammogram was nothing important, at worst some sort of cyst or benign tumor that would be removed easily. Still, we like to be prepared for the worst.

On the day of the biopsy, I waited for what seemed hours too long for a reassuring call from Rochester. When my father's voice finally came on the line, he told me the biopsy had been positive. The doctors felt certain they'd removed the entire small tumor and that the cancer had not metastasized. However, without being awakened from the anesthetic, my mother already had undergone a modified radical mastectomy, plus the beginnings of a breast reconstruction procedure.

I was stunned. The first shock was the realization that my mother actually did have cancer; although I'd known intellectually that it was possible, emotionally I had denied the possibility. The second was that her treatment had already been determined—along what seemed to me the most extreme line. Although I was relieved to hear that Mother's prognosis for full recovery was excellent, I wanted to know why the doctors had removed her entire breast. Had they considered doing a less invasive lumpectomy with radiation instead? And what about the kind of reconstruction I'd profiled for *Good Housekeeping*, which would have avoided the use of an artificial implant?

I felt my questions were inappropriate in a situation where decisions had already been made, where the surgery had already been performed, so I didn't press for answers. But I recall a surge of conflicting emotions over the next few days. The primary one was anguish that my mother had cancer. We could no longer kid ourselves that that spot on the mammogram meant nothing. Now my mother as well as my father had a potentially fatal illness; I realized I could lose both of them while I was still in my thirties. But in addition to a sense of pending loss, I felt impotent and guilty that I hadn't been in Rochester when my mother had had her surgery. And I felt frustrated and angry that my sister's and my attempts to participate in her treatment choices had apparently been ignored.

A short time later, another consequence of my mother's breast cancer hit home for me. During my annual physical exam, I told my doctor about her illness. His face took on a worried expression as he told me I would have to have a baseline mammogram immediately. He informed me that current research had indicated an hereditary aspect to breast cancer that had to be taken seriously. I would have to have annual mammograms and do monthly breast self-examinations—something I'd never bothered to do previously—as well. Suddenly this was not just my mother's health problem; it had become my own.

My first breast exam was thorough. It included a mammogram, which uses low-dosage X rays to detect cancer; ultrasound, which uses high-frequency sound waves; and thermography, which measures infrared radiation emitted from the breasts. Luckily, these tests revealed no abnormalities. Since that time, I have learned that my risk of breast cancer, while slightly greater than that of a woman with no close relatives who've had the disease, is still not terribly high. And I've learned that other factors besides heredity may have a greater influence on my chances of contracting the disease. At least eighty percent of breast cancer patients have no close relatives who've ever had breast cancer. The truth is that doctors still do not know what causes it.

So while I felt somewhat reassured as I saw my mother recovering from her surgery and as I got the results of my own exams, there's no doubt that a new concern had entered my life. Whatever the prognosis, the truth was that my mother had had breast cancer; although the doctors felt they'd removed it all, I now knew it could recur. In addition, as the daughter of a woman with breast cancer, I would have to be more diligent about my own breast care for the rest of my life; I was at higher risk.

I found myself reading and clipping articles about breast cancer, particularly about its hereditary aspects, and sharing them with my sister. I tried to remember to do breast self-exams every month, but frequently felt frustrated because my breasts tend to feel lumpy all the time. If I heard about a celebrity with breast cancer, or if a friend's mother or sister got the disease, I felt a kinship. This had happened in my family, too. It could happen to me.

An Increasingly Common Crisis

In late 1988, I attended an American Cancer Society (ACS) seminar for mothers, daughters and sisters affected by breast cancer—apparently the first gathering of its type anywhere in the country. Held at the Four Seasons Hotel in Los Angeles, the event drew an overflow audience. An ACS representative told me that within a few hours after a brief notice announcing the seminar had appeared in the *Los Angeles Times,* the society had received five hundred calls from women wanting to attend. The calls continued for days after the attendance list was filled. "I had women begging me to let them come, saying, 'This is my story. Nobody's ever let me talk about it before,'" the representative told me.

Clearly there were thousands of women in the area who were worried about the breast cancer that had invaded their families. Sadly, many of them felt they were alone in their concern, that they had no one to talk to about their feelings.

Since that day, several similar meetings have been held in other West Coast locations, and there are promising signs that the idea is beginning to spread eastward. Mothers, daughters and sisters everywhere have been affected by breast cancer; the need for this kind of information and support knows no regional boundaries.

It's understandable that women are worried about themselves and their relatives being hit by breast cancer. Despite ongoing medical research in this area, the disease is increasingly common in our society. A decade ago, one in every thirteen women could expect to get it in her lifetime; now it's one in every ten. In addition, the mortality rate among women over fifty, the group most likely to get breast cancer, has been growing steadily since 1973.

Breast cancer strikes a hundred and fifty thousand American women each year. Some forty-four thousand of them die. Every year, that's sixteen thousand more deaths than the combined total for the first seven years of the AIDS epidemic, or almost as many American deaths as were claimed in the entire Vietnam War. The frightening fact is that breast cancer kills more women each year than any other affliction except lung cancer and cardiovascular disease.

Women with breast cancer have daughters, sisters, granddaughters, nieces, mothers—all of whom quickly discover they're at increased risk of contracting the disease themselves. A common scenario seems to be that a couple of times each year some new research on breast cancer receives publicity. We're told that caffeine is bad for us, or maybe that glass of wine with dinner, or perhaps the birth control pills we've taken. Then a couple of weeks later, another study is released that contradicts the first.

All of this adds up to increased stress in the lives of not only breast cancer patients but their at-risk female relatives as well. We try to protect ourselves, but sometimes that seems an impossible goal. It's easy to feel helpless and hopeless.

In listening to the women who attended that ACS seminar, I began to realize just how far-reaching the negative effects of this emotional stress can be. I heard stories of women who had made major life decisions—which man to marry, which career to follow, when or whether to have children—based on their virtual certainty that they would someday fall victim to breast cancer. I heard other women tell of suffering from guilt, from sexual problems, from negative body image as a result of their mothers' having had breast cancer. Some became hypochondriacs. Others indulged in the self-deluding notion that it couldn't happen to them; in some way—personality or breast size or health habits—they were different from their mothers, a fact they wanted to believe would protect them from this dreaded scourge.

How distressed a woman was didn't seem to relate to how long ago her kin had been struck by breast cancer, either. Some women spoke of their mothers dying of the disease as far back as forty years earlier; they were still suffering from fear, guilt, anger, a sense of isolation. It was that sense of isolation—the idea each woman seemed to have that her feelings were unique—that this seminar attempted to address. Looking at this roomful of women, I could see that they were *not* alone. The problem was that no one had ever told them their feelings were entirely normal, and were shared by thousands of other mothers, daughters and sisters.

Although we have available to us a glut of often conflicting information and advice about breast cancer, I soon discovered that there was virtually nothing on the emotional and psychological effects of breast cancer in the family. Women who could not attend a seminar such as the one sponsored by the American Cancer Society had nowhere to turn for information, for reassurance, for help. With the exception of a very small number of research studies, it seemed no one had really ever talked to female relatives of women with breast cancer about their lives and their feelings and attempted to pass on that information to the public. I decided to try to fill that gap.

I began talking with women of all ages—mothers, daughters, sisters, grandmothers, granddaughters—whose families had been hit by breast cancer, some only in the previous few months, others as long ago as forty-five years. Some families had had a single occurrence; others had seen breast cancer strike in several generations or in each of several sisters. Some women had been hit by the disease while still in their twenties; others had been well past menopause. I talked with about an equal number of women who'd had breast cancer themselves and women whose relatives had been stricken. Several women fit into both categories: they represented the second or third generation in their families to have the disease. In a handful of cases, I talked with daughters who had been diagnosed with the disease *before* their mothers had.

Despite the variety of women I interviewed, however, I found that certain feelings were virtually universal among them. Breast cancer represents loss: of health; of a portion of the body; possibly of life; sometimes of a beloved relative; of lifelong notions about femininity and female sexuality; certainly of peace of mind. Most of the women I spoke with went through the successive emotional stages mental health experts identify as common to any loss: denial, depression, anger, and finally acceptance. Some never had reached that final stage; they still were stuck in one of the first three and trying to work their way out.

Among the women I interviewed, virtually all of them had been frightened, sometimes terrified, and most had felt alone in their ordeals, as though no one else could possibly understand what they were feeling. Because they had felt so isolated, I found that many of these women had never before verbalized how they felt about breast cancer, what effect it had had on their relationships with their mothers and sisters, and what they thought about their own risk of having the disease. All of these women were willing to share their stories in the hope that they could spare others some of the anguish they had experienced. Their names have been changed to protect their privacy.

I also talked with mental health experts and medical professionals to help me put my conversations with these women into perspective. It is my hope that this book will help other women with breast cancer in their families—women like me—feel less alone as we cope with this increasingly common family health crisis.

The Importance of Breasts

Breast cancer is terrifying to women for more than its potential as a cause of death. Other cancers, heart attacks, strokes, traffic accidents, natural disasters—these all can kill us, too. In fact they can be far more deadly than breast cancer that is detected early. Yet we are seldom as terrified of these other scourges as we are of breast cancer.

The special significance of breast cancer, of course, is that it attacks the most visible symbol of our female gender. Our breasts suckle our young, it's true, and the loss of a breast is traumatic on that basis alone. But we've also been socialized to see our breasts as an essential part of our femininity and our sexuality. So unless we can overcome this cultural conditioning, having breast cancer may mean we feel we've lost our basic femininity and sexuality.

Susan Brownmiller, in her book *Femininity*, writes that breasts "are the most pronounced and variable aspect of the female anatomy, and although their function is fundamentally reproductive, to nourish the young with milk . . . it is their emblematic prominence and intrinsic vulnerability that makes them the chief badge of gender. Breasts command attention, yet they are pliable and soft, offering warmth and succor close to the heart. . . . Breasts may be large or small, droopy or firm, excitable or impassive, and variably sensitive to hormonal change, swelling in pleasure or in discomfort or pain. Breasts are an element of human beauty. Breasts are subject to can-cerous lumps. Breasts are a source of female pride and sexual identification, but they are also a source of competition, con-fusion, insecurity and shame."

It's no news that America is a culture obsessed by sex and by women's breasts as sexual objects. Every day we are inun-dated by advertisements, television programs, motion pictures, magazine photos and articles celebrating the importance of breasts. Whether the current fashion is for large breasts or small, the breasts themselves are never unimportant.

Large bosoms were seen as essential assets to women after World War II and into the fifties, with actresses such as Marilyn Monroe, Jayne Mansfield and Jane Russell setting the norm. During that era, as I was approaching adolescence, I can well remember the importance of that first brassiere. The girls who graduated early from undershirts to training bras (although I could never really figure out why one's breasts needed training) felt very grown up. Unless, of course, they became too well endowed. Then they became the objects of the boys' demeaning leers. The girls who remained flat-chested felt somehow inad-equate as females. But none of us for a minute believed breasts were unimportant.

In the sixties and seventies, flatter chests became the style; thin women who could go braless without jiggling represented the norm to achieve. The media hyped near-anorexic figures such as Twiggy's as "feminine" and "girlish." We tried to diet ourselves into skeletal shapes—but skeletal shapes that still had breasts.

The eighties saw a return to the full-breasted look, with models who had cleavage, such as Cheryl Tiegs and Christie Brinkley, achieving superstardom. Toward the end of the decade, *Life* magazine used the hundredth anniversary of the brassiere as an excuse to run a cover story featuring pages of photos of women's semi-clad bosoms. *Self* magazine ran an article titled "Breast Obsessed" and *Vogue* told its readers that breasts were important as a "gift to men" to make up for the women's movement.

Because our culture places such a heavy emphasis on breasts, a woman who loses one or both of hers to cancer can easily feel she has become "less of a woman." In fact, many of the daughters I interviewed told me that their mothers had used a version of that phrase to describe how they felt about their bodies after breast cancer surgery. Certainly our society does little to reassure them that their femininity and their sexuality originate in their minds, not in their breasts.

I Am My Mother and My Mother Is Me

When a daughter, particularly a young one, sees her mother go through a crisis of any kind, she commonly sees it as her own, if not intellectually, at least emotionally. When we are infants, we believe our mothers are extensions of ourselves. After all, we begin life as part of Mother's body, and that symbiotic relationship is difficult to break.

Gradually we learn to separate from her and become individuals, but female babies never break away from the mother as completely as male babies do. To become masculine, to demonstrate appropriate male behavior, young boys must learn to identify with the father. As females, we continue to identify with Mother, who models appropriate feminine roles. So the line between her and us can easily remain far more blurred than the line between her and our brothers.

To the infant, breasts represent nothing less than actual survival. Babies normally become attached to Mother's breasts. Wendy Schain, Ed.D., a psychologist practicing in Bethesda, Maryland, Washington, D.C., and Long Beach, California, points out that "the breast is the [infant's] first contact with the world. It is the initial establishing component of the relationship between mother and child, either through breast feeding or cuddling against the breast during bottle feeding."

Breasts are our primary symbol of motherhood, of nurturing. Sprouting breasts of our own as we mature becomes a mark of our achieving womanhood, of our becoming even more like Mother. Buying that first brassiere is seen as a rite of passage from girlhood into womanhood. As Dr. Schain points out, our mothers usually went with us to get the first bra. Mother teaches us how to buy the bra, how to wear it, and by example, how to be a woman. To be like her is to become a woman.

We and our mothers are alike physically and behaviorally; sometimes we feel as though we are one person. So what happens when Mother's breast, the symbol of her femininity, her sexuality—indeed, of nurturing and motherhood itself—is attacked? We identify with her and her loss, sometimes completely.

Daughters whose mothers have lost a breast or who have died of breast cancer frequently see themselves as destined for the same fate, says David K. Wellisch, Ph.D., chief psychologist of the adult division of the Neuropsychiatric Institute at the University of California, Los Angeles. In his practice with cancer patients and their families, he sees some daughters who insist that *when* they get breast cancer (not *if* they get it), they will have the same treatment their mothers had, even though that kind of surgery may no longer be practiced. Whatever Mother had, he says, such daughters feel they also must have. They are unable to see themselves as completely separate people with different bodies and different lives.

Although Dr. Wellisch's examples represent an extreme, every daughter feels some level of identification with her mother, no matter how young or how old the daughter is when cancer strikes.

Sisters and Breast Cancer

We are also likely to identify strongly with a sister struck by breast cancer. A sister is someone with whom we've grown up, one with whom we may have shared a bedroom, our clothes and the secrets of emerging womanhood. Even if sibling rivalry was the main theme of our relationship as children, we are seldom unaffected by a sister's life.

It's also true that our sisters' genes are even more like our own than our mothers' genes are. We receive only half of our genetic makeup from our mother; the other half comes from our father. Because she shares the same parents, *all* of a sister's genes are similar to our own. So if there is indeed a strong genetic link to some kinds of breast cancer and the disease strikes a sister, we may feel certain that we're next.

A sister's breast cancer may also cause her to lean on us for help in a variety of ways. I spoke with women who were called upon to take over a sister's work load, others who cared for their sisters' children, and one who directed her sister's medical care. Even those who lived far from their sisters at the time breast cancer hit suffered for their sisters and for themselves.

The Risk of Breast Cancer

As I researched this book, I asked women to estimate their chances of someday getting breast cancer; I was surprised by the number who felt that this fate was a virtual certainty for them. Medical studies indicate that the increased risk ranges from twice as high for a woman with a sister or a mother with late-in-life unilateral breast cancer to as much as fourteen times as high for some women who have both a mother and a sister with early bilateral breast cancer. Yet even among those whose risk is highest, no woman is certain to get the disease. I spoke, for instance, with one woman who had three sisters with breast cancer; two had died of the disease. Yet she and her three remaining sisters were completely symptom-free, and no women in her family's earlier generations had ever had breast cancer.

One of the goals of this book is to present a *reassuring* picture of risk to as-yet-unaffected daughters and sisters. Statistics can be confusing if we don't know how to interpret them correctly. Most of us think, for instance, that if the average person has a one-in-ten chance of getting breast cancer, then someone like me, whose mother got the disease in one breast at age sixty-one, would have about a two-in-ten chance. If we follow this line of reasoning, the woman mentioned above, who had both a mother and sister with early bilateral breast cancer, would have a fourteen-in-ten chance. That's obviously impossible. Trying to interpret the kind of statistics we read, such as that one-in-ten figure, and applying them to ourselves requires additional information, which will be provided early in this book.

In addition, we should realize that early detection and new treatment techniques mean our world need not end even if we do fall victim to breast cancer. The disease no longer necessarily means death or even significant disfigurement. And it certainly does not dictate a loss of femininity.

In fact, some of the most inspiring stories I heard were those of daughters who did suffer the fate of their mothers, but who used their battle with cancer as an opportunity to change their entire lives for the better. One such woman told me, "Having breast cancer is the best thing that ever happened to me," and she meant it. Without it as a catalyst, she felt her life would have remained the series of negative events it had been for the previous forty-five years. Using the disease as an excuse to make changes, she says she's the happiest she's ever been.

The book that emerged from my research does not purport to answer all of a woman's questions about breast cancer and the current medical treatments. There are many excellent books available to teach us about the disease itself, many of which are listed in the appendix. My goal has been to offer information about the experiences mothers, daughters and sisters commonly have when breast cancer strikes in the family.

Relative Risk is divided into three sections. The first explores the question of how great a risk each woman has of someday having breast cancer. It also takes a look at what medical experts think may cause the disease, and at what we can do to ensure that a future cancer will be detected in time to save our lives, and possibly our breasts as well. Finally, this section includes advice from medical experts about how each of us can live a healthier life. After all, a woman who is in otherwise good health has the best chance of surviving an assault by breast cancer.

In the second and most expansive section, I have included, often in their own words, the emotional and psychological experiences of mothers, daughters, and sisters who told me how breast cancer had marked their own and their loved ones' lives. Observations and advice gathered from a number of mental health professionals who are pioneers in counseling women affected by family breast cancer are offered here as well.

Finally, the third section summarizes the kinds of support the women I interviewed said they wanted and needed from their closest female family members. This portion of the book offers ideas for opening channels of communication between generations as well as assistance for mothers, daughters and sisters who may be facing breast cancer for the first time.

The appendix includes a reading list of books and other publications that offer detailed medical information about breast cancer as well as other books that may be helpful. A list of

organizations to which readers can turn for breast cancer information and support services is included there as well.

Little did I foresee at the time of my father's phone call that
it would set me on a journey resulting in this book. But I'm
glad I took it. It offered me an opportunity to learn more about
a dread disease that strikes at every aspect of women's lives;
about the biological and emotional ties between mothers and
daughters as well as those between sisters; and about my own
mother, my sister and myself.

CHAPTER 2

Personal Risks

TWENTY-NINE-YEAR-OLD Kim's mother recently had a mastectomy for breast cancer. No other members of her family have ever had the disease. Yet because of her mother's cancer, Kim estimates her own chance of someday having the disease to be about eighty percent.

Thirty-five-year-old Becky is also the daughter of a woman with breast cancer. One of Becky's three aunts has had the disease as well. Becky believes there is probably a sixty percent chance that she, like her mother and aunt, will someday have breast cancer.

Other daughters and sisters of women with breast cancer have told me that they feel virtually certain they will someday have it. Many say they feel doomed because of their family history. The truth, however, is that these women—along with many other daughters and sisters who have breast cancer in their families—are vastly *over*estimating their own chance of contracting breast cancer.

According to the American Cancer Society, the *average* American woman now has a ten percent chance of having breast cancer during her lifetime. Even this figure is largely misunderstood and thus leads women to feel they're more likely to get breast cancer than they really are. According to medical geneticist Patricia T. Kelly, Ph.D., of Children's Hospital of San Francisco, most such risk figures are "couched in terms that are more applicable to a public health concern than an individual woman's concern." For instance, Dr. Kelly says, "everybody knows that the average woman's risk of breast cancer is ten percent. This is a figure that was developed by epidemiologists who were interested in public health concerns for the most part."

Specifically, the one-in-ten figure means that, under prevailing conditions, a white baby girl born today will have a ten percent chance of having breast cancer sometime during her lifetime—*if* she lives to be a hundred and ten years old. She will have only a two percent chance of getting the disease by the age of sixty and a six percent chance by the age of seventy, Dr. Kelly says. Because most women will not reach the age of a hundred and ten, we can see that the average woman's risk of breast cancer during her lifetime is actually less than that ten percent figure.

Caucasians are slightly more likely to develop breast cancer than are other racial groups, and the descendants of Eastern European Jews are slightly more likely to get the disease than are other Caucasians. Scientists are not certain why, although one probable reason is genetics. In addition, most breast cancer research has been done on groups of white women. Scientists attempt to make their subject pools as alike as possible so as to minimize the factors that could affect the ultimate outcome of their experiments. So if, for instance, they want to study the effect of diet on later breast cancer occurrences by comparing two groups of women with different diets, they will try to have each group as much like the other as possible (in age, number of children the women have, family history of cancer, race, etc.) so that diet will be the *only* variable. If the study group was all white and the comparison group racially mixed, the scientists wouldn't know whether any differences in the results were due to the different diets or to the racial differences between the groups.

Another point about statistics that Dr. Kelly likes to make is that many risk figures are meaningless because they're presented in an incomplete form. For example, saying that a particular woman's risk of getting breast cancer is fifteen percent means nothing unless we have a time frame within which to place that risk. Does this woman have a fifteen percent chance of getting the disease in the next ten years, or by the age of fifty? Or is fifteen percent her risk to age one hundred and ten? If the last possibility is the correct interpretation, the woman likely will feel far less threatened than if we're talking about a more imminent deadline.

Another important factor is that women are living longer today. Many experts say that the increase in the incidence of breast cancer can be attributed largely to this fact. In previous generations, many women died young, either in childbirth or of contagious diseases. Now women are living into their sixties, seventies and eighties—ages at which they are more liable to develop cancers of several kinds, including breast cancer.

While daughters like Kim and Becky tend to inflate their own chances of getting breast cancer because their family members have had it, it's true that both are believed to have a somewhat higher risk than women with no family history of the disease. The question is how much higher. In order to put this risk into context, you must realize that about eighty percent of women diagnosed with breast cancer have *no known family history of the disease.* That leaves about twenty percent who have mothers, sisters or more distant relatives who have been afflicted.

According to the National Cancer Institute, those of us with a family history of breast cancer generally fall into one of two categories. The first is quite rare and includes certain family groups in which susceptibility to cancer appears to be genetically transmitted through either the father's or the mother's side of the family.

According to Dr. Susan Love, M.D., director of the Breast Center at Faulkner Hospital in Boston, this accounts for about five percent of all breast cancers. "There's a dominant gene and practically every woman in every generation gets it. . . . Usually the women who get this kind of breast cancer get it at a young age, and often it's in both breasts," she says. "So one way to get a clue that you might have a genetic kind is if your mother and sister both had breast cancer pre-menopausally and in both breasts."

Scientists have discovered a way to trace the gene that is believed to carry susceptibility to breast cancer in these cancer-prone families. A blood test can be given to women in these families to discover whether they carry the specified gene. The NCI reports that the gene that confers susceptibility has not itself been isolated. However, it can be tracked in some of these families because it travels in tandem with another gene, one that codes for the enzyme glutamate-pyruvate transaminase (GPT). The blood test is designed to tell whether women carry the GPT gene and its companion, the susceptibility gene. If they do, it is estimated that they have a fifty percent chance of developing breast cancer by the time they reach fifty and an eighty-seven percent chance by the age of eighty. In contrast, female family members who do not have the gene have no increased risk of breast cancer. This test is useful only for these rare families, however; it has *no* application to the general population.

The far larger group of us who have breast cancer in our families may have inherited not a dominant gene but more "a tendency," says Dr. Love. "It may be that what's inherited, rather than a gene, is a tendency to get your first period very early, which makes you higher risk. Or maybe it's the tendency to late menopause. Or maybe for cultural reasons everyone in the family has a late first pregnancy, or everybody eats a high-fat diet. So there are a lot of factors mixed in, both cultural and genetic, which may make breast cancer more common in your family. . . . In that situation, it's harder to predict what your risk is." But Dr. Love says that it would not be much greater than that of the general population.

Scientific research is continuing worldwide in an attempt to isolate whatever genes might give us a tendency or predisposition to breast cancer.

Ruth Dworsky, R.N., M.P.H., director of the High Risk Cancer Clinic at USC/Norris Cancer Center in Los Angeles, points out that we need to learn more about how environmental factors influence whatever genetic makeup we have. For instance, Dworsky says, "maybe radiation activates some genes or turns off some other genes. Each individual is unique. Their whole genetic makeup is unique as well as their environmental input. When you consider how complex that is to learn . . . Do we really know what 'normal' is, when you think about it? But we are proceeding along that line very rapidly." Researchers seem to be closing in on the gene or genes that may predispose us to breast and other cancers.

Dworsky does not expect that a blood test as simple as the one to identify the gene that carries the hereditary disease Huntington's chorea will ever be developed to predict breast cancer. Along with a blood test that might reveal a genetic tendency toward cancer, she expects that we will still have to consider such factors as each woman's family history of breast cancer, her own history of breast disease, any exposure she may have had to radiation, the medications she has taken, and her hormonal levels.

Doctors and scientists have been working for years to identify the factors that predispose women to breast cancer. The final determination about what factor or combination of factors "cause" breast cancer has not yet been made, nor has the perfect formula to weight the known and the suspected risk factors been devised. We don't know yet, for instance, why, among five sisters, two may develop the disease while three others do not. Nor do we know why eight of ten women diagnosed with breast cancer have no family members who have had it, while in other families women in every generation seem to be hit.

We don't yet have positive proof of the roots of breast cancer and we can't yet predict with certainty which of us will someday have the disease. However, being aware of the factors the experts believe are or could possibly be involved in breast cancer may help motivate us to take certain precautions with our health. And it may help alleviate some of our fears by putting our personal risk into a more appropriate perspective.

Major Risk Factors

FAMILY HISTORY

As noted above, most researchers believe that a family history of breast cancer definitely puts female family members at increased risk. In certain cancer-prone families, it can be an extremely significant factor, while in more typical families, female members may be only slightly more susceptible to breast cancer than are women with no family history.

Medical geneticist Dr. Patricia Kelly collects data from her clients on all kinds of cancer in their families when she prepares breast cancer risk analyses for them. If members of our family have had other kinds of cancer, these cases, as well as those of breast cancer, may put us at higher personal risk. "There are patterns," Dr. Kelly says. "There are groups of cancers that seem to travel around together."

These include the female cancers. For instance, one woman told me that her grandmother had had uterine cancer, her mother ovarian cancer and her sister breast cancer. This woman may well have a high risk of getting breast cancer herself, even though her family history includes only one case of the disease.

How many of our relatives have had cancer and how closely related they are to us is another component of the family history risk factor. Incidences of cancer in first-degree relatives—mothers, daughters and sisters—are the most significant, while cancer in grandmothers, aunts and paternal relatives are less so. In addition, having just one relative with breast cancer generally means we are at lower risk than if two or more family members are affected.

The age at which our relatives developed their cancers and whether they were found in one breast or both can also be important information. There was a time when researchers felt that breast cancer developed after a woman had passed menopause meant that her relatives were not at a much increased risk. However, Dr. Kelly says that whether the breast cancer developed pre- or postmenopausally may not be as important as it was once thought to be. "Refinements of earlier studies are showing that we need to take a woman's older age of diagnosis as seriously as a young age of diagnosis," she says. "It's more important to take into account patterns in the family, whether other cancers are present in the family and other things." Determining whether we belong to one of those rare cancer-prone families is now felt to be more important than the ages at which our relatives got breast cancer.

Of course family members have more in common than their genes. We tend to share multiple environmental factors as well. So it's possible that some clusters of cancer in families may not have a genetic base at all. They may be the result of a yet-to-be-discovered aspect of the environment. Or they may be a result of a genetic predisposition in combination with environmental factors.

AGE
All women, whether they have a family history of breast cancer or not, are at increasing risk of getting the disease as they grow older. For example, nearly eight times as many women develop breast cancer in their seventies as in their thirties. The National Cancer Institute identifies breast cancer as "primarily a disease of aging."

PERSONAL HISTORY OF BREAST DISEASE
Having had breast cancer puts a woman at higher risk for getting it again. A woman who has already had breast cancer in one

breast has a five times greater risk of developing it in her other breast than a woman in the general population has of developing a first breast cancer.

According to the NCI, having noninvasive breast diseases, either lobular carcinoma in situ or noninvasive ductal carcinoma, also raises a woman's risk of developing invasive breast cancer. San Francisco registered nurse Kerry A. McGinn, author of *Keeping Abreast: breast changes that are not cancer,* says these conditions are defined as breast tissue changes "in which very atypical cells are localized; that is, they may press against adjoining breast tissue but they have not penetrated (invaded) it nor spread beyond the breast."

Other kinds of breast disease also carry a somewhat increased risk of later breast cancer, the NCI reports, but this does *not* include the frequently diagnosed "fibrocystic disease," which carries with it no increased risk of breast cancer. For years women have worried that because they are prone to the kind of lumpy breasts often labeled fibrocystic, they are likely to get breast cancer. This is simply not true. Since as long ago as 1984, the NCI has attempted to reassure these women. Yet many of them still are frightened needlessly by the inaccurate comments of their friends and family on the subject. Even some doctors are guilty of perpetuating the terrifying myth that fibrocystic disease is a precancerous condition.

In fact, Dr. Susan Love points out that autopsies have shown that a full *ninety* percent of women have what might be described as fibrocystic disease. Dr. Love explains that fibrocystic disease "really is a garbage term; it has no precise meaning. It means different things to different people." To clinicians, she says, it may mean any noncancerous breast complaint, including lumps, pain, swelling and tenderness. Pathologists may define it as any of "about twenty different entities which are found in anyone's breast." And radiologists reading a mammogram may see it as "dense breast tissue, which has nothing to do with the pathological entities or the clinical symptoms."

The NCI reports that one study has found that decreasing

caffeine intake may reduce the symptoms of pain and lumpiness often called fibrocystic disease; another study indicates that taking vitamin E could help reduce these symptoms. However, until further research is done to confirm these observations, the NCI urges women to follow their own doctors' advice.

AGE AT ONSET OF MENSTRUATION
The younger we were when we had our first menstrual period, the greater our chance of someday developing breast cancer. The NCI reports that women who were fourteen or older when they had their first period have a twenty percent less chance of someday getting breast cancer than women who were younger than twelve do.

AGE AT MENOPAUSE
The later a woman experiences menopause, the greater her chance of developing breast cancer. According to the NCI, women who reach menopause when they are more than fifty-five years old are twice as likely to develop breast cancer as women who are less than fifty at menopause.

The combination of early menstruation and late menopause as risk factors, according to the NCI, "might suggest that the duration of reproductive life is a significant factor; on the other hand, the combination might underscore the importance of a factor common to these two periods. One such factor is irregular ovulation or menstrual cycles in which ovulation does not occur."

AGE AT FIRST CHILDBIRTH
Having given birth to a child before the age of eighteen is known to lower the risk of a woman's later developing breast cancer. According to the NCI, such a woman's later risk of breast cancer is only one-fourth as great as that of a woman who gives birth when she is nearing thirty. In addition, the woman who waits until she is over thirty to have her first baby is at slightly greater

risk of someday getting breast cancer than if she'd never given birth at all.

Although it was once thought that breast-feeding a baby was a protection against breast cancer, this is no longer believed to provide any advantage.

RADIATION EXPOSURE

Women who have been exposed to excessive radiation from a variety of sources are known to be at increased risk of developing breast cancer. For example, a recent study by Dr. Nancy G. Hildreth of the University of Rochester School of Medicine and Dentistry found that exposure to medical X rays during infancy places women at a significantly higher risk of developing breast cancer in their thirties. Dr. Hildreth's study was based on a long-term follow-up of women treated with X-ray therapy shortly after birth for enlarged thymus glands. These women were found to be four times more likely to develop breast cancer by the age of thirty-six than were their sisters who did not receive the X-ray treatment.

Similarly, Japanese women exposed to radiation from the atomic bombs dropped on Hiroshima and Nagasaki were also found to have an increased rate of breast cancer. This was particularly true of women who had been children or teenagers at the time of the bombings.

The low doses of radiation used in modern mammography developed to diagnose breast cancer have *not* been found to be dangerous. In fact, a 1989 Canadian study of thirty-one thousand women found that the benefits of mammography for detecting breast cancer far outweighed any risks posed by radiation from these exams.

Possible Risk Factors

While there is consensus among experts that the risk factors detailed above are genuine and verifiable, a number of others remain controversial. As of mid-1990, studies of these factors remained contradictory or inconclusive. However, pending more definitive findings, we may wish to consider the following factors.

BODY SIZE AND SHAPE

A number of studies have shown that women past menopause who are obese (defined by the American Cancer Society as more than forty percent overweight) have an increased risk of breast cancer. On the other hand, the National Cancer Institute says that premenopausal breast cancer seems to be more common among thin women.

An interesting study published in 1990 correlates body shape with an increased risk of breast cancer. Although the study requires confirmation by other researchers, its preliminary results seem to indicate that how much fat women accumulate on their bodies may be less important than where they gain it. The study's principal investigator, Dr. David V. Schapira, associate professor of medicine at the University of South Florida, reported that "apple-shaped women" are at higher risk of getting breast cancer than "pear-shaped women" are. Apple-shaped women are defined as those who tend to gain weight in the abdomen, while pear-shaped women are those who gain pounds in their thighs and buttocks.

Dr. Schapira and his colleagues compared breast cancer patients with a control group, classifying their body shapes by computing their waist-to-hip ratios. To compute these ratios, the researchers divided a woman's waist measurement by her hip measurement. A waist-to-hip ratio of .77 to .80 was considered to be mildly apple-shaped. A ratio higher than .80 was classified as very apple-shaped. Ratios from .73 to .76 were called mildly pear-shaped, while those below .73 were considered very pear-shaped.

The researchers suspect that hormones may be responsible for any increased breast cancer risk in apple-shaped women. Apple-shaped women have higher levels of circulating estrogens, according to Dr. Schapira. For as-yet-unknown reasons, he says, higher estrogen levels appear to increase the risk of breast cancer. In addition, abdominal fat cells are known to be larger and more metabolically active than fat cells in the thighs and buttocks, he said.

DIET

Although many researchers believe that there is a connection between a diet high in animal and other fats and breast cancer, the research necessary to prove this definitively has not yet been done. It may be years before such research is funded and completed.

In January 1988, the National Cancer Institute canceled the Women's Health Trial, an experiment designed to see whether cutting dietary fat in half would lower the rate of breast cancer in high-risk patients. The study, budgeted at $130 million, was criticized as too expensive. Critics also argued that women might not report their fat intake accurately and that the study's hypothesis was shaky. Advocates of the study charged that sexism was the reason for the cancellation. They pointed out that the government had already funded a $115 million study based on the same hypothesis that attempted to learn whether reducing fat and cholesterol would lower men's risk of heart disease.

What we do know is that there is at least the suggestion of a link between high-fat diets and breast cancer. For instance, when Japanese women moved from Japan to Hawaii and Westernized their diets to include more fat, their rate of breast cancer rose. Additionally, in Japan proper, while the average woman's fat intake rose from only twenty-three grams a day in 1959 to fifty-two grams in 1973, the rate of breast cancer rose thirty percent.

Several small studies have indicated that there is a connection between dietary fat intake and breast cancer as well. For instance, researchers at the Karolinska Hospital in Stockholm, Sweden, studied two hundred and forty breast cancer patients and found that those patients who had eaten a typical Western diet, high in fat and low in fiber, tended to have larger tumors that contained estrogen receptors. The study, published in 1989, also indicated that women with smaller tumors tended to have drunk less alcohol, although alcohol was not a strong enough factor to be considered statistically significant.

Although several earlier studies attempted to link alcohol consumption and breast cancer, Dr. Patricia Kelly points out that there is no proven connection between moderate consumption of alcohol and the later development of the disease. There are, she says, studies that show female alcoholics have an increased incidence of breast cancer, "but we don't know if that's because of the alcohol or because of their poor diets."

There is even less indication that caffeine is guilty of causing breast cancer. Some women who suffer from fibrocystic breasts report gaining a measure of relief from their often painful breast lumps when they cut the caffeine from their diets. However, many physicians believe there isn't even a demonstrable reason for this effect. Moreover, there is no scientific link between fibrocystic breasts and breast cancer.

We may wish to eliminate alcohol and caffeine from our diets for many reasons, but protection against breast cancer has not been proven to be among them.

ARTIFICIAL HORMONES

Natural estrogen is present in all women's bodies. Manufactured by the ovaries during our reproductive years, estrogen levels fluctuate from a low point just before each menstrual period to a high point at the time of ovulation. After a woman goes through menopause, her ovaries no longer manufacture estrogen. At this time of life, the body's only natural source of estrogen is from another hormone, androstene dione, which is manufactured by the adrenal glands. Androstene dione is converted to estrogen by enzymes in other body tissues, particularly fat. Thus overweight women past menopause have more estrogen in their bodies than slimmer women do.

Scientists have long known that estrogen promotes the growth of certain breast cancers. In the 1960s, researchers discovered that they could prevent the growth of breast tumors in female animals by depriving them of estrogen and that they could promote the growth of such tumors by supplying them with estrogen. As a result of this research, an early treatment for breast cancer included removing or destroying the patient's ovaries to reduce her body's supply of estrogen.

Today that treatment is no longer used, but tamoxifen, an estrogen-blocking drug, is now prescribed for many women who have breast cancer as part of their postsurgical treatment. In addition, women who have had breast cancer are advised against taking any kind of artificial estrogen.

We know that either natural estrogen or artificial estrogen supplements can promote growth in an already existing breast tumor. What remains controversial, however, is whether estrogen can cause the actual birth of such a tumor.

When we examine the known risk factors for breast cancer, two of them—early onset of menstruation and late menopause—appear to confirm that estrogen could indeed play a role in causing cancer. Both early menstruation and late menopause are related to a woman's having a longer-than-average reproductive life cycle. The longer her reproductive life cycle—the time during which her body has high levels of natural estrogen—the higher her risk of developing breast cancer. A third element, obesity, ties in as well. An increased risk of breast cancer in obese postmenopausal women has been found. Obese women have higher levels of estrogen because of the role of body fat in manufacturing estrogen after menopause.

Additionally, it's important to note that most breast cancers discovered in premenopausal women are faster-growing than those found in women past menopause. The natural estrogen present in younger women's bodies is thought to promote the growth of their tumors, while the much lower level of natural estrogen present in older women causes their cancers to grow more slowly.

Several studies have attempted to confirm or refute a connection between artificial estrogen supplements and breast cancer. Unfortunately, they often contradict one another, leaving physicians and women undecided about whether the benefits of taking estrogen supplements outweigh the risks.

Many women and their doctors testify that artificial estrogen can have beneficial effects. It is a component in birth control pills, which remain the most effective temporary means of preventing pregnancy (other than abstinence from sexual intercourse). Estrogen is also the major ingredient in medications prescribed for uncomfortable or health-threatening side effects of menopause, which may range from hot flashes to osteoporosis and diseases of the cardiovascular system.

If artificial estrogen should someday be proven to promote breast cancer, however, many women, particularly those of us who already are at increased risk of getting the disease because of our family history or other factors, may well regret having taken it. The risks of breast cancer may, at least for some of us, outweigh the benefits of these supplements.

The jury is still out, but periodic research studies have kept the controversy about estrogen supplements lively. Three studies released in 1988, for instance, suggested that birth control pills could increase a woman's risk of breast cancer. Publicity surrounding these studies caused great concern among many women, but most physicians called for further research to confirm or refute these findings.

However, a 1989 study published in *Obstetrics and Gynecology,* the official publication of the American College of Obstetrics and Gynecology, came to the opposite conclusion. This project attempted to determine whether women who have a family history of breast cancer are more likely to develop the disease if they take birth control pills. The researchers compared a group of women with breast cancer who also had a first-degree relative with breast cancer to a control group of cancer-free women with a similar family history. The results showed that taking birth control pills had no effect on the development of breast cancer. Neither the length of time that a woman took the pills nor the length of time she took them before becoming pregnant had any demonstrable effect on her developing breast cancer.

Somewhat greater concern surrounds the estrogen replacement therapy for the side effects of menopause, which some experts estimate is prescribed for one-third to one-half of menopausal women in the United States. Women past menopause are already more likely to develop breast cancer than are women taking birth control pills, merely because of their increased age. Some recent studies indicate that the taking of estrogen supplements may further increase menopausal women's risk of breast cancer.

One highly publicized study that caused concern in both women and their physicians was released in mid-1989. A joint effort of Swedish and American researchers, the project followed some twenty-three thousand Swedish women who were taking various forms of estrogen therapy. Their rates of breast cancer were compared with those of a control group of women from the same geographic region who did not take estrogen supplements. Estradiol, a type of potent estrogen used in this study, was found to be associated with a doubled risk of breast cancer. Estradiol is not widely prescribed in the United States, however, which led many critics to discount the study's importance for American women.

Yet this study also found that women who took a combination of estrogen and progestin (an artificial form of the female hormone progesterone) for more than six years were 4.4 times more likely to develop breast cancer than were women not taking hormone supplements. American doctors have been prescribing estrogen in combination with progestin for many years because the use of estrogen alone has been found to be related to an increase in uterine cancers. This Swedish-American study also showed a correlation between how long a woman had taken estrogen therapy and her risk of breast cancer. Some American women are placed on these supplements permanently when they reach menopause, a practice that someday may be reevaluated.

Because long-term hormone therapy may carry with it a significantly higher risk of breast cancer than short-term therapy, many more years of research may be necessary before a final consensus is reached in the medical community. The National Cancer Institute and other organizations continue to study the subject. In the meantime, women and their doctors are left to weigh the benefits and risks of artificial hormone supplements for themselves.

STRESS

Even though there is no hard evidence that stress causes breast cancer, a growing number of researchers believe that stress can reduce the effectiveness of the body's immune system and make people more susceptible to various kinds of disease. For women already at increased risk for breast cancer because of their family history or other factors, stress may someday be found to be a factor in their contracting the disease.

Many experts in psychology express a personal belief that stress plays a role in determining which women get breast cancer. They cite anecdotal evidence of women whose breast cancer was discovered soon after some psychologically stressful event in their lives, such as divorce, the death of a spouse or their children leaving home. Or they talk about the great number of women with breast cancer who have been lifelong caretakers, always putting the needs of others before their own. The theory is that these women suffer so much stress from repressing their own needs that their immune systems are compromised, leaving them vulnerable to breast cancer. Some proponents of this idea believe the fact that cancer strikes in the breast—the symbol of female nurturance—is particularly significant. They feel that disease in the breast can be interpreted as the result of the patient's mind finally refusing to allow her to continue "feeding" other people at her own expense.

However, critics of these theories point out that most women survive catastrophic life events without getting breast cancer, and that the caretaker profile fits a majority of women—and some men—in our society, not just those with breast cancer. Currently, according to Jimmie Holland, M.D., chief of psychiatry at Memorial Sloan-Kettering Cancer Center in New York City, there is no proof that stress causes *any* kind of cancer.

Still, many observers, including New Haven cancer surgeon Bernie Siegel, M.D., who teaches at Yale University, and authors Norman Cousins and Joan Borysenko, believe that further research into the connection between the human mind and the human body may someday provide that proof.

Individual Risk Analysis

This list of known and possible risk factors for breast cancer helps illustrate how difficult it really is to calculate our own chances of someday getting the disease. Correctly weighing each factor in juxtaposition with all other factors requires specialized training.

Many of us would feel relieved if some simple formula was available that would easily assess our risk, or if there was a blood test that would tell us once and for all whether we carry the "bad genes" that predispose us to the disease. If our risk turned out to be less than we feared, we would be able to rest easier, to feel reassured. On the other hand, if our fears were confirmed, we might opt for more frequent mammograms and exams or even for a preventive mastectomy. Additionally, knowing a specific risk factor might help decide such questions as whether to take hormone supplements. For most of us, knowing the facts is better than not knowing. Someday a formula or blood test undoubtedly will be available. Until then, estimating our vulnerability is difficult if not impossible for laypeople.

Dr. Patricia Kelly says that a woman should not attempt to assess her own risk any more than she should attempt to diagnose her own strep throat. We are too close to the situation to be able to be objective, she says. In addition, the process is just too complicated. For those of us who want to know, however, professional risk analysis services are quickly becoming available at medical centers throughout the United States. One such service is run by Dr. Kelly at Children's Hospital of San Francisco. Others are available at Long Beach Memorial Medical Center and the Susan G. Komen Breast Centers in Dallas (see Appendix).

One recent study by researchers at the National Cancer Institute resulted in a formula designed to help medical professionals predict a woman's chances of developing breast cancer in the succeeding ten to thirty years. Published in late 1989, the study followed a group of white women who underwent medical breast exams annually. The rather complex formula devised by the NCI researchers uses only a woman's age and four risk factors to predict her chances. The risk factors include the age at which the woman began menstruation, how many of her first-degree relatives have had breast cancer, her age at the birth of her first live child, and the number of negative breast biopsies she has had.

Using this formula, science editors at the *Los Angeles Times* calculated the chances that two fictional forty-year-old women would contract breast cancer in the next thirty years. The first woman, Abby, has no first-degree relatives who've ever had breast cancer. She began menstruating at age twelve and has had one breast biopsy, which was benign. She has never given birth. The *Times* science editors calculated Abby's chance of getting breast cancer in the next ten years to be 10.1 percent, about average for American women.

Barbara, the second fictional woman, is at higher risk. Like Abby, she has had one breast biopsy that proved benign, but she also has both a mother and a sister who've had breast cancer. In addition, Barbara had her first menstrual period before she was twelve. All of these factors increase her risk of breast cancer. On the plus side, Barbara gave birth to her first child before she was twenty, which helps to lower her chances slightly. The *Times* editors found that Barbara's risk of breast cancer in the next ten years is 39.8 percent, about four times as high as the average woman's.

According to Mitchell H. Gail, head of the epidemiological-methods section at the National Cancer Institute and a co-author of the NCI study, a case like Barbara's is highly unusual; she is a woman who should be under intensive medical observation so that if she does develop a breast tumor, it can be removed immediately.

Although many experts consider the NCI formula to be helpful, it may not include enough risk factors to be completely accurate. For some high-risk women, it may actually underestimate their chances. For instance, a woman without sisters whose mother, aunts and grandmother all had early bilateral breast cancers would be at extremely high risk by any analysis. Using the NCI formula, however, only this woman's mother (the only first-degree relative listed) would be taken into account in calculating her risk. This woman's probability of getting breast cancer might well figure out to be approximately the same as my own. Yet, in my case, my only relative to have the disease is my mother, and she had it postmenopausally in one breast.

Some experts also point out that the NCI formula fails to consider such factors as diet, alcohol consumption and use of artificial hormones, all of which we may someday find to be important. In addition, it is useful only for women who have had annual medical checkups over a significant period of time. Dr. Kelly says of the formula, "It's really a model. I don't think it's anything yet that can be applied in general clinical practice. I think people who have the most questions are going to want information based on more specifics than this can include."

The service Dr. Kelly has provided at Children's Hospital of San Francisco since 1983 is more individualized, taking into consideration more data than the NCI formula. It is typical of the services that are becoming available at a number of cancer centers. Her initial clients, Dr. Kelly says, were only women with family histories of the disease and women who had already had cancer in one breast and who were worried about their chances of getting it in the remaining breast. Soon, however, women with no family history were using the service. Dr. Kelly says they were worried about such things as having lumpy breasts, taking birth control pills, eating the wrong foods and not having given birth by the age of thirty.

If a client has already had breast cancer, Dr. Kelly reviews with her the pathology report on her tumor. "Usually no one sits down with a woman and reviews her pathology report and tells her what it means and what it doesn't mean," she says. "Women are used to hearing, 'Oh, we got it all. Don't worry.' [But] they worry. So I think it's very useful for everyone in the family to learn what the pathology report means, to the best of our knowledge, if they want to hear it."

The Cancer Risk Analysis Service at Children's Hospital of San Francisco features a minimum of three one-hour visits between each client and Dr. Kelly. At the first session, the client fills out a questionnaire designed to elicit how she feels about the threat of breast cancer in her own life. This prevents miscommunication, Dr. Kelly says. Often, for instance, while a client may understand intellectually that "modern-day mammograms can find a breast cancer when it's quite small, her emotional reaction might be that breast cancer equals death." Without determining in advance this client's exaggerated feelings about the disease, Dr. Kelly says, she might well be "talking about breast cancer—I mean a minimal breast cancer with an excellent prognosis—and every time I say breast cancer, she's thinking death. We're not communicating." So a medical geneticist must understand the client's beliefs and fears about the disease before undertaking a risk analysis.

At the first session, Dr. Kelly also takes the client's family history and determines which medical records she wishes to order. Whenever possible, she orders pathology reports on all family members who have had cancer of any kind.

At the second session, more background information is shared and misconceptions about breast cancer are discussed with the client.

Between the second and third visits, all available medical records are collected. Dr. Kelly has managed to retrieve medical

records from as far back as 1939 and from many foreign coun-
tries. Although some doctors and medical facilities discard old
medical records after an arbitrary number of years, many keep
them indefinitely. The Mayo Clinic in Rochester, Minnesota,
for example, has kept the medical records for all of its patients
since its founding in 1889. Medical records are vital for breast
cancer risk analysis because they contain the facts about the
specific cancers the client's relatives have had and about how
advanced these cancers were at the time of diagnosis. Often
the information clients have believed through the years turns
out to be incorrect. Sometimes, for instance, family members
will believe that a grandfather died of stomach cancer when he
really had pancreatic cancer, or that an aunt died of lung cancer
when her disease had actually originated in the breast.

For example, Dr. Kelly tells of a young woman whose grandmother, mother and aunt died of breast cancer very quickly
after being diagnosed. The grandmother's medical records were
unavailable, and when the mother's and aunt's records were
retrieved, Dr. Kelly learned that their cancers were already
three and four centimeters in size at the time of diagnosis. The
client was astounded. She knew that her mother and aunt had
been watching for any signs of breast lumps because of the
grandmother's illness. She had always believed her mother and
aunt had died despite their vigilance, which made her feel quite
hopeless about her own chances of survival should she get the
disease.

However, with the medical records in hand, augmented by
Dr. Kelly's interpretation of them, this young woman began to
have a new outlook. She realized that more advanced technology
now makes it possible for breast cancers to be found when they
are much smaller than three or four centimeters, at a time when
a patient's prognosis is still very bright. This client began to
believe that she was not necessarily doomed to die of breast
cancer as her grandmother, mother and aunt had.

Accurate risk analysis "gives people hope," says Dr. Kelly.
Without it, "some people will say, 'Why should I bother to

examine my breasts? My mother did everything she could and look at what happened to her.' "

By the third session with a client, Dr. Kelly has analyzed the data she has collected and has computed individualized risk figures. At this time, these figures are presented and the client is encouraged to ask for any other information she feels she needs to help her make informed decisions about her own future. "With information," Dr. Kelly says, "people become stronger and can act like adults. Without information or with confusing information, people become like children and expect other people to make decisions for them."

Thirty-year-old Eve agrees with that sentiment. Her older sister had breast cancer at the age of twenty-nine and her mother got it at fifty-five. Worried about her own vulnerability and unsure what to do to protect herself, Eve had Dr. Kelly analyze her personal risk of contracting the disease. She found that the experience allayed much of her fear.

The first two risk analysis sessions were used mainly for information-gathering purposes as well as for answering some of Eve's questions. In addition to her mother's and sisters' health histories, Eve was able to provide at least some information about all her relatives in several previous generations—including their ages at death and their causes of death. Although she was unable to obtain medical records for her maternal great-great-grandmother, Eve learned from family members that she was the one other woman in her family who had had breast cancer. However, Eve says, "her breast was removed and she lived to be ninety years old."

Eve's family seems to have been plagued by various kinds of cancer, a fact that frightened her. In addition to the three women with breast cancer, she says, "my grandma died of pancreatic cancer, my grandmother on my dad's side died of leukemia, my cousin died of Hodgkin's disease, and I had an uncle who died of either pancreatic or prostate cancer. We tended to say, 'Oh, my God, cancer is all over our family!' "

Eve obtained medical records for her maternal grandmother

(the one who died of pancreatic cancer) as well as for her mother and sister. Dr. Kelly found a particularly useful piece of information in the grandmother's records: the fact that she had had a mammogram and breast biopsy shortly before her death. The results were negative. Eve had worried greatly that her grandmother might have had undiagnosed breast cancer as well as pancreatic cancer, but now she knew the reassuring truth.

Eve was presented with a breakdown of her personal risk of getting breast cancer by decades. "Between thirty and thirty-nine, I have a one percent risk of getting breast cancer," she says. "Between forty and forty-nine, it's a seven percent risk; between fifty and fifty-nine, eight percent; and from sixty to seventy-plus, four percent."

In order to find her risk for the remainder of her lifetime, Eve totals all of those percentages, finding that she has a twenty percent remaining lifetime risk, a figure with which she says she can live. In addition, she learned that as she ages, part of that risk is "used up." For instance, when Eve reaches age fifty, her remaining lifetime risk will drop to twelve percent, because the figures for her thirties (one percent) and her forties (seven percent) will no longer be applicable. She will already have lived through those years.

Overall, Eve says she's glad she went through the risk assessment process. "The main point was to take the statistics and explain what they really mean to me," she says. "It was a matter of giving me the facts, but also showing me that the facts aren't as horrible as I was thinking." For her, Eve says, having obtained this information has made "the difference between thinking, 'When I get breast cancer, this is what I'll do,' and 'If I get breast cancer, this is what I'll do.' That's a big difference."

DNA Banking

Most cancers appear to be the result of environmental factors acting upon a person's genes. With breast cancer, as with certain other kinds of cancer, the genetic factor is stronger in some families than in others.

A new method of identifying the genes that can increase our risk of developing some cancers has been developed. Called restriction fragment length polymorphism (RFLP), or gene probe, the method analyzes each individual's genetic material (DNA). While RFLP is now available for certain rare cancers, it has not yet been refined for breast cancer. However, with scientists working on it worldwide, such a test is expected to be available in the near future.

In the meantime, many cancer centers, including Children's Hospital of San Francisco, are banking DNA samples from family members so that their DNA can be used in the future. The test, which uses DNA obtained from small blood samples that are then stored for future use, requires DNA samples from several family members. Researchers expect that by means of the RFLP method and DNA banking, it will soon be possible to determine whether a child or grandchild of a person with cancer is at increased risk of developing the disease because of genetic factors.

According to Children's Hospital of San Francisco, DNA banking is appropriate for families in which at least two members on one side have cancer, some members from at least two generations are available to donate blood for DNA extraction, and at least one family member with cancer is still living. Banking the DNA ensures that it will be available when tests are perfected and the DNA is needed to assess the risks of younger or yet-to-be-born family members, even if those with cancer are no longer living.

Most of us who have mothers, sisters or other relatives with breast cancer will find an accurate assessment of our personal risk to be reassuring. With knowledge, we can make rational decisions. And making our own decisions allows us to regain a sense of control over our own lives. With the truth as a tool, we no longer need be ruled by fear.

CHAPTER 3

Necessary Precautions

SHORT OF SURGICALLY REMOVING all of a woman's breast tissue, we do not yet have a guaranteed way to prevent her getting breast cancer, whether she has a family history of the disease or not. Indeed, some women with strong family histories and an unrelenting fear of breast cancer have opted for preventive mastectomies. Most of us, however, won't choose such a drastic solution. We'll have to take our chances, just as our relatives did.

Yet while we cannot prevent breast cancer, the outlook is far from bleak. Someday an immunization against breast cancer may well be developed. In the meantime, we can feel reassured that it's possible today to cure the disease if it does strike us, often without the mutilating surgery our mothers or sisters may have had. What that requires is the earliest possible detection of cancer cells in the breast. We have the necessary tools. It's our own responsibility to use them.

In addition, there are general good health practices we all can follow so that if we ever do get cancer, we'll be in the best possible physical and emotional condition to fight its spread.

Early Detection

We can use a number of techniques to find breast cancer in its earliest form, and if it's found before it begins to spread, the prognosis for survival is excellent. The National Cancer Institute reports that eighty-five to ninety-five percent of women with early breast cancer will survive at least five years after diagnosis. Most of them will have no recurrence of the disease.

When breast cancers are discovered in the earliest stages, a far less radical surgery will often suffice. Many of the daughters with whom I spoke remembered the extensive surgery their mothers had had many years before. They recalled their mothers suffering heavy scarring and discomfort following surgery. Because the old techniques were so mutilating and caused so much pain, often both mother and daughter were psychologically traumatized. And because breast cancer in the past was often so far advanced before it was discovered, many of these women died in spite of surgery.

Frequently, daughters of breast cancer patients had grown up terrified that the same surgical techniques would be used on them if they someday developed the disease. Luckily, that's highly unlikely. The early surgery for breast cancer, known as either the Halsted radical mastectomy or the radical mastectomy, was indeed quite mutilating. Pioneered in the late nineteenth century by Dr. William S. Halsted of Johns Hopkins University, this procedure involved removing the patient's entire breast, skin surrounding the breast, pectoral (chest) muscles and axillary (armpit) lymph nodes. In Dr. Halsted's day, the prognosis for women with breast cancer was poor. Because good diagnostic tools such as mammography did not exist and few women were taught to examine their own breasts, most patients had large tumors by the time the cancer was diagnosed and they had surgery. The NCI reports that today surgery would probably not even be attempted on a woman whose breast cancer was this far advanced.

The Halsted radical mastectomy left the patient with a sunken chest wall and the possibility of developing both swelling in her arm and stiffness in her shoulder. However, because it was feared that anything less extensive might miss cancer cells that had spread from the tumor site, this procedure became the standard treatment used by most surgeons for well over half a century.

The NCI says that the extended radical mastectomy, an even more extreme surgical procedure intended primarily for tumors located between the nipple and the breastbone, was performed by some surgeons in the 1950s and 1960s. In this procedure, the surgeon would remove the internal mammary lymph nodes, which are located beneath the breastbone, and a section of the rib cage in addition to the tissues removed in the Halsted radical. In a few cases, he or she would take out the lymph nodes above the collarbone as well.

Today we can be thankful that breast cancer surgery is far less extensive and mutilating. We now have detection methods that allow cancers to be found when they are much smaller and far less likely to have spread beyond the tumor site. We also have available such additional treatment measures as radiation therapy, chemotherapy and hormonal therapy to further inhibit the spread of the disease. And, equally important, the late Rose Kushner and other women prodded surgeons into reevaluating their techniques and convinced them that less radical surgeries would offer patients the same chance of survival.

A medical writer, Rose Kushner found a lump in her own breast in 1974. When she began investigating her options, she discovered that the Halsted radical mastectomy remained the treatment of choice. She also learned that most doctors employed a one-step procedure. A woman would be anesthetized before the breast lump was removed for biopsy. If the lump was found to be malignant, the surgery proceeded immediately and the patient woke up to find that her breast had already been removed.

In doing research on the topic, Kushner discovered that there were other options in breast cancer treatment, including less radical surgeries. She fought against the one-step mastectomy procedure as well, arguing that women needed time after a breast cancer had been diagnosed to find the best surgeon to do the procedure. In her own case, she approached eighteen surgeons before she was able to find one who would agree to remove just her breast lump. Today the techniques for which Rose Kushner fought are in common use. Dr. Bruce A. Chabner, director of the division of cancer treatment at the NCI, once said of Kushner, "She is probably the single most important person in leading to this major change in breast surgery. I don't think the public would have accepted it or even known about it if she had not been so persistent in her efforts."

Because of the work of progressive surgeons and women like Kushner, as well as early detection techniques, a woman who has breast cancer today likely will face a much less invasive surgery. Modern surgical techniques include the following:

Modified radical mastectomy. In this procedure, the entire breast is removed, as well as the *pectoralis minor* muscle, but the major chest muscles are left intact. Some or most of the axillary lymph nodes are removed. Women treated in this manner do not exhibit the sunken chest and hollowness beneath the collarbone caused by more extensive surgeries and are also less likely to have arm swelling and shoulder stiffness.

Total mastectomy. As in the modified radical mastectomy, in the total mastectomy the entire breast is removed. However, no chest muscles are taken out and most or all of the lymph nodes are left intact.

Quadrantectomy. In this procedure, the surgeon removes the quarter of the breast that contains the tumor, along with the overlying skin, the sheath covering the major pectoral muscle, the entire minor pectoral muscle and the axillary lymph nodes. Radiation treatment is used as a supplement for this surgery.

Partial mastectomy. Also known as *segmental mastectomy*, in this procedure the surgeon cuts out the tumor plus a two- to three-centimeter wedge of normal tissue surrounding it. In addition, a portion of the overlying skin and the underlying membranes that envelop the breast and chest muscle is removed. Radiation therapy is used in conjunction with this surgery.

Lumpectomy. Also called *local excision* or *tylectomy*, this technique is the least disfiguring. The tumor is removed, along with a small margin of the tissue that surrounds it. The overlying skin and underlying membranes are usually left intact. The axillary lymph nodes may also be left intact. If they are removed, a separate incision in the armpit is made. The patient undergoes radiation therapy after surgery.

In 1988, citing recent studies, the NCI alerted doctors to consider using additional therapy following surgery and radiation for women with early stage breast cancer and no signs of cancer in their lymph nodes. These studies had shown that women were likely to benefit from chemotherapy or hormonal therapy following their primary treatment. Previously, women whose lymph nodes showed no sign of cancer were seldom given any additional therapy, but about thirty percent of them suffered a recurrence of their cancer. The use of additional therapy is designed to prevent those recurrences.

The outlook for women with breast cancer today is far brighter than it was for their mothers and grandmothers, particularly if we use the early detection techniques available to us. The American Cancer Society and the National Cancer Institute recommend that all women, particularly those at higher risk because of a family history of breast cancer, do a monthly breast self-exam, have a regular physical exam by a medical professional and use mammography after the age of forty. Some physicians recommend that women with a family history of breast cancer start having regular mammograms at a younger age.

BREAST SELF-EXAMINATION

Unfortunately, many women feel inept when they try to do a breast self-examination (BSE), complaining that they're not sure they would recognize a breast tumor if they felt one. Because of this, or because they're afraid they might find something wrong, many women told me that they do not do breast self-exams. Others said they don't feel they need to do BSE because they have annual mammograms, which they believe would detect a tumor long before they could feel it with their fingers.

While mammograms often enable doctors to find a tumor before it is large enough to be felt by touch, a full third of the breast cancer patients with whom I spoke found their own malignant lumps through BSE. Many of them had had recent mammograms giving them a clean bill of health. This is not an unusual situation: for unknown reasons, some tumors simply aren't detected through mammography.

Women must learn how to do BSE as soon as they have breasts to examine. Mothers should school their adolescent daughters in the technique so that the daughters become familiar with the normal contours of their own breasts. It's only by knowing what feels normal for each of us that we'll recognize important changes.

It's also vital that we realize about eighty percent of breast lumps are benign. Just because we find a lump or bump does not mean we necessarily have breast cancer; it merely means we should have it checked by a physician.

For women who are unsure of their technique, information about and individual instruction in how to do a breast self-exam is available from the American Cancer Society (see Appendix). The ACS has demonstration models of breasts available so women can practice BSE. I found this kind of model very useful as a training tool. The lump I detected in one felt very much like a tiny round stone about the size and hardness of a shotgun pellet. I found it helpful to see how firmly I had to press my fingers against the breast model in order to feel the "tumor." Running my fingers gently over the model's surface clearly did not provide sufficient pressure. As a result, I've changed the way I do my own BSE, and I feel more confident that I would find a lump if one was there.

BSE should be done monthly. It's probably easiest for menstruating women to do it at the end of each menstrual period. That's the time of the month when breasts are usually the least sore or tender. Being consistent about the time of month also allows us to examine our breasts while they are in roughly the same stage each month, thus ensuring that change can be detected more easily. Women who are past menopause or who are not menstruating for other reasons might choose a particular day of the month—the first, the fifteenth or any other—and consistently perform their BSE on that day.

MAMMOGRAPHY

Mammography is an X-ray technique that allows visualization of the internal structure of the breast. It can detect many non-palpable cancers. In addition, doctors can detect changes in the breast tissue that might signal the early stages of cancer by comparing a current mammogram with an earlier one.

Radiation doses delivered by modern mammograms are so low that they are deemed safe by the ACS, the NCI and other medical organizations. The ACS says that radiation doses delivered in mammography should not exceed one rem; many radiologists say that it's fairly easy to take a mammogram using only about a fifth of that dosage. Overall, the breast cancer risk from each mammogram is extremely low, no more than the risk of lung cancer from smoking half a cigarette.

Although not every malignant breast tumor can be located through mammography, it is a very useful addition to BSE and medical examination. Unfortunately, most American women do not take advantage of it, and as a result, their breast cancers are not detected as early as they might otherwise have been. The National Health Interview Survey done in 1987 showed that only thirty-seven percent of women aged forty and over had ever had a mammogram. And the American Association of

The following technique for BSE is recommended by the National Cancer Institute:

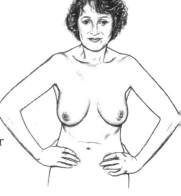

1. Stand before a mirror. Inspect both breasts for anything unusual such as any discharge from the nipples or puckering, dimpling or scaling of the skin.

The next two steps are designed to emphasize any change in the shape or contour of your breasts. As you do them, you should be able to feel your chest muscles tighten.

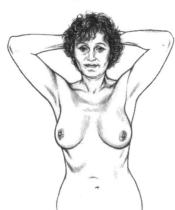

2. Watching closely in the mirror, clasp your hands behind your head and press your hands forward.

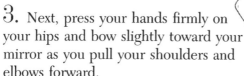

3. Next, press your hands firmly on your hips and bow slightly toward your mirror as you pull your shoulders and elbows forward.

Some women do the next part of the exam in the shower because fingers glide over soapy skin, making it easier to concentrate on the texture underneath.

4. Raise your left arm. Use three or four fingers of your right hand to explore your left breast firmly, carefully and thoroughly. Beginning at the outer edge, press the flat part of your fingers in small circles, moving the circles slowly around the breast. Gradually work toward the nipple. Be sure to cover the entire breast. Pay special attention to the area between the breast and the underarm, including the underarm itself. Feel for any unusual lump or mass under the skin.

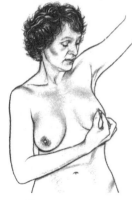

5. Gently squeeze the nipple and look for a discharge. (If you have any discharge during the month—whether or not it is during BSE—see your doctor.) Repeat steps 4 and 5 on your right breast.

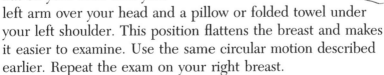

6. Steps 4 and 5 should be repeated lying down. Lie flat on your back with your left arm over your head and a pillow or folded towel under your left shoulder. This position flattens the breast and makes it easier to examine. Use the same circular motion described earlier. Repeat the exam on your right breast.

Retired Persons reports that more than half of American physicians fail to recommend routine mammograms to their female patients. As women with a family history of breast cancer, however, we can't afford to wait for our physicians to recommend such a vital test: if they don't suggest we have mammograms, we must demand them.

Many experts recommend that high-risk women have a baseline mammogram by age thirty-five. A baseline mammogram offers a standard against which future mammograms can be judged, allowing doctors to detect any changes in the breast tissue from year to year. The National Cancer Institute says that age forty is early enough for the average woman to have her first mammogram, but many of the women I interviewed began these tests earlier, sometimes as early as age thirty. This was particularly true if a relative had been diagnosed with breast cancer at a young age or if the person had naturally lumpy breasts. However, because the breast tissue of young women tends to be very dense, mammograms before the age of thirty are unlikely to be useful and are seldom recommended.

After the baseline mammogram, the NCI says that women should have a mammogram every one to two years until they are fifty, and every year thereafter. Daughters and sisters of breast cancer patients are generally advised to have these tests annually. Of course, if any suspicious lump or thickening is detected in the breast, a mammogram is indicated.

The cost of a mammogram ranges from about fifty to two hundred dollars. Twenty-five states now require that private insurance companies pay at least part of the cost for their subscribers, and legislation has been introduced in Congress to have the procedures covered by Medicare.

USC/Norris Cancer Center's Ruth Dworsky says that many women avoid having mammograms at least in part because they do not know what to expect. They often fear the test will be painful or dangerous. "Mammography is the most important tool we have today," she says. "Yet you have these women who

are so scared that they won't go." Her mission is to educate
them so that they lose their fear.

There is no need to be frightened of radiation exposure from
a mammogram that is administered correctly. While the effi-
ciency of mammography facilities around the country can vary,
the American College of Radiology now has developed a cert-
ification program to assure women that they are choosing a
competent and safe one. A list of local certified facilities can be
obtained by calling the federal government's Cancer Information Service at 1-800-4-CANCER.

Having a mammogram is not painful, either. The test is at
worst momentarily uncomfortable. Here's what it's like. The patient, undressed from the waist up and wearing a gown with a
front opening, stands before a large X-ray machine. The technician, who is usually a woman, positions one of the patient's
breasts on a small platform. She then lowers a paddle device
onto the breast, briefly compressing it and holding it steady
while she takes the X ray. These few seconds while the breast is
sandwiched between the platform and the paddle are the only
time when the test may be at all uncomfortable. Most of this discomfort can be avoided if the patient schedules her mammogram at the time in her monthly cycle when her breasts are least
likely to be tender, swollen or sore. As soon as the X ray is taken,
the paddle automatically raises and the breast is released.

The technician then repositions the same breast to take a
second picture from a different angle. Usually two views are
sufficient, but a third may be taken if the patient's breasts are
unusually large, her breast tissue is dense, or the mammogram
is being done to investigate a suspicious lump.

When the mammogram of the first breast is completed, the
technician will repeat these steps for the second. It's that simple.

When we consider the advantages of mammograms, particularly for women like us, who have a somewhat higher risk of
breast cancer, there's really no reason not to be diligent about
having them on the recommended schedule.

MEDICAL EXAMINATION

A breast examination by a physician should be part of a regular medical checkup. Basically, this procedure is similar to a breast self-exam, except that it is done by the physician, who is specially trained in detecting breast abnormalities.

How frequently this kind of exam is performed may vary. Most of us find it convenient to get it done at the time of our annual physical exam or Pap test for cervical cancer. Others may wish to see a doctor more or less frequently. Of course, if you detect any unusual lump during your monthly BSE and it doesn't disappear after your next period, you should see a physician immediately.

During an annual physical exam is a good time to get training in the correct method to examine your breasts if you're not certain you are doing it correctly. Also, immediately after such an exam is an excellent time to begin doing BSE if you haven't yet made it a habit. At the time when the doctor has pronounced your breasts to be free of disease, you can rest assured that any lumps or bumps you yourself feel are likely to be normal breast tissue.

USC/Norris Cancer Center's Ruth Dworsky reports that many women are afraid of doctors or are not comfortable with their own physicians, so they avoid medical exams. She, like many of the other medical professionals with whom I spoke, urged women to become better health care consumers. If we're uneasy with our particular doctor, we simply must find another, one in whom we can feel confidence. Among the services Dworsky provides at the High Risk Cancer Clinic is to help women find doctors who listen to their concerns and who exhibit both medical competence and caring. Many of the women she sees find they feel more comfortable with a female physician.

No matter how they locate a doctor they like, all women, particularly those with a family history of breast cancer, *must* have a regular breast examination by a physician.

General Good Health Practices

According to former U.S. Surgeon General C. Everett Koop, if we spent a third of the effort on preventing health problems that we do on trying to cure or repair them, we'd be far ahead. He estimates that some seventy percent of premature deaths might be postponed if the person took preventive measures, while only fifteen percent can be postponed "by repair" once the damage has been done.

Dr. Koop's comments are not specifically aimed at preventing breast cancer. However, following his guidelines can help give us a healthier, higher quality life if we never suffer from the disease. And if we do get breast cancer, having an otherwise healthy body can help us survive it.

Koop's plan for a healthy life includes the following advice:

- Don't smoke.
- Drink alcohol only in moderation.
- Exercise appropriately for your age.
- Avoid stress.
- Follow an appropriate diet.

In addition to these pointers, those of us at risk for breast cancer may wish to consider carefully whether, for us, the detriments of artificial hormone supplements might outweigh the benefits.

Let's take a closer look at each of these pieces of advice.

DON'T SMOKE

Although there is no evidence that smoking per se causes breast cancer, there is ample proof that it is a primary cause of the number one cancer killer of women, lung cancer. (Breast cancer is the number two cancer killer of women.) Smoking also causes cardiovascular diseases.

If we someday find ourselves fighting breast cancer, having damaged our bodies by smoking will hinder our chances for full recovery. Both the anesthesia necessary for surgery and the chemotherapy frequently prescribed as a follow-up treatment for breast cancer place a great strain upon the heart and lungs. Because smokers have already overburdened theirs, they have reduced their chances of surviving these vital parts of breast cancer treatment.

The lungs are also among the sites to which breast cancers often metastasize. Weakening our lungs under these circumstances simply makes no sense.

DRINK ALCOHOL ONLY IN MODERATION

Studies attempting to find a correlation between moderate alcohol consumption (generally defined as not more than two to three average-sized drinks a day) and breast cancer have been contradictory at best. According to medical geneticist Patricia Kelly, "a significant link between moderate alcohol consumption and breast cancer has not been shown."

Still, we know that drinking more than moderate amounts of alcohol overburdens various organs of the body. Excessive drinking over time can damage the liver. Like the lungs, the liver is a common site for metastasizing breast cancer.

So clearly women at risk for breast cancer should limit their consumption of alcohol to moderate amounts, if any.

EXERCISE APPROPRIATELY FOR YOUR AGE

Exercise offers a number of benefits, including improved cardiovascular health, assistance in controlling body weight, and stress reduction. In addition, early results of a new study done by the Institute for Aerobics Research in Dallas show that exercise may reduce cancer risks as well. The researchers followed groups of both men and women for eight years, categorizing them as low fitness, medium fitness or high fitness. After allowing for various other health-affecting factors, including age, cholesterol levels, smoking behavior, weight, blood pressure and family history of heart disease, the researchers found that women's death rate from all causes was almost twice as high in the least fit category as in the medium fitness group.

Applying these early results to the general population, researchers expected to see sixteen of each ten thousand low-fitness women die of any type of cancer each year, while ten women in the medium-fitness group and only one in the high-fitness group would succumb to the disease annually.

This particular study will undoubtedly be compared with others before exercise is validated as a cancer preventive. However, this good news can help spur those of us with a family history of cancer to be physically active, something we already know we should be.

AVOID STRESS

We don't yet have scientific proof that stress *causes* breast or any other cancer, but many physicians and mental health practitioners believe that stress can overburden the immune system, making us susceptible to various diseases, including breast cancer, and that proof of this connection will eventually emerge.

What we do know is that stress is no fun. It greatly impairs our quality of life. So whether it causes malignant breast tumors or not, stress is to be avoided.

Ironically, those of us who have a family history of breast cancer may feel highly stressed simply because of our family background. Many daughters and sisters of breast cancer patients told me that if stress causes cancer, they are in serious trouble: their lives are filled with stress because of concern about their ill relatives and worries about their own inherited health risks. They want to stop obsessing about breast cancer, but often they just don't know how.

Others told me that they feel they've journeyed beyond that kind of compulsive worrying to a kind of calm acceptance and an enjoyment of their lives. The most common route to this end was their finding a forum in which they could discuss their feelings about breast cancer. For some, that meant talking to family and friends. For others, it required individual psychotherapy. And for an increasing number, being part of a support group of women with similar family histories provided that setting.

Women who want assistance in handling their feelings about breast cancer in the family can contact their local chapter of the American Cancer Society. If no groups are available, they might volunteer to help their ACS chapter form one. Additionally, Los Angeles marriage and family counselor Ronnie L. Kaye, M.F.C.C., suggests that those who can't find a local support group to join might form one of their own and share the cost of a professional therapist to serve as moderator among the members.

There are a number of excellent guides for reducing the stress that we all suffer in modern life. Typically they include such sound advice as maintaining a program of physical exercise; meditating; getting organized and delegating responsibility; and maintaining supportive social relationships. These pointers are useful for everyone, particularly for those of us who must live with the added stress of breast cancer in our families. Once we take steps to deal with the stress in our lives, we'll begin to feel healthier—both emotionally and physically. And maybe someday we'll find that by making this effort we've actually helped ourselves avoid ever having the disease we all so greatly fear.

FOLLOW AN APPROPRIATE DIET

As detailed in the previous chapter, there is no consensus about the specific role of high-fat diets in causing breast cancer. However, we do know that a diet high in fat and low in fiber is not ideal for other reasons. This Western style of eating has repeatedly been linked to both cardiovascular disease and bowel cancers, and it's likely to be a cause of obesity as well.

Obesity is known to be a breast cancer risk factor for women past menopause. Because fatty tissue helps the body produce estrogen as we age and because estrogen spurs the growth of breast cancer, we'll be better off if we maintain a reasonable weight throughout our lives.

Dr. C. Everett Koop's idea of an appropriate diet does not mean we can never eat a steak or put a dollop of sour cream on a baked potato. What it *does* mean is that we can't eat those foods every day. For most Americans, it requires increasing our consumption of fruits, vegetables and whole grains and reducing the amount of animal products and other fats that we consume.

For most of us, following such a sensible, low-fat, high-fiber diet and combining it with a program of moderate exercise will maintain our body weight within normal boundaries. We'll feel better and we'll be helping to avoid breast cancer in our later years at the same time.

WEIGH THE RISKS OF ARTIFICIAL HORMONES

We know that estrogen makes existing breast cancers grow more quickly. So taking estrogen supplements of any kind, whether in birth control pills or for symptoms of aging, is clearly not indicated for women who already have the disease.

What worries many women with a family history of breast cancer, however, is the possibility that they could unknowingly have the beginnings of a tumor. If so, taking any kind of estrogen supplement could accelerate its growth. A second source of concern is the possibility that someday we'll discover proof that estrogen supplements can cause breast cancer in susceptible women.

As detailed in Chapter 2, research on the role of female hormones on breast cancer is continuing, but it may be years before there is consensus in the medical community about whether the benefits of hormone supplements outweigh the risks. In the meantime, it seems prudent for those of us already at higher risk for breast cancer to gather all the information we possibly can before we decide whether to take estrogen pills for any reason.

In this area, as in every other, we need to become better-educated medical consumers. We must learn to take control over and responsibility for our own health care. We, after all, are the ones with the most to lose.

It's possible, of course, that we could follow all of these good health practices religiously and still find ourselves someday facing breast cancer, as our mothers or sisters did. Still, having a personal health regimen can help us feel we have some control over our own fate.

If we *do* get breast cancer, we have the resources to discover it early enough to ensure that medical treatment can save us.

We can make sure we're in otherwise excellent health, which will increase our chances of survival as well.

And if we're lucky enough to avoid getting breast cancer, we will have given ourselves an added bonus of good health.

The truth is, we have nothing to lose by following these guidelines—nothing except a feeling of helplessness and a lot of emotional turmoil. And we may have a great deal to gain. We may well gain a happy, healthy future. We may well stand to gain our very lives.

Part II

The Emotional Effects

CHAPTER 4

Like Mother,
Like Daughter

MARILYN BOARDED AN AIRPLANE and escaped to Ireland. Barbara developed psychosomatic breast pains. Paula became obsessed with superstition. And Jessica became incapable of emotional closeness, even with her husband. Unable to recognize and deal with the fears generated in them when their mothers were struck by breast cancer, these daughters reacted to their family crises in negative and often self-destructive ways.

Fear, of course, is a natural reaction to any life-threatening disease, and breast cancer creates additional anxiety because the breast is an obvious symbol of femininity. It's entirely normal for a woman who learns she has breast cancer to be terrified of mutilation, of surgery, of pain, of possible death. And daughters whose mothers are stricken naturally fear being abandoned and are afraid that their mothers' fate someday, almost by definition, will become their own.

But many daughters do not realize that such feelings are to be expected. They suppress their anxieties in an attempt to deny that the cancer exists or that it is potentially deadly or that it concerns them in any way whatsoever.

Being the First to Leave

Marilyn, who was nineteen when her mother was diagnosed with breast cancer, remembers literally running away from the situation. "When my mom first told me, I didn't want to deal with it. I left for Ireland. I had been planning the trip for a long time and she didn't try to make me feel guilty for going." So Marilyn grasped at the opportunity to avoid the situation and packed her bags. Subconsciously she was abandoning her mother before her mother could abandon her.

It was the day of her mother's mastectomy when Marilyn climbed aboard that Ireland-bound jet, hoping to leave her mother's problems behind. Marilyn simply refused to think about what was happening back in the States, not even telling her traveling companion about the family crisis. If she didn't talk about it, maybe it wasn't really happening.

"I hadn't had any experience with breast cancer," she says, "so I didn't know if people could live through it. I knew it meant getting rid of the breast and I thought, 'Oh God, that's so horrible.'" The idea of breast cancer's striking the mother she loved and depended upon was simply too much for this teenager to handle. So she pretended it hadn't happened by throwing herself into a journey to a place thousands of miles from home.

Marilyn says she felt that if anyone could survive breast cancer, her mother, Lucille, could. Yet one of the reasons she was so terrified was that the mother who'd been such a rock-solid support to her throughout her life wasn't handling her own terrors at all well.

Lucille concurs with Marilyn's recollections. "I had prided myself that I probably would live to an old age," she says, because of the excellent health habits she had always maintained. She was only forty-six and had no family history of breast cancer, so she was not prepared for such a completely unexpected diagnosis.

"At the time, I felt really unstable," Lucille says. "I didn't want to deal with reality." While trying to decide between having a lumpectomy followed by radiation or a modified radical mastectomy, she spent long days lying on her bed weeping. Then, the night before her surgery, she recalls "playing music real loud. I love Neil Diamond and I had his music blaring. I was vacuuming the house and I was crying. I remember the kids being very scared and not wanting to deal with me. I just needed to stay busy," and vacuuming served that purpose. The attendant noise and Lucille's frantic activity also helped her avoid any emotional confrontation with Marilyn, who was busily preparing for her escape to Europe.

Lucille says that she gave Marilyn's exit her blessing and "I probably did mean it, because I knew she was really having a hard time. I thought I'd rather have her be away than standing over my bed crying, not knowing what to say and being miserable."

Even in the depths of her own grief, Lucille was aware of her daughter's emotional turmoil. "My impression was that she was not able to deal with it, that she went into denial and didn't want to talk about it. At the time, I was having a hard time talking about it myself because I cried so much. . . . I was very sad and very vocal about being sad . . . feeling I was going to lose something so valuable that I didn't know if I could survive it."

Why Daughters Depart

While Marilyn's escape to Ireland was perhaps the most obvious physical withdrawal I encountered in my talks with mothers and daughters, it was unique only in the distance she traveled in attempting to deny her fears. Several mothers told me that their daughters refused to come to the hospital to see them before or after the surgery was done. One explained that her fifteen-year-old had just broken up with her first boyfriend and her daughter's obsession with her own problems became a shield against sharing her mother's. Others told me that their daughters had used excuses ranging from work commitments to school exams to avoid being around them during their illness. Understandably, many of these mothers were confused and hurt by their daughters' seemingly callous actions.

Withdrawal from the mother and her breast cancer is particularly common among teenage daughters. This is the time when it's most difficult for a daughter to deal with her mother's needs of any kind; a life-threatening illness such as breast cancer simply makes this period that much harder. Counselor Ronnie Kaye explains that the teen years "are the time of breaking away from the family. [The family home] is supposed to be stable and provide a platform for you to dive off into the world and all of a sudden, [when the mother gets breast cancer,] there's no platform there. The rebel feels pulled, yanked back into the family. So how do you break that pull? You pull much harder, you get outrageous pulling in the other direction."

Kaye, who has survived two episodes of breast cancer and has a daughter of her own, has counseled both breast cancer patients and daughters whose mothers have had breast cancer. She points out that despite their efforts to break free of family bonds, teenagers are secretly very vulnerable to abandonment. "They don't want to be babies anymore. So it's very horrifying for a girl who's getting very sassy and saying, 'I can move out of this environment and I can relate to my peers and I can leave my family behind because they're so old-fashioned,' to suddenly have the covers ripped off and see her own vulnerabilities there." Such a daughter, Kaye says, is likely to feel overcome by "infantile . . . feelings." Underneath the daughter's bravado is "basically a three-year-old child saying, 'Mommy, Mommy, don't leave me.'"

A typical way teens try to cover up those feelings is to avoid the family problem altogether, as Marilyn did, to pretend it doesn't exist, to run as fast as possible in another direction. The problem is that human feelings never stay completely buried; they eventually emerge, often in a self-destructive form.

The Reality of Abandonment

For most daughters today, the fact that their mother has breast cancer does *not* mean they will be abandoned. With early detection and modern treatment methods, women have an excellent chance of surviving breast cancer. It has been five years since Lucille had a mastectomy, she recently completed breast reconstruction surgery, and she believes she and Marilyn are bonded more strongly than ever.

The full impact of her flight to avoid her mother's cancer hit Marilyn one morning as she awoke in an Irish bed and breakfast hotel. Suddenly she felt overwhelmed by a sense of isolation. She couldn't wait to return home, to be there for her mother, to face reality. Today mother and daughter have long since talked through their fears about breast cancer and their feelings about each other, with happy results.

Despite today's improved prognosis for most breast cancer patients, however, the fear a daughter feels that her mother won't survive breast cancer is far from irrational. This disease still kills more than forty thousand American women annually, many of them the mothers of daughters. Yet dwelling on such anxieties does little more than create additional stress in our lives. When we admit we are frightened, talk about how we feel, and become educated about breast cancer, most of us will feel our terrors subside and our emotional equilibrium reestablish itself.

Understandably, the daughters I spoke with who had the most trouble with persistent fears were those whose mothers had not survived breast cancer. Some of the mothers had died as early as a few weeks after the cancer was diagnosed and others had survived for as long as twenty years, battling several recurrences. Because these daughters' fears were so deep and so repressed, they often emerged disguised as totally different anxieties or physical illnesses. Their terrors included fears of intimacy, of childbirth, of having their breasts touched, of dying at the same age their mothers did.

Those of us whose mothers are surviving breast cancer often suffer, at least temporarily, the same kinds of anxieties, although they may be less severe. And unless we face them honestly, they tend to surface in negative physical and emotional ways.

Denial Hurts

Barbara was six when her mother first was struck by breast cancer and seventeen when metastasis of the disease claimed her mother's life. Barbara recalls that as a little girl, she took the situation in stride. "I remember going to the hospital to visit [my mother], but I had no understanding of what she was in there for, no fear. I mainly remember that she would save her pudding for me when I'd come to visit. I don't think I had any bad feelings that I was going to lose her at that age."

Barbara and her mother were extremely close, "best friends," she says, all through Barbara's adolescence and into her teen years. When her mother's cancer recurred and she died, Barbara simply didn't accept it. For eleven years, until she was twenty-eight years old, Barbara says she "kept her alive. When my mother died, I barely shed a tear. I didn't go to the funeral. I kept pretending it didn't happen.

"I had no family members to help me. My father worked nights and my little brother was out with his friends. I was all alone in the world. My only way of thinking I could survive was to pretend it hadn't happened. If I had let myself collapse on the floor and grieve at the time, I think I was afraid there would be nobody to pick me up.

"So for eleven years I would talk about my mother in the present tense. [My husband] thought she was some kind of God. I'd go shopping and see a dress and I'd say, 'Mom looks good in this color.' My husband knew there was something wrong, but he didn't make a big thing about it. Someone with more psychological knowledge would have said, 'You need to get to a doctor.'"

It was when breast cancer struck another family member,

her maternal grandmother, that Barbara's suppressed terror finally began to emerge. "I wasn't [consciously] fearful of breast cancer," she explains, "until my grandmother got it. All of a sudden it was boom! Oh, my God, I'm scared." Barbara's grandmother died shortly after her diagnosis; she'd long avoided medical care, and by the time she sought it, her breast cancer had spread widely throughout her body.

During her grandmother's illness, Barbara says she remembers "screaming and crying at her on the phone, knowing she had breast cancer, screaming like I'd never done before. Something within me was not right. I can't even explain it. I was really horrible to my grandmother."

Barbara soon found herself sitting at her desk at work, weeping uncontrollably. "My boss said, 'Go see a doctor *now*.' He gave me the name of a counselor, and the minute I started to talk to her, I began crying about my mother." Her grandmother's impending death had triggered Barbara's repressed feelings about her mother's illness and death from the same disease. As Barbara describes it, she had "a mini–nervous breakdown" during this time.

"There was a period there for six months to a year," she recalls, "when I would have panics at night. I would wake up and cancer would jump into my mind. I would get pains in my left breast, at the side where my rib cage is. My mother had lost her left breast, but at the time I wasn't conscious of which breast it was."

When her grandmother was near death, Barbara flew east to be with her and found her breast pains severely intensified. "I started having horrible pains and I started taking sleeping pills [to make it through the night]." Barbara consulted with several physicians who told her there was nothing physically wrong with her breast, that the pain was simply a manifestation of her fear of contracting breast cancer as her mother and grandmother had. One doctor even suggested that she have a preventive mastectomy, a procedure where most of the breast tissue is removed and replaced by silicone implants, Barbara says, "because my mother had breast cancer and because my fears were so great. He told me he was going to do one on his own wife because her mother had had breast cancer, too, and she was afraid."

However, Barbara didn't accept that advice. Instead, she continued her therapy and now says with enthusiasm, "The best thing I ever did for myself was to have that nervous breakdown and work through my grief about my mother. As much pain as I suffered . . . I have grown leaps and bounds. I feel like a totally different woman."

Barbara's breast pains recur occasionally. "If I watch cancer programs, I get breast pains," she says, "but I'm trying not to be obsessive about it. My therapist thinks once I work through some more [repressed] issues, the pains will go away."

Anything Could Happen

Like Barbara, Paula now realizes that the fears that took root in her childhood have dominated her life in unfortunate ways. Now in her mid-thirties, Paula has been in psychological counseling off and on for half a dozen years. Her mother's death ten months after breast cancer surgery has had a powerful and long-lasting effect on Paula's life.

When she was seven, her thirty-five-year-old mother had a radical mastectomy. Like Barbara, Paula says that she "didn't know what was going on. All I knew was that my mother was going into the hospital for an operation. I didn't know she had cancer." But the child observed that her mother returned from the hospital lacking one of her breasts.

Tragically, Paula's mother could not cope with what she considered her body's mutilation. "My mother was very pretty and I think she grew up being told this was the most important thing about her. So she didn't have any resources," Paula says. "My mother didn't work, so she really didn't have any distractions and she didn't have any feeling of self-worth other than that she was supposed to be pretty. I heard from my father that she was having a hard time getting older anyway. On her thirtieth birthday, he said she had kind of fallen apart."

The loss of her breast was a blow this vain woman could not survive emotionally. Her self-worth was tied up in her physical appearance, an attitude reinforced by both her husband and her own mother. "My father is a drinker," Paula told me, "and I think that he probably started drinking more heavily" after the cancer diagnosis, so he was no real help during her mother's crisis.

Neither was Paula's grandmother. She remembers the older woman's reaction upon seeing the mastectomy scar: "My grandmother was not very good about it. I heard her say to my mother, 'Oh, you'll never be the same.' Then, on another occasion, she said, 'Can't they do anything about that scar?' " Such thoughtlessly critical remarks rubbed salt in an already depressed woman's psychic wounds.

In the early 1960s, when Paula's mother underwent her surgery, there were few support systems for breast cancer patients. The words "breast cancer" were seldom spoken in public, families kept the disease a secret, emotional support from outside the home was scarce. When she came home from the hospital following the surgery, Paula's mother slipped deeper and deeper into depression.

Over the next few months, she twice tried to commit suicide by swallowing sleeping pills, although Paula didn't realize what had happened until years later. "After she had the surgery, all she did was sleep. She took sleeping pills and she slept all day. She would get up to eat dinner. We had a housekeeper at that time because my mother couldn't do anything and somebody had to watch me."

Eventually Paula's father committed his deeply disturbed wife to a mental hospital; shortly afterward, she killed herself. Once again, Paula was not told what had happened. "I was just told she died," she says. "I thought she had died from the operation."

Understandably, this situation was terrifying to a child. From little Paula's point of view, the world had become a horrifying place, one where a parent can suddenly leave and never return, one where another parent can quickly become a drunk, one where anything terrible can happen at any time.

Mind Games

As most daughters do, Paula strongly identified with her mother, even though, unlike Barbara, she never enjoyed a particularly close relationship with her mother. As a small child, Paula had no idea how to deal with her terror, so she repressed it. But her fears soon began to surface in a variety of destructive ways. The first was an attempt to control her world through superstition. "After my mother's death," Paula explains, "I became horribly superstitious of certain numbers and certain things. I became obsessed." She quickly became frightened of the number 3. "I was paralyzed with terror if I had to do something three times. If I had to go somewhere three times, I couldn't go, or else I'd have to go and come back quickly and go a fourth time. I would lie awake at night terrified if I'd done something three times."

Years later, Paula's therapist suggested to her the possibility that a 3 turned on its side could resemble breasts or the letter M, which could stand for either *Mother* or *Maureen,* Paula's mother's name. Another explanation might be the common superstitious belief that bad things—deaths, natural disasters, airplane crashes—tend to happen in threes.

When Paula developed breasts of her own, she could not stand to have them touched. Subconsciously, like Barbara, Paula feared sharing her mother's fate. Because she couldn't express that fear, it came out in physical ways. "I had a boyfriend I lived with for five years," she says, "and it used to annoy him because my breasts were hypersensitive. I felt physical pain [when he'd try to touch them.]" She never realized the connection with her mother's disease and death until years later, when she read a newspaper article about daughters of women with breast cancer that cited psychosomatic breast pain as a common complaint among them.

Paula's first mammogram was a frightening ordeal for her. "I went to a new gynecologist when I was thirty-one or thirty-two, and he said since I have a family history of breast cancer, I should have a mammogram. I made the appointment a month in advance and I didn't really think anything about it. But when I actually got to the hospital, I became terrified. I went into a cold sweat. I was just horrified." Her mammogram was completely normal, but that hasn't stopped Paula from suffering periodic bouts of paralyzing fear.

"I never consciously think about getting breast cancer until I feel a lump or something and then I go into a panic," she says. On one such occasion, Paula said she "imagined that my whole arm hurt." She had a surgeon check out the tiny lump she had found. He told her it was nothing and it disappeared in a few weeks.

Like many daughters whose mothers have died, Paula couldn't picture living beyond age thirty-six; her mother hadn't. "I just haven't made any plans past thirty-six," she says. When we spoke, she was thirty-five and hoping that reaching her next birthday would mean she'd faced her terror and conquered it. Paula feels that it is time for her to finally struggle free of the fears born more than twenty-eight years ago, when her mother left for the hospital and returned without her breast . . . and without the will to survive.

"If I Love You Too Much, You'll Leave Me"

When teenage Jessica lost her mother to breast cancer, she made a subconscious vow never again to be emotionally vulnerable to another person. If she cared too much about anyone, she knew she risked inviting the terrible pain of abandonment back into her life. And that was just too frightening.

"I'm a very closed person," Jessica admits today. "I don't really discuss my feelings or emotions. I was sixteen [when my mother died] and I didn't have anyone to talk to then." Jessica remembers sharing her feelings only with her dog, "who was my best friend, but she died when I was eighteen. I've learned that it's just easier to keep everything inside."

It may be easier, but Jessica's husband, Joe, doesn't think it's better. After seven years of marriage and two children, he became so frustrated by his wife's remoteness that he urged her into therapy.

"I'd never met anyone I wanted to share my life with until I met [Joe]," Jessica says, but, she admits, "there's still a lot he doesn't know and I don't share.

"I always felt if I got too close to someone or opened up and let them know how I was feeling, they would leave. If I loved someone too much, they'd desert me." So Jessica continues to hold back, keeping herself aloof from too much potentially painful intimacy.

"If You Love Me Too Much, I'll Leave You"

Another vital aspect of Jessica's self-imposed detachment is her certainty that she, like her mother and her mother's mother before her, will die of breast cancer at a young age. "To me," she says, "getting breast cancer and dying is inevitable. I know it's in my family, and in my mind, I'm gonna get it." In view of this belief, she feels she will only hurt her family more if she allows them to become too attached to her. She feels destined to do to her own husband and children what her mother did to her.

A major complaint of Joe's—that Jessica has no personal goals, thus forcing him to decide the family's course of action unilaterally—has its roots in Jessica's conviction that she is doomed. "I just don't make many decisions," she admits. "My husband says he's always told me what his goals and dreams are and I never tell him mine. I don't even think about having goals, because I don't think there is going to be time for all of that.

I don't even want to think about it; I'm just afraid. [I don't want to be hoping] that I have time to do something that I don't."

"If It Happened to Mom, It Will Happen to Me"

Jessica's fear that she will end up a victim of breast cancer like her mother and grandmother is a very common one among daughters of women who've had the disease. UCLA Neuropsychiatric Institute's Dr. David Wellisch "sees daughters who say, 'I'm simply doomed to get this.' It's like they're so identified with the mother that the separation and individuation in their own mind isn't even present."

Often, daughters' fears of contracting breast cancer are wildly out of touch with reality, Dr. Wellisch says. He points out that "most daughters have had mothers with unilateral, postmenopausal breast cancer," which puts their risk just fractionally above that of a woman with no breast cancer in her family. "But this has nothing to do with how they experience this thing psychologically." He's seen women with low risk be "just tormented with the idea that they're going to get breast cancer." On the other hand, he cites one client whose risk is extremely high. Yet "she's not tormented by that notion; she lives with it. So the biological risk does not correlate with the psychological effects."

Medical geneticist Patricia Kelly has observed much the same phenomenon. She told me about a research project she'd done on women's beliefs and health practices concerning breast cancer. Under the auspices of the University of San Francisco, Dr. Kelly interviewed women whose mothers had had breast cancer and found that many of them had expected for years to get the disease themselves. Because of this certainty that they were destined to have breast cancer, they'd frequently altered their lives in radical ways.

"They told me terrible stories," she said. "One woman said she never would have married her husband—she knew he was boring when she married him—but she knew that when she got breast cancer and was dying, he would take care of her. Another said that she had wanted to be a missionary, but she didn't want to die alone in a foreign country, so she stayed here. Other people told me they'd lie in bed as children saying things like, 'Please God, I know I'm going to die of breast cancer, but not this year.' People told me of homes being disrupted, lives being really ripped asunder."

Some of these women, Dr. Kelly says, were already in their sixties and seventies and still physically healthy, but their entire lives had been changed by their fear that they were doomed to share their mothers' fates. With education about their true risks, which were far lower than they envisioned them to be, Dr. Kelly believes they might have led far happier lives. "I think it makes a difference" to know the real risk, she says, "because there is nothing more scary than the unknown. I think the more people know, the more relaxed they can be."

Reflected Fear

Daughters' natural fears can be either soothed or exacerbated by the ways in which a mother handles her own emotions when breast cancer strikes her. For instance, Marilyn, the daughter who fled to Ireland, believes that her own fear was worsened by her mother's terror, demonstrated by extended crying jags. From Marilyn's perspective, not only had a frightening, life-threatening disease struck her family, but the one person she believed she could always count on—her mother—appeared to have lost control and fallen apart.

Happily, Marilyn's mother soon recovered her equilibrium and returned to being a strong support for her daughter. But not all mothers are so successful. Paula's mother slipped into a depression from which she never recovered. Today a large portion of Paula's terror of breast cancer results from her fear that she would not be able to cope with it any better than her mother. "I really feel that, if I got it, I'd probably just kill myself," she admits. She's afraid she's destined to follow the entire path that her mother set so many years ago, even though today's medical treatment of the disease is generally far less invasive than the radical mastectomy her mother underwent.

Psychologist Ronnie Kaye says that often a mother's fears are communicated nonverbally to her daughter. She tells of a mother in one of the breast cancer support groups she supervises. This woman had been having trouble adjusting to her changed body after a mastectomy and "her overriding concern was that her [twelve-year-old] daughter shouldn't see" her mastectomy scar. The mother told the group of women, all of whom had had breast cancer themselves, "I don't think she'd better look at me; I don't want to scare her."

"Her anxiety created a distance between her daughter and herself," Kaye says. "What was fascinating was that a daughter who used to barge into her mother's bedroom [unannounced] all of a sudden was knocking. And the mother hadn't even said, 'Honey, please knock.'"

Kaye explains: "The daughter was picking up the mother's terrible discomfort—though nothing had ever been communicated to her verbally—and was respecting it. She was agreeing tacitly, 'Yes, we need this distance; it will keep both of us safe.' When the mother no longer needed the distance and had worked through her issues and was feeling good about herself again, the daughter just barged into the bedroom" once more. The girl no longer worried about whether her mother was dressed. So, Kaye says, many messages are exchanged "on a level of communication that isn't verbal. Nothing gets said, but it's like everybody's antenna are out."

In this case, the problem was quite simple and soon solved. But many mothers never deal with their own fears successfully and continue to communicate them to their daughters in many ways. For instance, several of the women I spoke to told me that their mothers had overprotected them and their health when they were children, undoubtedly as a result of their own bouts with breast cancer. "My mother was always bundling me up the minute the temperature dropped to sixty," one said.

"She'd be afraid a headache was brain cancer, or a sniffle was tuberculosis." This kind of hypochondria can leave a permanent mark on a daughter, causing her to continue the tradition of exaggerating even her most minor physical symptoms.

Los Angeles marriage and family therapist Sandra Jacoby Klein, M.F.T., who specializes in the emotional effects of illness, says that how the mother deals with her breast cancer treatment can affect how the daughter feels about herself and her femininity as well. "If the mother has had a mastectomy," Jacoby Klein asks, "how does she now dress? How does she see herself as a woman? What are her male-female relationships? Is she comfortable with herself? It may start with the breast, but it encompasses the role of womanhood."

How much the daughter fears contracting breast cancer herself can depend greatly on how well the mother coped. If the mother expressed the attitude that she was "no longer a complete woman," as many women did in the days of radical mastectomies and secrecy about the disease, her daughter is likely to be more fearful than if the mother continues to live a full life, one that includes normal sexuality.

How the mother modeled femininity for her daughter before the breast cancer struck is also important, Jacoby Klein says. "If the daughter is taught that her femininity is in her mind and in her stance and in her personality, it doesn't matter if she has one breast or twelve. But if she's taught that she's supposed to dress a certain way to show herself or not show herself and then a breast is affected, her whole sense of sexuality is threatened."

Jacoby Klein speaks not only as a therapist but as a breast cancer survivor. "Both my daughters were very young, five and seven, and my son was three when I had the [modified radical mastectomy] surgery," she says. "I was single at the time, recently divorced. Their father came and stayed at the house while I was at the hospital. They were confused about this, but they were allowed to see the bandages and we talked about what was happening at different levels throughout the time. I re-married, so they never thought there was anything about my being sexual or being with men that was in any way affected by having one breast or two breasts, because that was never an issue."

UCLA's Dr. David Wellisch has found that teenagers are most severely affected by a mother's breast cancer. "I think their own emerging sense of femininity would be most threatened by a mother who'd had a mastectomy and had been altered in that way. It's the female equivalent of male castration anxiety at its height."

Conquering Fear

The first step in exorcising the fear is to recognize that it exists. The mental health experts with whom I spoke all reinforced the idea that it's entirely normal to be afraid when cancer strikes our families; it would be abnormal *not* to be fearful.

As the women's stories included here illustrate, fear can take a variety of forms, some of which are not readily recognizable—denial of reality, superstition, physical pain, depression, sleeplessness, and an inability to trust oneself and others, to name a few. Yet it's only after we're able to admit we're afraid that we can take the next two essential steps: to communicate our fears and to check them against reality, which puts them into proper perspective. With this three-step process, we can begin to conquer our fears and live a full, productive, happy life.

It's in those families where problems are not discussed or where they're kept secret that people have the most trouble recognizing and overcoming fear. Among the daughters I interviewed, those who were the most terrorized were those to whom no one had ever explained what was happening to their mothers. The family crisis was the family secret. Thus these daughters had had no opportunity to talk about their anxieties or to put them into perspective. In most cases, what they imagined was far worse than reality, and the more they kept it inside, the more it grew and became distorted.

Child psychiatrist Margaret Stuber, M.D., of UCLA's Neuropsychiatric Institute explains that parents make a terrible mistake when they try to keep the truth about something like a mother's breast cancer from their children. If a crisis like this is not handled openly, she says, the children are "going to think that it's something really dreadful that they can't know about, or that they're being punished in some way, or that this is all really mysterious, so anything could happen."

Not only will such children imagine something worse than the reality, says Dr. Stuber, but the secrecy regulation robs them of any "relief from anxiety, because no matter what you say to them [later], they're not going to believe you because you lied to them before." Children whose parents try to protect them in this misguided way quickly learn that they can't trust people "and that almost anything can happen and no one's going to warn them in advance."

Paula, for instance, thought that her mother's death was due to the mysterious operation she'd undergone. As a child, Paula lived in a world where a parent could disappear without explanation and never return. It's easy to see why she became a terrified little girl obsessed with superstition. Additionally, after her suicide, Paula's mother was seldom mentioned by her family again; it was almost as though she'd never existed. Little Paula quickly learned that her mother was a taboo subject. So it wasn't until years later—years filled with the most exquisite terrors a child's imagination can invent—that Paula realized what had stolen her mother from her.

Jessica, too, came from a family where no one told her the truth about her mother's disease and pending death. Her father and brothers tried to protect sixteen-year-old Jessica, the baby of the family, from the facts, with unfortunate results. "My mother went to have a biopsy and I was the only one who stayed home," Jessica told me. "My father called that night and said everything was fine, she was okay. And then my mother got on the phone and started crying. I had no idea what was going on. The first thing she said was, 'I'm no longer a woman.' That's the way she dealt with it. It's like she gave up because of what had happened to her.

"Even all these years later, I don't know all the details," she says. "I knew that my mother was sick, but no one told me how severe it was. In fact everyone kept telling me she was okay, she was getting better. She was the only one who tried to tell me. She'd wake up from a half sleep and start to cry and say, 'I'm going to die like my mom did.'

"I'd get hysterical and call my dad and confront him with it. He'd say, 'Just kind of laugh at her; she doesn't know what she's saying.'" Even on the day her mother died, Jessica's family insisted that everything was all right.

The lesson Jessica learned from this painful experience was that she couldn't trust either her own senses or what others told her. And a world in which one doesn't know who or what to trust is terrifying. Today Jessica is trying to overcome that early conditioning in therapy; with luck and work, she'll eventually overcome her fears and learn to trust once more.

Even in such cases as Paula's and Jessica's, where fears took root a long time ago, communicating those fears to someone years afterward can help eradicate them. Counselor Sandra Jacoby Klein says that sometimes it can actually be easier to achieve this goal if the mother, like Paula's and Jessica's, has died. "Then we can do some role playing," she explains, with herself playing the part of the mother. "I ask the daughter, 'What would you have liked to have said to your mother? What would you have liked your mother to have said to you?' We can do some drawing or imagery and get to what the woman is really carrying with her that feels so bad. Sometimes the [daughter] and I doing it together is enough."

The same technique can be used if the mother is alive but unwilling to discuss breast cancer with her daughter. Or if the mother is willing, Jacoby Klein says, the daughter can confront her directly, allowing both women to complete the important unfinished business in their own lives.

Another technique Jacoby Klein frequently uses in her therapy practice is letter writing. The daughter can write out her feelings and questions. "We read back what the woman has said to her mother, what's going on underneath. Sometimes we mail the letters, sometimes we don't. Occasionally we find the mother really wanted an opportunity to talk to the daughter and didn't know how to do it."

Jacoby Klein recommends the use of "I statements" to make this kind of communication nonthreatening. The daughter might say, for instance, "This is really important to me. I would like to know. If it's something you would like to talk to me about someday, I'd like to listen."

Or at the time a crisis hits, a daughter might say to her mother, "I'm afraid you're going to die, Mom." By putting her fear into words, she can discuss with her mother the feelings both have and can become closer in the process.

A daughter is often as frightened by the thought of what her mother's body will look like after the mastectomy as by the idea of her mother's death itself. A check of reality can help alleviate this fear, too. Many daughters have never seen the results of their mothers' surgery; once again, what they imagine is usually far worse than the reality.

For their part, mastectomy patients often fear that they have become physically repulsive as a result of their surgery. Counselor Ronnie Kaye remembers her own apprehensions in that regard and how her nineteen-year-old daughter was able to help her overcome them. About six months after her modified radical mastectomy, Kaye says, "I was in a bathing suit, getting ready to go to the beach and I stopped by [my daughter's] room. I said, 'By the way, would you like to see what my surgery looks like? I asked her that to give her plenty of room to say, 'Not really, Mom.' But the truth was that I needed her to look at me. That had been one of my issues—who will look at me?—because I had several girlfriends who wouldn't. Even if I could accept myself, [I wondered], would anybody else accept me with this altered body?

"So she said, 'Yes, I would.' I showed her what my surgery looks like and she said, 'Mom, that's actually very nice.'" Her daughter's matter-of-fact reaction helped Kaye regain her self-confidence. She felt less fearful that others would reject her.

However, Kaye warns that both mother and daughter must be willing participants in such a confrontation. "I've heard a lot of very brutal stories about mothers who in their need would rip off their shirts and say, 'Here, look!' Of course their children, some of them very young, would freak out. I've seen these daughters years later, where they've held on to this memory and it has a brutal quality to it."

It's important for women in this situation to realize what their mothers were trying to do, Kaye says. The mother "didn't intend to be brutal; she was coming from someplace else. But the daughter's experience was 'Oh, my God, I didn't ask for this. I shouldn't be forced to see it.'"

If the daughter has a need to see but her mother is either unwilling to be seen or has died, education can help alleviate her fear. Kaye recently showed a poster-sized photograph of a nude, smiling mastectomy patient at a one-day seminar for breast cancer daughters. One daughter who viewed that photograph told me, "I actually was pleasantly surprised. I really thought it was going to be gruesome and I almost didn't look. But it wasn't bad at all."

In her smaller, multiple-session groups for daughters, Kaye often demystifies fears of mutilation by showing the participants who wish to see it the results of her own mastectomy.

As we have seen in Chapter 2, virtually no one is certain to get breast cancer, and heredity is only one of many factors. The feelings of doom common to many female relatives of women with breast cancer are unnecessary and can be mitigated by education. A small amount of anxiety can be helpful if it spurs us to do monthly breast self-examinations and to have periodic physical examinations and mammograms. But the cancer phobia that many daughters experience is both irrational and psychologically damaging. It can be reduced greatly through learning the facts about risk.

When the myriad fears spawned by breast cancer are recognized, communicated and checked against reality, they lose their power over us. There's nothing strange or wrong about being afraid; at times we all are. With knowledge and the courage to grow, we can achieve a measure of gratifying peace and can live our lives to their fullest.

CHAPTER 5

Why Me?

ANGER IS THE EMOTION many women tend to have the most trouble recognizing and expressing. We're taught from infancy not even to feel, never mind express, anger. In response to similar situations, little boys are taught to get angry, little girls to cry. Yet all human beings feel anger. It's a natural emotion.

When breast cancer hits us and our families, it's entirely normal to be frustrated and angry. The disease itself is not fair, and the havoc it wreaks is not fair either. It deprives everyone. We have every right to be angry.

Many of the mothers and daughters to whom I spoke told me it had taken them years to recognize their anger, particularly if it was directed at what they felt were inappropriate targets: each other, God, the men in their lives, or their doctors. Yet when it wasn't acknowledged, the anger remained, buried and festering. Sometimes it erupted sporadically and painfully, causing these women lasting regrets. And frequently, when the anger did emerge, it was misdirected at themselves.

From Anger to Depression

Anger has plagued twenty-five-year-old Amy since she was thirteen. That was when her young, vivacious mother was diagnosed with breast cancer. She died just nine months afterward. In therapy years later, Amy discovered that she had long been angry with her mother, with her father and with fate for stealing her youth. But because expressing that anger seemed neither safe nor "nice," she had turned it inward, where it resulted in her being depressed for years.

It was just before Christmas when Amy's mother's cancer was confirmed. At first Amy and her younger brother, Tom, were told nothing about the family crisis. But Amy remembers that her parents were out of the house more often than usual and that "they were getting a lot of phone calls back from the American Cancer Society and doctors. There was a weird feeling, these really ominous tones to that Christmas."

In early January, just before Amy's mother entered the hospital for surgery, she took her children aside and told them she had cancer and needed an operation. Amy was given no further details. "We didn't know what she had. I remember when she was in the hospital, I used to wonder what would be taken away from her. I remembered Teddy Kennedy, Jr., had a leg removed; I'd read about that. I used to think, 'Could it be a leg?'

"Then we went to see her in the hospital. She was wearing a robe and I was really looking at her, searching to see what could have been removed. I noticed there was a space where her breast should have been. I realized, because I remembered about Betty Ford, that my mom had breast cancer."

Yet Amy never discussed the cancer with her mother; she intuitively knew such questions would not be welcome. As counselor Ronnie Kaye says is common among daughters, Amy kept her need to know buried. The atmosphere at home when her mother returned from the hospital confirmed Amy's suspicions, too. Before the surgery Amy's mother had not been particularly modest around her children, but now she screamed at them to get out if they entered her bedroom or the bathroom while she was dressing.

The breast cancer was kept secret from outsiders, too. Amy says, "There was a bizarreness to my mom's illness. We had a housekeeper who'd been a nurse. My mom became bloated [after she began chemotherapy treatments] and she couldn't eat. What she did eat, she would always throw up. She had stopped menstruating, too. The nurse interpreted this as my mom's being pregnant. It was really ironic. For my mom, [dying] was a nine-month process.

"I remember my mom telling me that this nurse had gone to my father and said, 'I think your wife's pregnant,' not knowing what was really going on. But still we couldn't tell [the housekeeper/nurse] what was wrong, and she was living in our house."

Each of her chemotherapy treatments made Amy's mother ill for days on end. The household was chaotic and Amy was severely affected by witnessing her mother's rapid deterioration. She retains vivid memories of that time. One is of a special occasion when her mother treated herself to a haircut at an expensive beauty salon. Amy's mental portrait is of her mother's lush dark hair being shampooed in this posh place, resulting in "handfuls of her hair coming out in the sink."

Food presented a problem because Amy's mother could eat very little. "I remember getting angry at her because she would eat like a child," Amy says. "I would make her a sandwich and she'd eat only the bread and not the crust. Or she would just eat sugar cookies. She would have to drink from a straw. I remember once she didn't drink from the straw and she dribbled. I got so upset with her." Feeding her mother became a frequent task for Amy.

Her face registering her anguish, Amy says, "I remember thinking then, Why do I have to be my mother's mother at age thirteen?" As a blossoming adolescent, she was filled with resentment of the cancer that was stealing both her mother and what was left of her own childhood.

Toward the middle of the several months of chemotherapy treatments, Amy's rage at the situation became almost unbearable. "My mom's illness took over our family," she recalls. "She would get her chemotherapies on a Friday and that weekend would be destroyed. We'd hear her throwing up. I used to hate that." Amy felt trapped and ignored. All the family's energy was going toward trying to alleviate her mother's pain; there was none left for her.

"One day I wrote [my mom] a hateful letter. I wrote, 'Stop feeling sorry for yourself.' It was a really nasty letter. That night she came to me and said she was so sorry; she felt so bad." It took Amy a dozen years before she could forgive herself for inappropriately expressing the anger that any thirteen-year-old in her situation would have felt.

On the day her mother died, Amy overheard a comment that haunted her for years. "My aunt was at the hospital with us. We were all in the waiting room crying. My aunt said to my father that my mother had known about [her breast] lump for many years" but had done nothing about it. Could it have been her mother's own negligence that had killed her?

Many years later, Amy went back to that hospital and retrieved her mother's medical records. "That blew my mind away," she says. "It really helped me understand what had actually happened. . . . I remember my mom was a really private person about her body and she hated gynecologists. After she had my brother, she never went to see a gynecologist again. When I looked at the records, there would be all these appointments when she was supposed to see her gynecologist and [every one] would say, 'Canceled.'

"What I learned was that my mom went [for medical help] at the very end, when there was almost nothing they could do anymore." The cancer had already spread throughout her body. An additional piece of information Amy learned from the medical records was that "midway in her illness, my mom was prepared to die. It shows in the records, because she mysteriously asked for the chemotherapy to stop. She hated the surgery, she hated the chemotherapy, she hated it all."

After her mother's death, Amy says, her family really fell apart. She had never been close to her father; her parents had had a traditional marriage in which the father earned the living and left the child-rearing chores to the mother. With her mother gone, Amy felt she had no emotional support system whatsoever. It was too frightening to risk becoming angry with her father for not attempting to take over her mother's role. If she offended him, she feared she would lose the essentials that he *was* willing and able to provide—housing, food, money. So she swallowed her anger.

"I became incredibly depressed, for years," she says, "but I never realized what it was. On the weekends I would spend the whole day in bed, reading. I gained a lot of weight. . . . There was tremendous sadness. There wasn't any joy anymore. There was isolation and a real bleakness" to her teenage years.

Amy tried psychotherapy a couple of times, largely because of trouble she began having with her high school studies. But she couldn't quite make herself reveal her anger. "I'd kind of skirt the issues. I'd come into therapy saying, 'I feel really depressed and I think it has to do with my mom's death, which I've never gotten over.' " But then she'd clam up. She just wasn't ready to risk sparking the potentially explosive rage she was keeping inside her.

A year before we spoke, Amy finally became ready to take that risk. She went into double therapy: she joined a group made up of daughters of women who'd had breast cancer and had private sessions with a psychologist. "It was like we were dealing with a bomb," she says. "First there was my mom and her cancer and what I didn't know about that. Then we started to deal with my father. There were all these issues." And all of them, Amy feels, go back to the central core of bitter resentment caused by her mother's breast cancer.

Secrecy and Rage

Psychotherapist Sandra Jacoby Klein says that secrecy such as that maintained by Amy's family is one of the most common causes of bitterness in daughters of women with breast cancer. "There's a lot of anger," she says. "They don't feel trusted." Although the family may believe that keeping the truth from a daughter is merely protecting her from harsh reality, the typical child interprets this action to mean that she isn't trusted by those most important to her. Given this interpretation, the child begins to think her parents believe there's something terribly wrong with her. She can either accept this judgment, agreeing that she is unworthy of their trust and losing self-esteem in the process, or she can rail against what she feels is an unfair accusation. Ronnie Kaye adds that secrecy "is the biggest issue of all" among the daughters she has counseled. It haunts many throughout their lives.

Amy was forced to deal with her mother's fatal illness without anyone's having explained to her what was happening. In addition, she was pressured to say nothing to those outside the family about what little she did understand. These are unreasonable expectations, and she was justified in resenting their burden.

According to Amy, her mother withdrew from her friends because she "didn't want people to feel sorry for her." Amy also believes her mother was embarrassed that so private a body part as her breast had been affected. Even at the funeral, her mother's wish for secrecy prevailed. "We told people she'd had cancer," Amy says, "but we never said it was breast cancer. We still paid tribute" to her mother's desire to hide the truth.

Like Amy, Noreen was never told that her mother had breast cancer. This slight still hurts and angers her, even though it happened more than thirty years ago. Noreen was eleven when her mother had cancer surgery. "I was not really told much about it," she says. "I got most of my information from my own observations. I suspected what it was because I was a fairly bright kid and I read a lot. But nobody actually told me, and the message was 'Don't ask.'"

What hurt the most, Noreen says, is that her best friend confirmed her suspicions of breast cancer. "My friend's mother had told her what my mother had. I knew, but I hadn't been told. My friend's mother had told her. That hurt."

When Noreen was fifteen, she saw an article in a magazine about breast reconstruction surgery, "which was pretty new stuff at the time. I remember asking my mother whether she would ever consider it and she said, 'Oh, no, no, I would never do that,' and that was the end of the subject. [Her attitude] was, how did I come off asking her such a thing?" Noreen's attempt to be helpful and to discuss the subject of breast cancer openly was greeted only by her mother's own anger. "My mother had a great deal of difficulty in letting emotions out and in being direct," Noreen says today. "I suppose she thought she was protecting me," but instead she hurt and angered her daughter.

Dr. David Wellisch explains that families who deal with breast cancer through secrecy "make a horrible mistake. Protecting their kids is really protecting themselves. It's a projection onto the children of their own anxieties and inabilities to face emotions." If a mother talks to her child about her breast cancer, she'll be forced to deal with the child's reaction. By not telling the child, the mother is really trying to spare herself, not the child.

Occasionally a mother will share her secret with her daughter, but then burden the daughter with a request to keep it from everyone else. This happened to Laurel, whose mother forbade her to confide in anyone, even close family members.

Laurel was thirty-five and nursing her second child when her mother's cancer was diagnosed. She says her mother "waited to tell me until [the surgery] was all scheduled. I think she told me then only because her doctor said I should get a baseline mammogram." Laurel's mother interpreted the doctor's comment to mean that Laurel should have the mammogram *immediately*, which would require that she stop nursing her baby. In addition to her mother, two of Laurel's great-aunts also had breast cancer, and the mother was concerned that Laurel now was at increased risk.

Laurel's mother had to wait about four weeks for her surgery because of problems in scheduling the hospital and the surgeon. She told Laurel she wanted to avoid anyone's filling her head with horror stories during that interim, so she swore her to secrecy. Laurel wasn't even allowed to tell her three brothers that their mother was facing breast cancer surgery.

Her mother's demand made Laurel fume. She recalls, "I thought, Here's a time when people could be supportive of her if she'd only let them, just by letting them know what's going on. But she didn't want to do it that way. She waited until after the operation to tell anyone else, even her closest friends." Swearing her to secrecy was unfair, Laurel feels, because breast cancer now seemed a threat in her own life as well as in her mother's. Why, she was even being encouraged to stop nursing so she could have her first mammogram. "By my not being able to share my concerns with the people around me, I too was deprived" of emotional support, Laurel says. "I felt it was selfish of her. I did respect her wishes, but I let her know at the time that I was unhappy" about it.

Mothering Mother

A second issue that disturbed Amy and many of the other daughters with whom I spoke was the requirement that they switch roles with their ailing mothers. Amy was still a girl and not ready to trade the role of the child for that of the grown-up. She felt unfairly robbed of her childhood. Other daughters told me that they resented similar burdens, ranging from running the household for their ailing mothers to doing small chores for them that brought them into undesirably intimate contact with their mother's illness.

For instance, fifty-five-year-old Helen retains the memory of a personal chore she was asked to perform for her mother nearly forty years ago. "This little incident, I don't know why it stays with me," she told me. "When I came back from college and my mother had had her breast removed, for some reason she asked me to wash her nightgown and underpants by hand. She'd never asked me to do that. As I was doing it, I didn't like the job and I thought, Why did she ask me to do this? but I did it. It was such a foreign thing to me. Her pants were stained and I didn't like that. That stayed with me."

Ronnie Kaye says that forcing a young daughter into the mother's role is inappropriate, although it frequently happens when a mother is ill with breast cancer. It's appropriate, Kaye says, for a mother to say to her daughter, " 'I really need a hug from you,' because the child can give a hug. That's doable. But the child can't be the parent. That's a terrible burden. The child feels like a failure or very resentful." Such a child feels the mother is asking her to make her feel better, to cure her cancer, and that's not fair to the child.

Child psychologists say that children who grow up feeling responsible for their parents tend as adults to have difficulties with intimacy. The overly responsible child doesn't learn how to play, how to be spontaneous, or how to share in decision making.

All of those problems have plagued thirty-seven-year-old Tess, who was only a year old when her mother was diagnosed with breast cancer. Tess has no conscious memory of what her life was like before breast cancer struck her family, but she believes that it was markedly better. Relatives have told her that before her mother developed breast cancer, she was "a very happy, bubbly baby." Tess thinks that after the cancer episode, she "got real quiet and shy. That feels right. I can only remember myself being quiet and scared. I wanted to be this outgoing person, but I wasn't."

Tess relates a story her mother has told about "me in the crib in the living room. She was crying and saying that she was never going to see me grow up. I can just see myself looking up at her, thinking, What am I doing that she's crying? thinking that I caused it in some way." If this kind of scene had been an event that happened only once, it might not have caused so much trauma, but Tess's mother has played the invalid role for the last thirty-six years. "The reality was that she decided she was going to die," Tess says. "The energy in the house was pretty much death. How she made it through with that kind of an attitude, I don't know, but she did."

Because her mother abdicated her responsibility as a mother, Tess says, "I feel like I raised myself." And that still makes her angry.

Tess now realizes that her mother cannot deal with stress. She is also a very angry woman who "has to blame somebody. 'Things just don't happen' is her philosophy. It must be somebody's fault." Tess has often felt that she was the one her mother blamed. In her desire to make her mother happy again, Tess as a child tried her best to become her mother's mother, to be calm in response to her mother's frequent hysteria.

"When I was two years old," Tess says, "my mother put me in the bathtub to give me a bath. When she tried to lift me out, she couldn't. She'd had a radical mastectomy and she couldn't use her arm very well. When she couldn't get me out of the tub, she got hysterical. Somebody came to the front door and she asked them to lift me out. I asked her later how I reacted and she said, 'You looked at me as if to say, What are you getting so excited about?' So even at two years old, I was doing it. I could have started crying, but I knew not to."

Another representative incident sticks in Tess's mind. "I remember being about eight years old and waiting for my father to get home," she said. "I was riding a bicycle and I fell off in the driveway and got my face cut. It wasn't horrible, but it was bloody. I went into the house and my mother became hysterical. She started to scream at me, 'Why did you do that? What were you doing out there?'

"It was like she was angry at me. I remember being pulled by the wrist and being told, 'Now we'll have to take you to the doctor!' All this terrible, negative stuff.

"How I've dealt with that over the years is that I've had to take care of my mother's feelings. I've had to say to her, 'Everything's okay.' I've had to be stoic. Really, it would have been nice to be able to cry about it." Only in recent years, Tess says, has she realized that an emotionally stable mother would have comforted a child who fell from her bicycle, would have held her and reassured *her* that everything would be okay. The child would not have been expected to reassure the mother.

Another normal part of parenting that Tess's mother failed to do was to give her daughter essential information about the changes that would happen to her body as she grew up. Any discussion of female anatomy, it seemed, might lead to the subject of breasts and cancer, and Tess's mother would have no part of that. Tess was afraid to ask questions because she feared her mother's wrath.

"She never told me about menstruation," Tess says, which left her completely ignorant about it. When Tess got her first period, she remembers, "I didn't feel too good and I saw blood. I thought I was dying. I waited two days to tell my mother, figuring she was going to get hysterical and send me to the hospital. I used paper towels, toilet paper; it was horrible. When I finally got up the nerve to tell her, all she said was, 'Already?' Like I should know [what was happening to me]. My hands were shaking, I was so angry with her."

As a child, Tess learned to stay away from her mother and depend more on her father, whom she adored. "My mother was always negative; I don't remember her hugging me or giving me any kind of physical affection. But my dad, I was all over him, playing with his hands, his hair. And I remember every Sunday he would sit down and play the piano for me."

But when Tess was twelve, her father died suddenly of a heart attack. "My mother went nuts again," she recalls. "She got really caught up in how catastrophic it was. I don't think she was grieving for him, but for herself. She didn't pay much attention to me. I had to ask my aunt what to wear to the funeral. Again, it was a matter of me taking care of her. I remember sitting there in the funeral home. My mother was whimpering and I just wouldn't."

Tess was not without strong feelings, however. She was furious that it was her father and not her mother who had died.

She still feels that way. "I don't like her much," Tess says of her mother. "She's not my friend, she's somebody I got saddled with. I wish she was the kind of person who knew how to handle illness, because I think it would have made a lot of difference. My model for illness, for breast cancer, is horrible." Tess's biggest fear if she ever gets breast cancer herself is not that she will die; it's that she, like her mother, will "go crazy."

Because she had breast cancer, Tess believes, her mother "wasn't the mom. Emotionally, I was the mom. I call my growing up my personal holocaust. I don't know what it would have been like if she hadn't had breast cancer. I think maybe things would have been hard, but they wouldn't have been that bad. From everything I can tell, before that happened, things were very nice. But nobody knew how to deal with breast cancer."

Ronnie Kaye says that a situation such as Tess's is far from unique. Many daughters in the groups she's counseled feel their mothers have leaned far too heavily on them. "Can you imagine losing a mother without losing a mother?" Kaye asks. "Their mothers are still alive, but they're not available for any parenting at all. The role reversal is hopefully temporary, but sometimes not.

"So I see a sort of loneliness or despondency in the daughters because abruptly they lost parenting from their mothers and somehow they never got it back. If it's temporary, it's understandable. The mother is fighting for her life. But those fights don't go on for years."

A Mother's Anger

It's likely that Tess's mother was expressing her own anger by regressing into childhood after breast cancer struck her. She'd lost her own mother at a young age to an unknown disease. So when she became ill herself, she may well have decided that the burden of marriage and motherhood was too heavy; she'd never received adequate mothering herself. So she returned mentally to the dependent cocoon of childhood, where others were called upon to care for her. Once there, she never returned to adulthood.

While this kind of behavior is clearly disruptive to family life and scarring to the affected children, it can serve to remind us that all family members have a right to be angry when breast cancer or any other serious disease disrupts their lives.

Children such as Amy, Noreen, Laurel, Helen and Tess may resent unexpected changes in their lives, greater demands placed on them, perhaps the loss of their mothers and other consequent changes in the family structure.

Fathers and husbands may feel frustrated with the physical and mental changes in their wives, or enraged by the actual loss of them.

And the breast cancer patients themselves, of course, are facing the risk of their own death, unwanted surgical alterations of their bodies, physical pain, possibly the uncomfortable side effects of radiation or chemotherapy treatments, and any number of fears these things generate. At the same time, most of them feel they must make a strong effort not to overburden those they love. This ordeal can be a terrible load, one a woman with breast cancer may quickly learn to resent.

The anger expressed most commonly by the women to whom I spoke was a sort of general rage caused by their having been the target of a potentially fatal disease. "Why me?" most of them had asked, feeling at least temporarily enraged by the unfairness of their lives.

Others told me they were angry about specific issues related to their cancer. For instance, Gwen, a young mother whose breast cancer was diagnosed while she was nursing her first baby, said she bitterly resents the fact that she may have to forgo having more children. When she spoke to her obstetrician about her plan to have another baby, he told her about another of his patients, a woman who had undetected breast cancer when she became pregnant. The hormonal changes in her body apparently spurred the cancer's growth and it spread rapidly throughout her body.

Gwen got a second opinion: the doctor told her to wait three years after her chemotherapy treatments had ended before trying to get pregnant a second time. Still, Gwen isn't sure she should take that risk. If she should die, she asks herself, what will become of her baby daughter? And will she be able to give birth to a healthy infant or will her disease scar her child in some unforeseeable way? Being faced with making a possibly life-threatening decision about something as basic as giving birth makes her furious.

Another woman told me she's angry with her older daughter, who refuses to discuss the topic of breast cancer or techniques to detect it. "She's at high risk because of me, and because she's thirty-five years old and hasn't had a pregnancy yet. I've tried a million times to give her the information about how to take care of herself, but she's so stubborn, she just won't listen." This woman feels frustrated by her daughter's unwillingness to listen to her mother's advice and denial of her own health risk.

Other women nursed old hurts about daughters (or in a few cases, mothers) who had avoided them while they were having surgery or follow-up treatments. Such women may realize intellectually that the relatives they love simply couldn't deal with the disease, but that doesn't completely mitigate the pain of being shunned when they needed support. They felt that their family members, not they themselves, should be the ones to go the extra mile in such situations.

On the other hand, one woman told me that when she was diagnosed with breast cancer, her mother overreacted, becoming completely hysterical. "My mother's two sisters had had breast cancer and my mother lived her life in fear of getting it herself. She never did. But when I got it, she freaked out. She acted like I'd done something to cause it, like I'd gotten breast cancer just to make her miserable." This breast cancer patient found that each confrontation with her mother made her so angry that she finally refused to see or talk with her.

Such reactions are common and understandable. And every member of a family affected by breast cancer should recognize the right of other family members to feel frustrated, overburdened, and angry.

Loss of Control

A major reason we feel frustrated is because we feel we have so little control over such a life-threatening illness as breast cancer. We can't predict who or when it will strike. We can't control whether it will recur. We can't guarantee our own survival or that of our mothers. When we can't control the big things, like life and death, it's only human to put extra effort into trying to control the little things. They can be as obviously related to the problem at hand as the choice of medical treatment. Or they might be as seemingly unrelated as a daughter's dating habits, a husband's work schedule, or one's own weight.

Some of the rage that lingered the longest was aimed at doctors. Sometimes this anger seemed misdirected, people blaming physicians for being unable to perform miracles, but occasionally it was appropriately targeted. For instance, a pair of sisters whose mother had recently died of breast cancer told me of a botched mammogram that should have revealed the tumor three years before it was finally discovered. Jane, the older sister, has since become an X-ray technician, specializing in mammography. "I now sometimes work for the doctors who read [my mother's] mammogram and I really let them know about it," she told me.

In addition, both Jane and her sister, Lois, feel that the doctors who performed their mother's mastectomy gave her incomplete and tardy treatment. Jane says she's certain the cancer had already metastasized at the time the surgery was performed, but the doctors didn't catch it. They told the family that only "traces of cancer" were found in the lymph nodes and that a hormone blocker would be an adequate follow-up treatment. They failed to order a bone scan, which might have shown the cancer's spread; if that test had been performed before surgery, Jane says, immediate chemotherapy treatment might have been indicated. "I truly believe they messed up by not giving her the drugs right after the mastectomy."

By the time their mother began having severe pain in her ribs and the bone scan was finally performed, two months had passed. At that time, massive chemotherapy treatments were tried, without success. "The chemotherapy drug they gave her was an extremely heavy dose and it just about killed her," Jane says. "She barely made it through the first two days. It was unbelievable; she went from being sick to almost—right then and there—being on her deathbed."

Lois adds her own anguish: "The thing that really irritates me is that [hospital] specializes in cancer. So many doctors were in on the case. When you get a lot of people, you think everything's been done, but nobody really takes control." She cannot emphasize enough the importance of having one doctor in charge of a case.

Jane had been planning her wedding for months before her mother's cancer was detected. By the time her mother entered the hospital for chemotherapy treatments, the event was only a month away. The invitations had been sent, the wedding dress purchased, the caterers hired. Ten days before Jane's wedding, her mother died.

Jane went ahead with her marriage ceremony, explaining, "My mom wouldn't have wanted me to cancel and lose everything that I had planned for. I was devastated, believe me, but I didn't want everyone at my wedding going, 'Oh, that poor girl, I really feel sorry for her,' so I really put on a show. It was the direct opposite of what everybody expected. They thought I would fall apart, but I walked down that aisle beaming, a smile on my face you couldn't have believed."

Jane says she and Lois made it through the strain of their mother's funeral and her own wedding "in a state of shock." When the shock wore off, they discovered they were both livid about not only the medical treatment their mother had received but also the attitudes exhibited by the doctors.

"A lot of doctors don't see what the family goes through," Jane says. "They make their diagnosis—be it right or wrong—and that's it for them."

Lois adds her dismay that once the cancer's spread was found, the doctors kept giving differing estimates as to how long their mother would be likely to survive. "At first it was two years, then it was nine months, then a few months. I got used to them telling me so many different lines.

"I know they can't predict what's going to happen, but don't give us two years." It was barely three months from the time of her mastectomy to the time of their mother's death.

At the end, Lois says, the kidney specialist came into the hospital room and told the family that their mother's kidneys had stopped functioning. "I said, 'Well, then, we'll just keep putting her on dialysis, right?' And he said, 'You don't understand. There's nothing else I can do.' He said this right in front of her!" Lois remains outraged by what she sees as this doctor's insensitivity to her dying mother's feelings.

Many daughters told me they were angry about the medical treatment their mothers had received, frequently echoing their mothers' own feelings. This was particularly true if the mother had had breast cancer in the days of the radical mastectomy and the one-step procedure (which didn't end until the late 1970s), in which a woman would enter the hospital for a biopsy to detect cancer and wake up from anesthesia without her breast. Frequently women were not prepared emotionally for the surgery, and they almost always felt no sense of control over their own medical treatment. Many told me of having felt helpless and angry, and these emotions were often expressed by their daughters as well.

Luckily, the severely disfiguring (and often debilitating) radical mastectomy is no longer performed. In addition, most doctors now allow a woman to participate in the choices concerning her own treatment, if she wishes to do so. While inept and insensitive doctors certainly exist, I was encouraged to find that most of the women I spoke with were grateful to their doctors, who'd done their best to save a life.

Releasing Anger

It's perfectly all right for a woman, whether she has breast cancer herself or has to cope with its attack on a relative, to feel angry. Yet if she allows her anger to dominate the rest of her life, she may well become a bitter, neurotic person like Tess's mother. The key is to recognize and release the anger so we can get on with living the best possible life. Psychotherapist Susan Forward, Ph.D., cautions that the "things we're afraid will happen if we get angry are the very things that have a good chance of happening if we don't. When you repress your anger, you may become depressed or abrasive and other people may reject you as surely as they would if you were openly angry at them. Repressed anger is unpredictable—it can explode at any time. When it *does,* it is often uncontrollable. Anger is always destructive unless it is managed, especially if it has been allowed to fester beneath your conscious awareness."

Identifying the anger at the roots of our emotional turmoil is the first step, and possibly the most difficult. Often anger masquerades as something else, such as Amy's depression. Or it may manifest itself in compulsive behavior. For instance, one daughter told me that she'd become a compulsive overeater shortly after her mother had died of breast cancer some twenty-four years earlier. The youngest child in a family where expressing anger was considered taboo, she told me, "I've had a lot of depression. It's all from stuffing everything inside. Now I'm trying to learn to express my emotions in a healthy way instead of continuing to stuff them down with food."

Psychologist Dr. Wendy Schain theorizes that eating disorders are particularly common among daughters of women who've had breast cancer. Severe, life-threatening disorders such as anorexia and bulimia are thought to be the result of efforts to exercise some control over one's life. A girl or woman in the throes of these disorders feels that she must control her weight because she feels helpless to control anything else in her world. Such extreme behavior requires professional treatment.

If the anger isn't obvious to us, it may well be to others—family members, other women who've had breast cancer in their families, friends, psychotherapists. That's why it's so important to risk talking about our lives and our feelings with supportive listeners. Keeping our emotions bottled up never helps.

Once we realize we are angry and identify the reasons for this anger, there are a number of ways in which we can relieve our feelings. One is to take some kind of positive action to heal the emotional wounds. Amy, for instance, found that learning the truth about what had happened to her mother a dozen years earlier was extremely liberating for her. By going to the hospital where her mother had been treated and retrieving her mother's medical records, Amy was able to stop feeling like an angry thirteen-year-old who'd been deprived of vital facts. At long last, she was able to hold the truth—in the form of those medical records—in her hands.

Another positive action Amy took was to visit her mother's grave and "talk" to her there. Still resentful that she hadn't had a mother to guide her through her difficult teenage years, Amy often felt like a ship without a compass. But her therapist told her that death needn't separate her from her mom.

"I hadn't been able to go [to my mom's grave] since she died," Amy told me. "Then when I went, at first I couldn't find her grave and I got hysterical. To me it seemed so symbolic; she hadn't been in my life and now I couldn't find her. But then I went to the [cemetery's] office and they gave me a map."

As a child, Amy had been too young to bring her mother formal floral bouquets, but she had often brought her chocolates. "My mom loved chocolates." So when she visited her mother's grave, Amy brought a box of chocolates with her. She also carried a letter she'd written to her mother that clearly stated her feelings of abandonment and loss and grief. But when she found her mother's gravestone, Amy says, "I didn't feel I needed the letter. I just felt incredibly at peace. I ate chocolates at my mom's grave site and it felt really, really wonderful."

Now Amy says she feels as though her mother is back in her life. If she needs guidance in some area, she simply relaxes and tries to let her mother's advice "come through." One of the big issues for her was "how to handle men. So I went to my mom's grave to finally have it out with her about men. We had never had that conversation. I got this answer back immediately. She said to me, 'Don't even think about men. Be happy, write, graduate from college and the rest will come.' "

Whether this was Amy's mother speaking to her or Amy giving herself advice of which her mother would have approved is irrelevant. Once Amy was able to release her hurt and anger over being abandoned, her life began to proceed on course once more. "I've renewed an energy that's really been helpful," she says.

The techniques that Amy used, or similar ones, may help other angry daughters. As Sandra Jacoby Klein suggests, writing a letter spelling out our feelings can be liberating, even if it's written to a dead relative or is never mailed because the addressee can't or won't respond favorably. Just expressing our feelings is often enough.

If our mothers are still alive and not too ill to communicate, Jacoby Klein recommends using such nonthreatening statements of our own feelings as "I need to know the truth about what happened when you had breast cancer. I would like to discuss it with you if you are able." How our emotional needs are perceived by others often depends on how we state them. If we are overtly hostile, we will probably evoke defensiveness and anger in the other person, which will simply escalate the conflict. However, if we state our needs simply, without throwing blame, it becomes difficult to argue.

Sometimes, of course, those with whom we are angry simply

will not listen, no matter how we state the problem. Tess, for instance, told me about screaming fights she'd had with her mother whenever she broached the subject of breast cancer and her mother's secrecy about it. After the yelling subsided, her mother would always close the conversation abruptly with a statement such as "I guess you think I'm just a terrible mother," designed to make Tess feel guilty. Tess now tries to avoid having any contact with her mother.

But she is using another method to ease the continuing turmoil created by her chaotic childhood. The American Cancer Society sponsors group therapy sessions for daughters of women with breast cancer, which Tess is attending. In the safety of the group, she can talk with others who know exactly what she's experienced. In addition, the group sessions offer her an opportunity to check her perceptions and expectations against reality. "One thing [the group leader] made me understand," she says, "is that breast cancer does *not* make people go crazy. That was just my mother's way of dealing with it." Tess's way of dealing with her own life need not be like her mother's.

Psychotherapy in a supportive environment, whether it's in an American Cancer Society–sponsored group or in individual or group sessions, can be very helpful in dealing with anger. But it requires a willingness to examine old behavior patterns and beliefs, which can be painful. Amy told me about attending her first group session, where the group leader's discussion of vital issues evoked tears from several participants. "As we were leaving, one woman told me she didn't think she could go through this, that she probably wouldn't come back," Amy said.

"She was prepared to carry that sadness with her forever because she didn't think she could go through those eight weeks of hell to make the breakthrough. That woman was prepared to go through her life carrying this melancholy with her." In her own case, Amy was willing to endure almost any amount of pain to release her malignant anger. After being depressed for years, she wanted to change, no matter how difficult that might be.

It had taken Amy twelve years to work up the courage to take that step, but she's very glad she did it. "What I learned was that you can do it only when you're ready," she says. Today, Amy is in college and working toward a career, and she carefully protects her own physical as well as mental health. If *she* ever gets breast cancer, she vows, it will be caught early enough that her life can be saved.

Amy, like many other daughters of women with breast cancer, has finally faced and exorcised her internal demons. Her anger gone, she has learned to feel a peace with herself, her mother and her life.

CHAPTER 6

Lasting Regrets

ON THE NIGHT HER MOTHER DIED, Claudia hadn't been to visit her at the hospital all week; since then, she's been plagued by guilt over her failure to say good-by. Holly believed that losing her mother to breast cancer was her punishment for some unforgivable sin. Shannon felt disloyal because she had two healthy breasts while her mother's were being invaded by cancer cells. Because she had breast cancer herself, Lillian often feels responsible for putting her daughters at increased risk of getting it.

Regrets over something done or not done, said or not said, even thought or not thought, frequently haunt both women with breast cancer and their close relatives. Of course, guilt, whether it's justified or not, is an emotion that can accompany any life-threatening family situation. Even when our parents die of old age, we may well regret things in our past relationship with them. And because of the symbiotic ties between female family members as well as the fact that breast cancer may be inherited, the illness can prompt guilty feelings that are particularly lasting and debilitating.

Not having done enough for their mothers was an extremely common regret expressed by the daughters I talked with. It's one I've known myself. I've often felt guilty for not insisting that I fly to Rochester to be with my mother when she had her biopsy done. I've regretted relying on my parents' conviction that the surgeon would find no malignancy. As a result, by the time I realized that my mother actually did have breast cancer, her breast had already been removed. And instead of being at her side, where I might have offered her some support, I had been two thousand miles away.

I was an adult, however, and better able to deal with my regrets than many others who were only children when their mothers got breast cancer. Particularly plagued by guilt are those daughters who were teenagers when their mothers became ill. Often they suffer lifelong anguish for no reason; in fact they did nothing more than display the kind of self-centeredness common among teenagers.

Claudia was a typical sixteen-year-old—preoccupied with boys, clothes and friends—when her mother got breast cancer. She admits, "I didn't want to go home and take care of my mother. I wanted to be out with my friends." During the months her mother spent at home, Claudia says she "basically just kept her company and did a little bit around the house."

An added obstacle was that Claudia's father tried to "protect" both Claudia and her mother from the truth. Despite the doctors' bleak prognosis, he continually reassured both mother and daughter that full recovery was imminent. So Claudia had not been to the hospital all week when her mother died that Friday night.

"I wasn't even able to say good-by to her," she told me. "I was supposed to go to the hospital the next day," but by then her mother was dead. "I wasn't allowed to see the body," she says. "I'm Jewish and there was a closed casket. My father wouldn't even allow us to say our good-bys to her."

Feeling that she didn't do right by her mother has haunted Claudia throughout her adult life. "I feel guilty that I didn't know the truth and therefore wasn't able to console my mother or let her talk. She had all these feelings inside her and she couldn't talk to anyone because they kept saying, 'You're fine; there's nothing wrong with you.' "

Claudia's self-image has been scarred severely by her self-blame. "I feel like I'm a bad person because I wasn't there to help my mother," she says. "I look at things as though I was the bad person instead of looking at the actual circumstances."

Claudia's children have been helpful in shoring up her shaky self-esteem. When we spoke, she had a four-year-old daughter and an infant son. "To me, they're my whole world, my only source of love that no one can take away," she said. "They need me, so even though I'm a bad person, they still love me. I'm holding on to that because as long as I don't abuse them, they'll love me. I can't lose that."

When she was thirty-four, Claudia attended a one-day seminar for daughters of women who have had breast cancer. There a counselor spoke of the reactions typical teenage daughters have to their mothers' illnesses. "It sort of opened the floodgates," Claudia recalls. "It's like she was talking directly to me. Here I was sixteen and I'd gone through feeling I was selfish and wondering how I could have thought of myself when I should have been there for my mom and done all these things for her.

"I heard [the speaker] saying that that was a typical sixteen-year-old's reaction and there wasn't anything wrong with it. I went up to her afterward and I tried to talk to her, but I couldn't because I started crying."

Claudia is hard on herself not only for having exhibited an ordinary teenager's self-centered behavior but also for not intuitively knowing the truth despite her father's attempts to keep it from her. Holly had similar irrational feelings of guilt. Now in her fifties, Holly was seventeen and living at college, some fifteen hundred miles away from home, at the time that her mother's breast cancer was diagnosed. At the airport, ready to fly home for a school vacation, Holly phoned before boarding the plane "to tell my family how excited I was about flying. My aunt answered the phone. She usually wasn't there, so that was strange. But I still didn't know what was going on. When I got home, they told me my mother had had a breast removed. It had already happened. I had no knowledge of that whole hospital scene."

Holly's mother recovered for a time, but her cancer recurred four years later and she died when her only daughter was twenty-two. Holly says she didn't feel guilty about having been so far away from home while her mother was dealing with cancer. What disturbed her was the feeling that "here was my mom in the hospital, finding a lump, having a mastectomy, and I never *knew* it. I was doing whatever I was doing. . . . At the very moment she was having her breast removed, I could have been out having a good time.

"It was like I had failed her, but there was no way *not* to fail her. When your mother is having a serious operation, you should know or you should be there. You shouldn't not *know* that."

A year after Holly's mother died, her father became ill with leukemia and died very quickly. Within a year's time, young Holly had lost both of her parents to cancer. "Afterward, I thought there was something wrong with me," she said. "I mean, people twenty-three years old have parents! It was really strange, like I was somehow an aberration, like I deserved it for some reason. In some way, it almost didn't surprise me that this was happening to me." Like Claudia, Holly felt that she was in some way a bad person, deserving of punishment. Losing her parents seemed to be that punishment.

Children and teenagers often feel responsible for the bad things that happen to their families. Child psychologists explain that children believe the entire world revolves around them. So if something happens, the child thinks somehow she must have caused it.

Most of us outgrow that narcissistic stage of development without incident, but occasionally, if something traumatic happens in our childhood and we have no way to explore its true cause, we can be left with lasting scars. One daughter, for example, told me that as an eight-year-old, she'd been very angry with her mother, who was battling breast cancer. In her rage, the child sometimes wished her mother would die. Then her "wish" came true; her mother really did die. For years, this daughter was tormented because she secretly believed that her "evil thoughts" had killed her mother. She felt like a murderer.

Many children occasionally wish their parents were dead. That wish is a natural, and temporary, result of childish anger. But most people are adults, well past the stage where they believe they can "will" a person's death, before their parents actually die.

Too Much Responsibility

While Claudia and Holly both felt that somehow they hadn't done enough for their ailing relatives, that they hadn't "been there" for them, Elaine blamed herself for being less than perfect when she tried to help. Eventually Elaine lost her grandmother, her mother and her aunt to breast cancer, which has had a profound effect on her life.

When Elaine was fifteen and a sophomore in high school, her maternal grandmother moved in with her family. "My grandmother had an ulcerated tumor in her breast when she came to live with us, but she hadn't told anyone in the family," Elaine says. "I knew she had the tumor, because we shared a bedroom, but I didn't really know what having a tumor meant."

Elaine's grandmother didn't want to have surgery, so she asked Elaine to keep her condition secret. Elaine agreed, but she was uneasy. "I remember telling my grandmother on numerous occasions that she should tell my parents or go see a doctor and have something done about it," Elaine says, but her grandmother, who was in her late sixties, believed she would fare better without medical treatment.

Elaine felt torn. She wanted to honor her grandmother's wish and to keep her vow. Yet she also wanted her grandmother to live, and she suspected that her grandmother's avoidance of medical treatment was going to mean certain death. No matter what Elaine did, she was going to feel guilty. She agonized over what to do, confiding in no one. She was carrying a burden far too heavy for a fifteen-year-old's shoulders.

"Finally, after about a year, I just went and told my parents," Elaine says. "My grandmother immediately saw a doctor, went into the hospital and had the surgery. It was a Halsted radical mastectomy and it never healed properly. It always drained and caused her a lot of problems." Seeing how her grandmother was suffering, Elaine felt more and more guilty about having revealed the secret. "I thought, Well, maybe she was right in her thinking that the surgery would really just give her extra pain and discomfort."

Three years later, when Elaine was nineteen, her grandmother died. Elaine had tried her best to help, but she'd been unable to save her grandmother's life. Now she feared that, by setting in motion the events that led to the surgery, she simply had made her grandmother's last years more miserable.

When Elaine was in her mid-twenties and married with two children, she had what she saw as an opportunity for atonement. She and her family had been living on the East Coast and her husband had just received an offer for an overseas job. When Elaine called her family back in Chicago to tell them she would be moving to Europe, she learned that her mother had terminal breast cancer. "That day my mother had gone to the doctor and been told she had less than a year to live," Elaine says. "So we never really told her we'd been planning to go overseas. We made the decision to move back to Chicago and help my parents out.

"We lived less than two miles from them. I'm the family caretaker. I have two brothers and I'm the only daughter. I was actually highly experienced from [caring for] my grandmother and I was glad to have the opportunity to do something that I felt was personally gratifying to both my mother and me." Elaine was able to take care of the needs of her two small children, her husband and her dying mother at the same time—not an easy task but one she feels proud she was able to do. Yet putting so much energy into caring for others took its toll. Elaine feels her own emotional growth was inhibited as a result.

"Devoting your time to other people's problems and welfare has a tendency to take away from devoting time to your own self-development," she says. "I didn't recognize the fact that I had a lot of personal needs, so I neglected myself, thinking my first priority was always to help somebody else." Now forty-six, Elaine says she's still "sort of struggling" with her own growth issues. On occasion, she's found herself resenting the family members to whom she's devoted so much time. Then, shortly afterward, she will feel guilty for having those emotions.

Identifying with Mother

Another common source of guilt for daughters results from the natural identification of daughters with their mothers. If your mother loses a breast to cancer, you may not just fear that the same thing will happen to you; you may actually feel a sense of guilt, of disloyalty to your mother, if it does not. One reason for such a reaction, according to licensed clinical social worker Shirley Devol VanLieu, Ph.D., is survivor guilt. It's the same kind of emotion felt by the sole survivor of an automobile crash or a tornado—guilt over having survived while everyone else has perished.

Dr. Devol VanLieu, who practices on the Monterey Peninsula and in Tarzana, California, tells of recognizing this phenomenon in a woman who consulted her for advice about a breast lump. Shortly afterward, Dr. Devol VanLieu herself underwent a mastectomy, but her client's tumor turned out to be benign. "My client bought me this elaborate piece of jewelry," she says. "It puzzled me until we sorted it out together and discovered she felt guilty that I had cancer and she did not." Such a feeling of survivor guilt, Dr. Devol VanLieu says, can be far stronger in the case of two family members than in the case of friends or a clinical social worker and her client.

Shannon felt such guilt after her mother developed breast cancer. She was ten and entering puberty when her mother had a radical mastectomy. Because of her mother's illness, Shannon says, she grew up feeling "really uncomfortable with having breasts. First, because mine were healthy and my mother's weren't. And second, thinking that eventually mine were going to get cut off, too. I saw only the downside. I think it really had an influence on my self-image and my sexuality. I can't really say just how, but I know I have a definite discomfort."

Her mother's illness hit just when Shannon was most vulnerable. Psychologist Wendy Schain explains that "the most affected stage is puberty, when there's so much energy and attention focused on the development of breasts and there's so much anxiety and competition with Mom anyway."

Ronnie Kaye elaborates on the competition between mothers and their growing daughters. When their daughters move into puberty, she says, "on top of everything else, what the mothers feel is envy. Suddenly there's another woman in the house who gets to have both of her breasts while the mother may have lost one or both of hers." Some envy and rivalry is normal in any family because of issues related to aging, Kaye says. The daughter is becoming a woman just as the mother is starting to feel older and thus devalued in a society obsessed by youth and beauty. In a family where the mother has had breast cancer, these issues can become exaggerated.

Shannon intuitively may have been picking up her mother's anxiety concerning breasts and feeling responsible for causing the anxiety. Shannon's own breasts also developed early; there was no way to ignore them. She recalls a shopping trip with her mother when she was fourteen. The salesclerk commented that she looked at least eighteen. Shannon believes she looked older than she was because of her already fully developed figure. The clerk's offhand comment made her feel extremely uncomfortable, as though by having a womanly figure, she'd somehow hurt her mother.

The jokes her fellow adolescents frequently made about breasts were another source of shame for Shannon. "I was consciously aware of feeling guilty when people would make breast jokes, Dolly Parton–type jokes," she says. "I felt I couldn't laugh at them because if I did, I was being disloyal to my mom." She felt "real anger toward the people who were making these jokes. . . . It was just one more thing that made me feel cut off from mainstream society.

"I don't know if most young girls are terrorized by the development process or excited by it," Shannon adds, "but I just had a lot of fear and guilt and negativity associated with it because I felt like eventually I was going to end up like my mother."

Child psychiatrist Dr. Margaret Stuber says that a certain level of anxiety about the development of breasts is common among daughters of women who've had breast cancer. "They worry about what this means, whether they have to watch out for [cancer], and they think, I don't want to deal with this." A daughter who felt this kind of anxiety to an extreme degree, Dr. Stuber says, might "become anorexic so that she wouldn't physically mature and have breasts."

Shannon did not stop eating in an attempt to alter her body. She simply spent her early teen years trying to hide her large breasts, to pretend they were not really a part of her. She didn't date until she was in college, partly because she felt boys were attracted to her only because of her breasts. "I never really understood the fascination of men's attraction to the female breast," she says. "My association was so totally negative from an early age that I was really uncomfortable. Having large breasts and getting complimented on them [by men] was such an ironic message to me. I felt, What good are they? All they do is cause problems, and possibly death. I think there was guilt about getting complimented, too. It made me feel really weird."

It took her years, Shannon says, to begin to feel comfortable with her body. Part of that process involved checking out her perception that all men are obsessed with women's breasts. She entered a coed therapy group, where she forced herself to bring up the subject. "It was difficult to speak of things of a sexual nature with men in the group," she admits. But in doing so, she discovered what the men really thought about women and their breasts.

"We ended up talking about what men look for first in a woman. One man said he looked at a woman's whole figure. Another said he looked at her face. Another said he looked at her legs. That was a real positive experience for me. I thought they only looked at breasts; the guys I dated in college, that was their big thing."

Mothers' Guilt

Mothers, too, find plenty of opportunities to feel guilty. The form that guilt most often took among those I spoke with was the notion that by having breast cancer herself, a mother was somehow personally responsible for placing her daughters at higher risk. Dr. David Wellisch has seen such psychological torment many times in his clinical practice. "I saw the mothers so upset and grief stricken and guilty [that they were] almost unhinged with the notion that they may have genetically threatened their daughters," he told me. "It was bad enough that they themselves had this problem, but what seemed unbearable" was the thought that they might have passed it on to their daughters.

"The clinical presentation of that was the pacing of the mothers in my office," he added. Dr. Wellisch differentiates between levels of anxiety by noting that while bearable anxiety allows one to sit in a chair, unbearable anxiety forces one to pace. "And these were pacing issues for these women," he says.

Lillian knows that feeling firsthand. The mother of two adult daughters, she says the worst thing about her breast cancer is "the anxiety I feel about my daughters. Both of them are extremely high risk. They've not been married, they're in their mid-thirties, with no pregnancies, and they have a mother who's had breast cancer." Three months before we spoke, Lillian's only sister had also been diagnosed as having breast cancer.

Although it's been more than ten years since Lillian's mastectomy and she says her life generally is more fulfilling to her now than it was before she had breast cancer, she still feels "tremendous anxiety as far as my daughters are concerned. It's a subject I find very threatening. The statistics scare me."

Active in the American Cancer Society, Lillian works as a Reach to Recovery volunteer. Reach to Recovery is an American Cancer Society program in which volunteers who've had breast cancer surgery themselves undergo special training and later visit new breast cancer patients to offer them practical information and emotional support. Lillian is very knowledgeable about breast cancer research and extremely supportive of others in the work she does as a volunteer. Still, she told me that the thought of attending a mother-daughter seminar on breast cancer had been "too threatening" for her: she hadn't had nerve enough to go.

Lillian realizes she is not alone. She's seen other mothers in the support group she attends encourage their daughters to have prophylactic mastectomies as a preventive measure against breast cancer. "I think that's very sad," she says, "although the mother seemed to be behind the idea and relieved herself" when her daughter had this surgery.

Guilt and fear become mixed on this issue, of course. Women who have had breast cancer worry a lot about their daughters' chances of getting breast cancer, yet they also feel somehow to blame for their daughters' higher risk factors. It's almost as though they feel getting cancer was something they did to themselves.

At first glance, such a notion seems ridiculous. Surely no one *chooses* to get any kind of cancer. Yet some well-known doctors and psychologists propound the theory that we can help cure ourselves of cancer through positive thinking. Many women with breast cancer conclude that if their thoughts can help cure their breast cancer, then their thoughts must have caused it in the first place. They're consumed by self-doubt. Maybe they got breast cancer because they allowed their lives to be too stressful. Or because they repressed their own thoughts and desires while playing a caretaker role for others. Or because their personalities were too passive. Or perhaps they ate a bad diet or lived in a polluted city or failed to nurse their babies. Or—you can fill in the blank. These women learn to blame themselves for their cancer. And now, because *they* were foolish enough to become ill, they assume it is their fault that their daughters may someday suffer the same fate.

Many mothers feel "horribly guilty," says Ronnie Kaye. They believe they've "established a family history, that because they have this thing, they've created a risk for their daughters."

"Some of the mothers say, 'I gave myself breast cancer,' which is a notion I don't subscribe to. It can't just be that we're all creating it [in ourselves], because we used to be one out of fifteen women getting it and now we're one out of ten and [the ratio is] heading down." Kaye says, "I don't feel that women are running around giving themselves breast cancer, but I have women coming in saying that, and the guilt they feel toward their daughters is enormous. 'I gave it to myself and now my daughter can get it because of me' doesn't make sense, but that's how they feel."

At Memorial Sloan-Kettering, psychiatrist Dr. Jimmie Holland frequently sees the fallout of "the mind can cure the body" theories among her patients. Particularly hard hit are those women whose prognosis is for less than full recovery. The way such a "woman perceives this," she says, "is to feel, I really am a failure. I can't control the tumor. I got it in the first place and now I can't control it. What a failure I am. And that's an added burden" for the patient. She feels guilty as well as ill.

Dr. Shirley Devol VanLieu says that such negative reactions are the result of our culture, in which "people have a very difficult time separating responsibility from badness. For [patients] to know that they can affect their healing process [by altering their behavior] expands their choices and their options. But coming from a good-bad, right-wrong framework always includes punitiveness, and that has, unfortunately, the opposite effect." Because of our culture's propensity for blaming and punishing, Dr. Devol VanLieu says, we have a tendency to blame the victim; and the victim has a tendency to blame herself.

Dr. Holland told me, "A breast cancer patient stopped me in the hall yesterday to thank me for an editorial I wrote several years ago." In the article the patient had remembered, Dr. Holland had written, "Don't blame somebody because they got cancer and don't blame them if they're not doing well. It's unfair and it's an added burden." The patient wanted to let her know that she agreed and appreciated a public expression of that opinion.

"The data are very unconvincing to me that any personality type is more vulnerable to breast cancer, when you take into account the well-known risk factors like family history, having no full-term pregnancy or one very late in life—the known factors," Dr. Holland says, adding that "when you look at stressful life events like divorce or death and so on, there is no increase" in cancer of any kind when you study "large numbers of people. I don't think stresses of that kind relate to it."

If she already has breast cancer, can a woman change her prognosis for survival by some psychological means? Dr. Holland thinks that "the data are very poor indeed" that a woman can aid her recovery significantly by using some of the mental processes frequently recommended, such as picturing her immune system fighting her cancer cells.

The one psychological factor that Dr. Holland believes may make a measurable difference to a cancer patient's survival is social support. She cites, for example, a recent study published in *Lancet*, which involved "taking women with advanced breast cancer, working with them in a group, helping them deal with the situation. In no way [were the women told], 'You're going to live forever if you attend psychotherapy.'" These efforts, Dr.

Holland said, were apparently successful in helping these patients "to feel better, to control their pain better and to relate better with their doctors and families, because they were able to talk and face their situation more squarely. The women who had that participation, that kind of support, appeared to have survived longer."

Results of a similar study done by researchers at Stanford University and the University of California, Berkeley, were reported at the 1989 annual meeting of the American Psychiatric Association in San Francisco. Here, eighty-six women with metastatic breast cancer were divided into two groups and followed over a ten-year period. One group received only medical care while the other received medical care plus weekly group therapy sessions and lessons in self-hypnosis to help them control their pain.

By the end of the ten-year study, eighty-three of the original eighty-six women had died. However, the women who had received the psychological support lived an average of thirty-six and a half months, while the other group lived an average of less than nineteen months. The women who'd had the support of a therapy group had lived an average of nearly twice as long as those who received medical care alone.

Dr. Holland and other psychiatrists caution that such studies must be duplicated by other researchers to be considered definitive. However, Dr. Holland says, "we've seen that people who are elderly, who live alone and who are isolated have a greater mortality [in the case] of all diseases, so there may be some factor in social support that is important." But, she continues, there's no proof that psychotherapy or mental exercises of any kind can cure cancer.

Still, many women with breast cancer blame themselves for getting the disease and then for being unable to cure it. And if they are mothers of girls, they are very likely to blame themselves for putting their daughters at risk as well.

Control at Any Cost

Many of the women I spoke with, both women with breast cancer and their relatives, *wanted* to believe they could control the disease through some mental process. Daughters of breast cancer patients frequently told me they thought they were somehow safe from the disease because their personalities were so different from their mothers' or because they had learned from their mothers' experiences and were determined to live a different life-style. Frequently they had bought books espousing theories about the mind's ability to cure the body and given them to their mothers.

Women who said they had been cured of breast cancer often wanted to believe that they had been able to control the disease. This notion probably made them feel they would be safe if their breast cancer ever recurred. If they'd beaten it once, surely they could beat it a second time. Dr. Holland says that "we all want to believe" there's a connection between the power of the mind and the healing of the body. But she cautions that "it's very easy to say, when you're healthy and well, 'I knew all the time I was going to make it. I just *willed* it that way.' People don't give much credence to all the cancer treatment they got" after they've recovered. Still, Dr. Holland says, for the patient whose prognosis is poor, "that kind of nonsense doesn't help much."

Yet while medical treatment may be the most important factor, many physicians and mental health experts believe that emotional stress can damage the body's immune system. And a faulty immune system has a negative impact on health.

It's ironic. If we accept the theory that by thinking positively a woman can help cure her breast cancer, then making her feel she's to blame for becoming ill is obviously counterproductive. Certainly guilt is among the least positive of human emotions. So it seems to follow that a woman consumed by guilt over getting breast cancer and threatening her daughters genetically may well be worsening her own physical condition because of her mental anguish.

Relieving Guilt

We must learn to forgive ourselves for our real and imagined transgressions if we are ever to overcome guilt and achieve emotional peace. Often, a careful check of our perceptions against reality is the first step in this process.

For instance, women with breast cancer who study the probable causes of the disease eventually realize that there's no real logic to the idea that they gave it to themselves. And there's even less logic to the idea that they've done something to cause their daughters to be at higher risk. It's appropriate for a mother to feel sorry that her daughters might eventually have to go through the ordeal she has gone through, but she needn't feel responsible.

A reality check helped Claudia feel less guilty about her behavior toward her mother. Her turning point was when she realized she was not the only sixteen-year-old in history who'd been unwilling or unable to meet her dying mother's needs. When Claudia learned that her behavior, while not totally laudable, was simply typical for her age, she felt an immediate sense of relief. Maybe she wasn't such a bad person after all; maybe, in fact, she was just average.

Holly also finally realized that she was not guilty of the charges she'd lodged against herself. There was no way she could have known what no one had told her: that her mother was undergoing breast cancer surgery. The fact that she didn't have extra-sensory perception didn't make Holly a bad person. When she was able to look at the situation logically, she also realized that the deaths of her parents could hardly be her punishment for some unknown infraction. Cancer is a disease that can hit anyone at any time. The way a child behaves doesn't bring it upon her parents.

For her part, Elaine now sees that her grandmother put her in an untenable position by asking her to keep her breast tumor secret from other family members. No matter what decision she had made, Elaine would have blamed herself for making the wrong choice. Now, as an adult, she has learned to forgive herself for not being perfect.

One additional lesson Elaine has learned from her many family experiences with illness is not to ignore her own needs forever in the cause of serving others. In addition to nursing her grandmother and mother through their final illnesses, Elaine was later called upon to care for her father-in-law and a paternal aunt, both of whom died of cancer. More recently, her husband has had two heart attacks and subsequent cardiac bypass surgery and her sister-in-law has died of breast cancer, leaving behind two young daughters. At the time we spoke, Elaine told me that her own recent mammogram had shown a slight change in her breast tissue that her doctor will be monitoring carefully.

Elaine's life has been full of the stresses of caring for others and the deaths of her family members. But it's led her to a new philosophy about the heavy expectations we place on ourselves. "One thing I want to give to my daughter and my nieces," she says, "is a strong concern for their own self-development and interests in life. While they are caring for other people, [I want to let them know that] their own needs must be looked at and dealt with first. Only through personal strength can they give to others."

Elaine has learned that harboring guilt undermines personal strength, so she has stopped blaming herself for things beyond her control.

To be human is to be imperfect. We do what we can with what we have at the time. And although we later may regret the actions or words we choose in an instant of crisis, the past cannot be changed. Perhaps, if a careful examination of reality convinces us that we truly are culpable in some way, an apology will relieve our guilt. Depending upon the situation, an apology can be made in person, in a letter that may or may not be mailed, or at a grave site.

But we must learn to forgive ourselves, to stop dwelling on our shortcomings and to focus on developing our own personal strengths.

CHAPTER 7

Solitary Confinement

"I THOUGHT NOBODY could understand what I was going through," one daughter told me. "When my mother got sick, it made me feel weird, like I was different from all my friends."

"I was the only one I knew who didn't have a mother," another said, "and I didn't want people feeling sorry for me. So I didn't talk about it."

A third explained that she "couldn't tell my family's secret." She would have felt disloyal.

These daughters of women with breast cancer, like many I interviewed, kept their thoughts and emotions to themselves. Predictably, they felt at varying times fearful, angry, and guilty. But because they didn't talk to anyone about what they were experiencing, they were also very lonely.

Having breast cancer in the family can be very isolating, particularly when we try to keep outsiders from knowing about it. And even when we do risk being open with our relatives and friends, we sometimes find rejection instead of the support and understanding we need and want.

Children and teenagers, in particular, often feel ashamed when a mother gets breast cancer. They don't want to be different from their peers, especially in a manner that has sexual

127

undertones. UCLA child psychiatrist Dr. Margaret Stuber says that many children experience a real sense of shame when their mothers get breast cancer. Suddenly they are no longer like their friends, and they feel "contaminated." These negative feelings are frequently intensified by the taunts of other children, who are cruel to them, Dr. Stuber explains, in an effort "to deal with the fear that it could happen to them, too."

For instance, playmates of a girl whose mother has breast cancer may avoid her or treat her as though she is weird. A playmate is likely to have the natural "feeling that if this could happen to her, it could happen to me, too," says Dr. Stuber. "You can fight that feeling by making [the affected child] different from you in some way." Thus, a playmate might try to distance herself when a friend's mother gets breast cancer by saying, "That wouldn't happen to me because her mother is really stupid and that's why it happened to her." Or "They're just weird people, and that's why it happened to them. It wouldn't happen to me; my family isn't weird."

Dr. Stuber counseled one girl who was mortified by a schoolteacher's misdirected attempt to be kind. Dr. Stuber quotes the child: "My teacher announced that my mother had breast cancer in class and asked everyone to have special patience with me. I hated it." If this girl hadn't felt isolated from her classmates before the teacher's announcement, she certainly did afterward.

Often the young daughter of a woman with breast cancer will try to keep others from learning her secret by retreating from her old friendships. Or if her peers already know about her mother's having breast cancer, they may shun her because they feel threatened. Either way she feels isolated.

The desire to fit in with our peer group can last well into young adulthood. Lyn felt it at nineteen, when her mother's breast cancer was discovered. Four years later, she told me, "We'd been going through a lot of things around that time and I thought, Now Mom has breast cancer. That's just one more thing that puts a stigma on our family. If I could have joined another family, I think I would have."

Lyn now says she's ashamed that she ever wanted to change families, but she still feels somewhat stigmatized. When her mother had her mastectomy, Lyn says, "I got worried about my relationships on down the line, that if I got involved in a serious relationship with a man, I'd have to tell him that my mom had had breast cancer." What if that man rejected her when he found out? Yet despite her stated determination to reveal her family's secret to any future lovers, when I called Lyn to arrange an interview for this book, she was living with a man who didn't know about her mother's illness. She asked to talk with me while he was away from the house.

Later Lyn told me, "When I spoke to you, he wanted to know who was on the phone." Initially she didn't want to tell him; then she changed her mind. "I thought, This is crazy. I'm *living* with him, so I just told him. At first he really didn't take me seriously. He's met my mom and he said, 'She's so wonderful and outgoing and together. How is that possible?'"

Lyn convinced her boyfriend that she was indeed serious about her mom's having had cancer, but she denied that the reason she hadn't told him earlier was that she'd been worried about his reaction. "I don't know; maybe I'm scurrying past the issue again and not thinking about it," she told me. Lyn hadn't really planned to keep the information secret, but as she said, "Here's this person I really care about and I didn't tell him. Who knows when I would have brought it up?"

Now that she has shared her secret, however, it has brought them closer together.

Many daughters simply withdraw from their friends when their mothers' cancer is diagnosed. They crawl into a protective shell that others cannot penetrate. In effect, they reject others before they themselves can be rejected. And often they see this self-isolation as a form of loyalty to their mothers, a way to keep the family crisis private.

Amelia is typical. She was in the eighth grade when her mother became ill and died of breast cancer. "I remember there was this boy at school who liked me," Amelia, who is now twenty-five, told me. "For him to phone me had seemed so important, and he was phoning me a lot. But one day, when I realized my mom was dying, I just stopped the relationship. I never talked to him again because this was a family secret, a private secret, and I couldn't let him know what was going on.

"He'd come up to me afterward and try to be nice to me and I would just say, 'Hi,' and walk away. I think it was easier just not to be friends than to be friends and try to keep the secret."

Amelia says her closest girlfriends knew about her mother's death, but that "it was always awkward. Nobody knew what to say." Counselor Ronnie Kaye can appreciate the feelings of such a child. "These kids have nobody to talk to," she says. "They're afraid to confide in anybody because they don't think anyone else will understand and they're afraid of being abandoned."

Amelia felt branded, set apart from her peers. "Somehow for the longest time, wherever I was, somewhere in my subconscious was the thought, My mom's died. I've been through death. So even when I was laughing with people, I could never laugh wholeheartedly because there was that sadness in me.

"I think that because of my mom's death, I've had a problem with intimacy with people," she told me. "Part of it is because I'm afraid of getting hurt again. But another part is that there's this tremendous darkness inside me. I feel like I carry such a burden and it's ugly and it's difficult. When I was growing up, the issue with most of my friends was that their parents were getting divorced. I'm still the only one who has had a parent die." Until recently, Amelia felt certain that no one else could understand what she'd experienced. Her own life had been too different from everyone else's.

"Even today, I'll see my girlfriends have lunch with their moms," she says. "Their moms are so involved with their lives, and that hurts." Being around happy mothers and daughters reminds Amelia that she is an outsider, that her own mother is dead and she's completely on her own.

How we react to a crisis like breast cancer in the family depends in part, of course, on our individual temperament. Dr. Stuber says that "some children will withdraw, some will fight back, some will act out their emotions in various ways. They'll become rebellious and difficult at home or moody and irritable. Often they'll be angry with their mothers for having done this to them, but then they'll feel very guilty about that."

How our families have taught us to deal with our emotions greatly influences how well we cope. For example, those of us who have been taught that it's not okay to talk about how we feel often become the most isolated and lonely when illness and death strike. That is true of Veronica, who is from a stereotypical stoic New England family that disapproves of any display of emotion. Just twenty-one when her mother died of breast cancer, Veronica at forty-five is still suffering. Repressing her feelings for years, she says, has resulted in a lifelong loneliness, a feeling she's frequently tried to assuage with food.

It's only now, in therapy, that Veronica is remembering exactly what happened during the months her mother was ill. The youngest of four sisters and the only one still living at home during that period, Veronica says, "We were all very self-contained, isolationist kinds of people. We were all expected to cope by ourselves, and I don't think anybody asked me for support. It was something my mother took care of herself as much as she could."

Veronica's mother had a radical mastectomy, which left her with trouble moving her arm. Veronica describes the surgery as "a pretty brutal carving," but says that she never doubted it had cured her mother's cancer. "I didn't know enough about cancer to know it could come back. I just thought she had this terrible surgery and life goes on. No one expected much emotion about it because we didn't ever express much emotion. It was a stoic, coping kind of situation." In her family, you did what you had to do and didn't complain.

The surgery took place in the fall and Veronica returned to college soon afterward, assuming that life would go back to normal. But the next spring her mother was unable to attend an important event at Veronica's college. "I confronted her and she told me she wasn't well," Veronica recalls. "I asked what was wrong and all she said was 'It's more of the same.' It was a real shock to me. I just didn't expect it. I'd thought it was over and done with. I don't know how long she'd known . . . but nobody had told me."

By summer, Veronica was terrified that her mother might die, but she couldn't talk about her fear. "As a teenager, I was virtually alone, pretty much an only child," she told me. The sister nearest in age to Veronica was six years older than she was, and Veronica doesn't remember "living with any of them in the house very much. I never felt very nurtured. Everybody was kind of in their own little world. The messages I got were 'Don't make any waves. You're not supposed to be real needy. And you don't ask for what you need.' So of course I never did. I didn't know what I needed, anyway, so I didn't get it."

Veronica believes that her mother was more nurturing of her older sisters than of her. "By the time I came along, I think she wanted to get out in the world." Still, her mother was the one family member with whom Veronica ever felt any rapport. Her sisters were cold and distant and her father was a stern, strict man.

"I was a lonely kid and I cried a lot in my room," she says, "but I did talk to my mother. She was my mainstay in the family, the only one I felt I had. I remember thinking that she was a real buffer between Dad and the rest of us, and that if she died first, it would be awful."

Veronica's mother had lost her own mother when she was only fifteen. "She died of cancer, but I don't know what kind," Veronica says. "Nobody ever talked about it. Nobody ever shared more than they had to in my family, and we learned not to go digging." Still, Veronica remembers her mother's lament that her mother had died before they'd had a chance to become good friends. Now, Veronica says, "By God, the same thing happened to me. I was in a real painful time and I didn't get to a place where I felt happy enough with myself to get to know my mother."

As her mother's illness progressed, Veronica made a last-ditch effort to close that gap. At the end of her college term, she decided to withdraw from school and move back home to be closer to her mother. "It was a very strong drive I had, to be at home, and nobody seemed to question it," she says. "Now that I look back, it seems odd to me. I should have stayed in college. I should have kept on with my life, but I don't remember anyone encouraging me to do that." Ironically, her attempt to become more a part of her family by leaving school ultimately made Veronica feel even more like a misfit: her three sisters were all honors graduates of prestigious Eastern women's colleges.

Veronica couldn't talk to her family and she couldn't confide in outsiders, either. "Cancer was a secret. You didn't say the word in those days," she says. "People knew, but they didn't call it by name the way they would other diseases." In fact, when she was dying, Veronica's mother refused to go to the hospital where she'd worked as a volunteer. Instead, she insisted on going to another facility where no one knew her.

"My mother was in the hospital the last week of her life," Veronica says. "I saw her there once and I was so devastated by what I saw that I couldn't go back." On the day her mother died, Veronica was working downtown, but "nobody called me. I walked into the kitchen when I got home and saw my older sister cooking our supper. She said, 'Oh, Mother died today. Do you want peas or beans?' That sort of thing."

Veronica remembers going to find her father. "Dad was sitting in the den, poker-faced, watching TV. I went up and put my arms around him, which was about all I could muster, and said, 'We're all together now.' That was the most comforting thing I could think of to say, but it was really stupid, because we weren't together. I guess that's what I wanted it to be."

At the funeral home, Veronica says, "we all took tranquilizers so we could be jolly and happy and smiling. I remember, for the funeral, I didn't want to take a tranquilizer. I wanted my feelings to come through. When I saw a friend burst into tears, I did too. But one of my sisters came over and tried to hush me up and put me in a corner. She told me, 'You don't display your emotions this way.' I needed to cry and everybody was crying all over the place. Everybody except my family."

It wasn't until many years later that Veronica realized her desire to express what she was feeling was normal and that eating to keep her feelings "stuffed down" inside of her was not. By that time, she required psychotherapy to help her identify what she was feeling and talk about it, something her parents and sisters had never allowed her to do. "I've stopped even trying to be close to my sisters," Veronica says. "I don't feel I'm allowed to need them, and they don't need me for anything. If you have no needs going back and forth, there's no closeness."

Now when she looks at her father and sisters continuing to keep their own feelings bottled up and festering, she says she feels she's the "most emotionally healthy" member of the family. But to change, Veronica had to emerge from the sterile prison of her family and to risk revealing herself to others who would understand and support her.

Risking a Connection

In order to gain support, we, like Veronica, must risk connecting emotionally with others. We must take a chance and talk about our feelings. And that means we must be willing to risk rejection. Psychotherapist Ronnie Kaye knows from her own experience how that feels. "There's a terrible stigma," she says. "Somebody would find out that I was being treated for breast cancer and suddenly would turn around in a supermarket and walk away from me."

Such an experience is what every breast cancer patient fears. "I have patients coming to me for the first time saying, 'I feel like a leper,' " Kaye says. "They're not the ones who are cancer phobic. They can handle it if somebody else gets it. But when they get it, they feel like a leper. And they're afraid they're going to be treated that way. The word *cancer* conjures up a picture of horrible, painful death for many people. [If they have it], people feel unclean."

It's easy to see why breast cancer patients and their families can fear others knowing about their disease, and why they might expect rejection. Frequently enough, their negative expectations are fulfilled, but if they withdraw from others, making no attempt to connect with them, they risk isolating themselves completely. Therapist Sandra Jacoby Klein points out that patients often need to learn how to communicate with others about a subject as sensitive as breast cancer. "Frequently family members or friends avoid the patient or make ridiculous remarks. Patients then tend to withdraw or say, 'Well, it didn't really matter anyway.' It becomes easier not to communicate.

"Sometimes patients won't call friends back because they don't want people to pity them," she adds. "So they get into this erroneous thinking" and they end up alone. If women can learn to communicate about breast cancer, she says, they can learn "to ask for what they need."

The ideal way to open communication, Jacoby Klein says, might include a patient saying something like this to her family or friends: "I've gone through this experience [of having breast cancer] and I really would like to share my feelings with you. I'd like some feedback as to how you feel, how it has affected you, what you think about it, how you perceive me going through this. This is something that has affected both of us and I think it would be helpful if we could talk about it. But if you're not able to, I'll respect that."

Many women fail to ask for what they need, Jacoby Klein says, because they don't think they'll get it. But "there's also the possibility that they *will* get what they need. We have an equal chance to get what we want."

Even when our attempts to communicate with family and friends are thwarted, we needn't settle for loneliness. Emotional support can be found in places where we traditionally have not sought it. Ronnie Kaye, for instance, says that she made many new friends and discarded some old ones as a result of having breast cancer. None of us needs a friend who won't stand by us during a time of trial, and the sooner we know which kind we've got, the better off we are.

Support and a needed boost in self-esteem can be found among others who have shared our experience, Kaye says. "If you sit in a room full of good, solid people and every single one of them is dealing with breast cancer, how bad can we all be?" Such an experience helps a woman who's feeling like a leper check her view of the situation against reality. If she defines herself as unclean, what does that make the other women in the group?

Kaye recommends seeking inspiration from role models, people "who've been there and are terrific. Look for women who've maintained or increased their self-esteem" after having breast cancer. Dr. Shirley Devol VanLieu agrees. She says, "After my own surgery, I very much appreciated my Reach to Recovery contact, and I realized that one contact was not going to do it [for me]."

Because she wanted continuing contact with other women who'd been through her ordeal, Dr. Devol VanLieu formed her own group through ACS. "We called it the Mastectomy Assistance Program—MAP," she says. "I surrounded myself with other women who could say, 'My surgery was twelve years ago' or 'My surgery was twenty years ago.' In that way, in the group, we learned to shift our attitude." By getting to know women who had survived breast cancer for many years, the newer mastectomy patients begin to expect to survive themselves. Death from the disease no longer seems inevitable.

The same kind of help is often available for daughters of breast cancer patients. Amelia, for instance, is grateful for an ACS-sponsored group she attended. For the first time in her life, she found herself among others who understood precisely what she had experienced as an adolescent, among other women of all ages who knew just how it felt to have a mother undergo mastectomy surgery and to fear getting breast cancer themselves. Several of these women, like Amelia, had lost their mothers to breast cancer and were able to share their feelings with her. Suddenly, Amelia says, she no longer felt odd or alone.

Reading about others who have felt as we have, who have experienced similar events in their lives, does help us realize we are not alone. Still, reading about other women's experiences, while useful as a way to boost our self-confidence and change our attitudes, is a solitary act. We should then take the next logical step and risk exposing ourselves and our secret feelings to others. The easiest way to begin is to find others who will, because of their own similar backgrounds, understand what we have to say.

One way to locate such people is to utilize a cancer support system such as the American Cancer Society or an outreach program of a hospital specializing in cancer treatment. Such organizations may offer continuing support groups. If they don't, Ronnie Kaye suggests that women form their own groups with the assistance of such organizations. In most cases, these services are available free or at minimal cost.

For those who find entering a group to be too frightening, one-on-one contact with a trusted friend or relative or with a trained psychotherapist can provide a first step. The important thing is to take the plunge, to begin to talk about our feelings with someone in whom we can confide, someone who will understand. That accomplished, we will find ourselves no longer alone.

As counselor Kaye says, "I don't think there's anything as painful as unfinished business. Human beings have an intense need for closure. It's like a drive we have to finish things." And as long as we hold ourselves apart from others, hoarding our secrets, we will never find closure. We will never be able to live normal, open lives. We will forever condemn ourselves to loneliness. "Unfinished business is forever unfinished" until we deal with it, Kaye says. "It doesn't matter if it's two hours, two years or twenty years."

Luckily, however, it's never too late to recognize and deal with our feelings about breast cancer in the family. By taking a small risk, we can make contact with others who have had similar experiences and will understand what we have gone through. With their help, we can emerge from solitary confinement as stronger, healthier, happier women.

CHAPTER 8

Peas in a Pod

ANTHROPOLOGIST MARGARET MEAD once said that the relationship of sisters "is probably *the* most competitive relationship
within the family, but once the sisters are grown, it becomes
the strongest relationship."

Her sister, Elizabeth Mead Steig, added that a woman never
gives up her sisters. "You were born with them and you die
with them. Or they die and leave you, and you feel absolutely
discomfited."

Shortly afterward, Margaret Mead died of cancer.

When a sister has breast cancer, we are likely to feel many
of the same emotions as when a mother has it: fear, anger,
regret, loneliness—all of the negative feelings that accompany
loss. But there is one significant difference: a sister is almost
always a member of our own generation. We expect that our
parents will die at some point in our lives. But when a sister
has a life-threatening illness or dies, it challenges our own sense
of immortality. If this can hit her, we think, can I be far behind?

On the positive side, most of us are adults by the time a crisis
like breast cancer strikes a sister. If only because we're likely
to be older, we tend to be better able to handle the emotional
repercussions of a sister's illness than a mother's. Yet depending

upon our individual personalities and how close we feel to our sisters, we may well still be devastated.

Some women, such as Dallas socialite Nancy Goodman Brinker, feel they've lost their best friend when a sister dies of breast cancer. Brinker founded a research foundation in honor of her sister, Susan Goodman Koman, who died of breast cancer in 1980 at the age of thirty-six. Four years later, Brinker discovered a malignant lump in her own breast. Luckily, she found her own cancer early enough for successful treatment. Appointed to the president's National Cancer Advisory Board in 1986, Nancy Brinker now frequently speaks publicly about her life and devotes her time to the Susan G. Koman Foundation because she doesn't want other women to suffer the way her sister did.

All sisters may not be as close as Nancy and Susan Goodman were, but it's difficult to imagine a situation in which a woman would remain completely untouched by her sister's breast cancer. As adults, sisters may have their own separate lives and families, and indeed may even live thousands of miles apart, but the ties that result from children growing up together are binding.

The Family Curse

Forty-nine-year-old Rita knows that well. She grew up in the Midwest, a middle child in a family of seven sisters and three brothers. Since Rita was in her late thirties, three of her sisters have had breast cancer; two of them have died of the disease. As an intensive care nurse, Rita is accustomed to dealing with suffering and death on a daily basis. Yet when a member of her own family is affected, she's found that professional distance becomes impossible.

Her oldest sister, Myra, was the first to be diagnosed with the disease, Rita says. At first the family believed the cancer had been detected early and that Myra's radical mastectomy had cured her. But less than a year later, cancer was discovered in Myra's remaining breast and her health began to decline rapidly.

"I remember going down to see her the week before she died," Rita says. "I was thinking how bad she looked." Myra wanted to travel to an Arizona cancer clinic in a final attempt to find a cure. "I remember going out and buying her a suitcase and a special nightgown for the trip," Rita says, but she doubted that her sister would survive the journey. A few days later, Myra entered a local hospital and died at the age of fifty-four. She left a husband and nine children.

Myra was sixteen years older than Rita and, Rita says, "by the time I grew up, she'd already left home." But both sisters later ended up living on the West Coast, where they became good friends. "She could relate to me on a nurse level, too," Rita says. "I think it made her feel good to know that I really knew how she was feeling and where she was going."

During Myra's illness, another sister, Beverly, who was forty-nine at the time, found a lump in her breast. By the time she sought medical treatment in the small Pennsylvania town where she lived, Beverly's cancer had invaded both of her breasts, as well as her lymph nodes. She died shortly after Myra, leaving a husband and seven children.

At the time of Myra's death, Rita was only thirty-eight, and, she says, "Fifty-four seemed old to me. But now I'm forty-nine and I think about her a lot. She never really got to see any of her grandchildren."

Temporarily, the family saw Myra's illness as a random event. "When one sister has breast cancer in a family of ten," Rita says, "you can believe it's the luck of the draw. But when our second sister got it, we all became very panic-stricken and decided we'd have to alter the things that are known to be cancer-causing."

Rita and her remaining sisters tried to rationalize why both Myra and Beverly had been struck down by breast cancer. "We tried to find a common thread," Rita says. Yet none was evident. No women in previous generations of the family had had breast cancer. Neither Myra nor Beverly had been smokers or drinkers. They didn't even drink coffee. Both had given birth at a young age, although neither had nursed their babies. Rita believes that the high-fat, meat-and-gravy diet on which the entire brood had been raised may have had some influence, along with the fact that both Myra and Beverly were slightly overweight and had been under considerable stress in the last years of their lives. Still, no indisputable explanation could be found.

As she had with Myra, Rita became involved in helping to care for Beverly during her illness. She flew the three thousand miles to be with her sister on several occasions, and she managed to be there when Beverly died. "It was much, much more difficult with her in the sense that we'd already gone through it" with Myra, Rita says. The two sisters' deaths so close together, both from the same disease, had a severe impact upon the remaining siblings.

Rita vowed to be particularly vigilant about her own health; if she ever got breast cancer herself, she thought, she'd find it early and she'd get the best care. She would not die as her sisters had. Rita told herself that she had accepted her own increased risk and felt that she would be able to deal with it rationally, but she hadn't reckoned with her subconscious mind.

Am I Next?

When Rita eventually did find a lump in her own breast, she didn't react like an experienced intensive-care nurse; she reacted like any terrified woman who'd seen two sisters die of breast cancer. "I went into an absolute panic where, literally, I went to bed and pulled the covers over my head," she says.

First, Rita observed a bloody discharge in her bra. "Being a nurse, I know I should have run, not walked, to the nearest doctor," she admits. "But I was so panicky that I refused to believe it was there. For about a week, I absolutely denied it." Trying to tell herself that her eyes were playing tricks on her, Rita says she "was looking at it every five minutes," hoping to find that the evidence had disappeared. After several days of obsessively checking her bra for signs of blood, Rita's fingers located a "tiny little lump, the size of a pea [in her breast]. Having two sisters who died of breast cancer, the minute I saw that, I thought, This is it, this is my death sentence, this is how it's gonna be. I didn't even tell my husband."

Rita allowed more time to pass, continually reassuring herself: "I bet that lump isn't even there. This is just my mind playing games on me." One night in a restaurant where she and her husband were having dinner, Rita says, "I just broke down in tears. I told him what was happening and he said, 'My God, you've got to go to the doctor right now!'

"We were planning a trip to Alaska," Rita recalls, "and I remember thinking, I just can't deal with this right now. I'll deal with it when I get home. Classic denial. I couldn't believe myself. *Me,* of all people! I thought I was so strong about meeting things head on."

Luckily Rita had a physician friend at a San Francisco oncology clinic who specialized in needle aspirations of breast lumps. On her husband's urging, she called her friend, who told her to fly to San Francisco immediately; he would perform a needle aspiration of the breast lump and she would have a preliminary diagnosis within a few hours. After performing the test, the doctor told Rita he was "ninety percent sure" it was benign. He gave her permission to go to Alaska, but said she'd have to have a surgical biopsy when she returned.

After Rita returned, she took the time necessary to find a highly skilled surgeon with whom she felt comfortable to do the biopsy. Because of her family history of breast cancer, he "did what's called a segmental resection: he took a lot more tissue than they normally do and luckily it was benign."

Because of her own experience, Rita was able to provide direction for a third sister, Liz, who later found a lump in her breast. Liz flew in from her Denver home and saw the same surgeon who had done Rita's biopsy. Unfortunately, Liz wasn't as lucky. Her lump was malignant and she had a modified radical mastectomy. However, because Myra's and Beverly's deaths had alerted Liz to the dangers of breast cancer, hers was found early enough that it had not spread. She has now survived well past the five-year mark.

Rita believes that going through the terror of finding a lump in her own breast and finally being able to deal with it has purged at least some of her fear. "The doctor reassures me that if I do get breast cancer, he's sure they'll find it early. I get checked every six months, I try to check myself every month, and I have a mammogram every year."

Still, Rita would love to find some outside factor, some behavioral pattern her sisters may have had in common that she could blame for their breast cancer. "I'd like to be able to point to diet or [lack of] exercise," she admits. "Then I can think I won't get it because my eating habits are good and I exercise regularly. I wish that I had some real evidence it was something other than the hereditary factor."

Anger and Guilt

Gillian worries about the hereditary aspects of cancer, too, for her four daughters even more than for herself. Before her sister, Nora, was diagnosed with breast cancer when she was only twenty-eight, they had lost several other relatives to various kinds of cancer. "My mother died of ovarian cancer," says Gillian. "Her mother died of uterine cancer. Then right after my mother's death, her brother died of a brain tumor. My family really went through a lot."

Gillian's mother lived only twelve weeks after her ovarian cancer was found. "My sister and I pretty much spent most of our time at the hospital from the time we found out," Gillian says. "When we took her into the hospital, we thought she had congestive heart failure." Instead, the diagnosis was an advanced stage of ovarian cancer. "At that point, we were all so stunned. My mother had a ticket to go to Europe on a sabbatical. She was going to write a book and study for a while. We didn't know what hit us."

Adding to the burden, during this crisis Gillian's husband left her. Suddenly she was alone for the first time in her life, left with the responsibility for her dying mother and four teenage daughters.

Shortly after her mother died, Gillian says her sister "found a lump in her breast and went to the gynecologist. He tried to extract fluid, but couldn't. But he said it was nothing. Then she had a mammogram and they said it showed nothing.

"Nora was at UCLA at the time and she kept saying to me, 'Oh, Sis, when I carry my books I have a lot of pain and a shortness of breath.' She sensed something was wrong, but nobody would believe her. Everybody told her, 'Don't be neurotic.' " Nora was told she was "too young" to have breast cancer.

Like Rita, Gillian and Nora also had a friend who was a cancer specialist, a surgeon. Nora called and asked him to remove her lump as a favor to her. He told her to come into his office as an outpatient and he would perform the procedure. Nora went to the appointment alone because Gillian had a meeting that day and she too was convinced that her younger sister's lump couldn't possibly be malignant.

The next day the surgeon called Gillian at work and asked her to come to his office and to bring Nora and their father. "The second he said that, I knew," Gillian says. "Nora was so bright, she picked right up on it, too." The lump was indeed malignant. Nora had a lumpectomy, and an examination of her lymph nodes indicated that her cancer had metastasized. She had both chemotherapy and radiation treatments, a process Gillian remembers as "horrendous."

Because of her divorce, her job and her children, Gillian says she was not able to provide as much support to Nora as she would have liked. "I was drained from my mother's death," she says, "because a lot of what I had to deal with when she died were the feelings of my daughters, who'd adored her and were just devastated by her death, and their sudden panic that the same thing could happen to me. They were aware that my grandmother died extremely young and my mother died very young."

When her children learned about Nora's breast cancer, Gillian says, their reaction was that "their aunt was going to die. That's all they'd ever heard or seen [of cancer]. They knew that my grandmother did and my mother did and then my uncle. . . . So when Nora got it, they thought, Oh my God, it's just coming right through the family. They looked at me and were very frightened. So a lot of my energy was going back into my children at that point."

She did her best, Gillian says, "but I just had a hard time dividing my time to be there for all my daughters and also for Nora." As a result, "Nora became very angry, and the angrier she got, the more guilty and frightened I got. I couldn't really be there for her. I couldn't give her what she wanted. Nobody could."

Gillian and Nora had always been close. Although they were born nine years apart, into what Gillian calls different generations, and they lived very different life-styles, they always spoke daily by telephone. Still, Gillian feels that Nora, as a single woman with no children, did not understand the pressures a newly divorced mother of four necessarily feels. "It's taken a long time and a lot of talking, a lot of communication in areas that are very painful" for the sisters to work out the strong emotions that emerged during Nora's cancer treatment.

Gillian felt that Nora unfairly made her the target of her anger. "She was very angry that no one had taken her seriously and that the cancer had gone this far. She was angry that her mother was dead and that she had to go through this alone. She had a feeling of total abandonment. She felt sick, so she was edgy," Gillian explains. She took the brunt of Nora's rage.

"Another thing I realized is that the person going through chemotherapy is fighting for her life. Her entire world is what she's going through—the getting sick, the throwing up that's so awful. But the other person who isn't having chemotherapy, her daily life still consists of money problems, business problems, her children, her routine."

Gillian felt guilty whenever she became depressed about her own problems or even frustrated by a bad day. "I'd be trying to find a way to get to the hospital, to be there for my sister, and I'd feel, How could I get so upset with my problem? It always seemed so petty compared with what she was going through." Those hospital visits were a trial for both sisters. "I'm very sensitive," Gillian says, "and it was very difficult to go there and be yelled and screamed at. I had a very hard time with it, and Nora knew I had a hard time with it. It hurt so much."

The pressure was so intense that Gillian feels she fell apart. "I was trying to run a business and raise my children, go here and go there, to do what could not be done in a day and still get to the hospital to see my sister and be supportive for her.

"You want to be superwoman—the best sister, the best mother, the best employer—and you don't know how to balance everything." Predictably, because of the stress in their own lives, Gillian's children became more demanding than usual.

Luckily, Nora survived her breast cancer. Since that time she has formed a support group for young people with cancer and their families, making her personal ordeal the basis for helping others. The group also allows her to find support among other young people who truly understand what she's experienced because they've been there themselves.

Gillian says she and Nora are still working out their feelings about the ordeal of Nora's cancer, "but I think we've come a long, long way. I'm comfortable now talking to Nora about it." And Gillian feels that Nora has come to understand the problems in her sister's life much better.

Still, strong emotions creep back on occasion. For instance, seven years after Nora found her lump, she and Gillian appeared on a panel made up of breast cancer patients and their sisters. The public event triggered fears that Gillian thought she had conquered. "Being in a crowd, I found it was really hard to deal with the feelings that just came pouring out. One of the things that jolted me so much was [realizing] the recurrences that had taken place with so many of the sisters there, up to seven, eight, nine years later. That was very upsetting to me to listen to, and I think Nora's very aware that it could happen to her" again.

Gillian was so upset by appearing on that panel that she entered psychotherapy, which she feels has been extremely helpful. "I don't care who it is, I really believe that some therapy is needed when you've gone through something like this," she says. "You feel guilty even when you're off having a good time and someone [in your family] has cancer. It's hard to enjoy your good fortune as well. You can't win. I highly recommend therapy to sisters who go through this."

Gillian worries more about her daughters' health than about her own. She feels her risk of breast cancer is lower than Nora's because she has gone through four pregnancies, the first when she was only seventeen. In addition, she had a hysterectomy at a young age because of hemorrhaging, so she no longer has her ovaries or uterus. "I don't think about cancer [for myself] too much," she says, but adds, "I would think about it all the time if I still had my ovaries."

She urges her daughters to have regular checkups. "What I keep saying to them is that I now believe cancer can be cured; it's simply a matter of timing. I ask them to become friends with their bodies, to be very aware, to know every inch of their bodies."

Gillian has changed her diet to cut out meat and most fat and she has annual mammograms and does monthly breast self-examinations. "Somehow, I feel if I get breast cancer, I'll probably find it very early." Yet she adds plaintively, "If breast cancer is really connected to stress, I've got a real problem."

Shared Lives

Madeleine and Rachel have experienced many of the stresses that Gillian and Nora did. And because they live together and are partners in a small bakery-delicatessen business as well, their lives are even more intertwined.

The sisters have radically different personalities—Rachel is quiet and serious, Madeleine more volatile, outgoing and humorous. Yet each counts the other as a best friend with whom she seldom argues. They've learned to make allowances for their differences, but their experience with breast cancer strained both of them to their limits.

Madeleine found the lump in her breast when she was forty. "I'd just had a breast exam maybe three or four months before" and the doctor had found no lumps, she says. She'd never had a mammogram.

When she discovered the lump, Madeleine took immediate action. She went to see her gynecologist the next day and he did a needle biopsy, then sent her for a mammogram. She thought she was home free when the radiologist who read the mammogram told her that he saw nothing amiss and that she should return in five months for a follow-up exam.

"I might have come back in the five months or I might not," Madeleine says. "But the results of the needle biopsy came back the next week and they were pretty bad. I'm totally grateful to that doctor [who did the needle biopsy], because I feel like he saved my life. He said to my mother, 'I don't really know why I did that [needle biopsy]. I haven't done one in twenty years.' "

Rachel has her own recollections. Madeleine "told me right when she thought she felt something" in her breast. I felt [the lump], too, and I couldn't tell" whether it was anything to fear. Initially, Rachel says she was not worried because "my sister is a really nervous type. She gets worried before she has to. I figured it was nothing. Then, of course, I was really upset when we got concrete results."

Rachel says that although she's seven years younger than Madeleine, she's the one who was the more informed about breast cancer. "I was praying [her surgery] would end up to be a lumpectomy," Rachel says. "When that prayer didn't come to pass, then my next prayer was that the lymph nodes wouldn't be affected. At least that prayer got answered. But my sister is the kind who didn't even know she *had* lymph nodes. I'm the one who always read about breast cancer. I guess I was always afraid of it, just as a woman."

The sisters have since discovered that they have a family history of the disease. There are no known occurrences on their mother's side, but three of their father's sisters had breast cancer, and a daughter of one of those sisters had it as well.

Madeleine's treatment was a modified radical mastectomy followed by a year of "light chemotherapy," she says. "They promised me I wouldn't get sick [from the chemotherapy], but I did." She missed about two days of work with each of her monthly treatments, which meant that Rachel had to pick up the slack at the bakery.

The cancer could not have been discovered at a worse time for the sisters. Right before Madeleine found the lump, both of their bakers, their only two employees, quit. Rachel, whose son at that time was three years old, was getting a divorce, and the housekeeper who had cared for the little boy also left.

While Madeleine was hospitalized for her mastectomy, Rachel says her mother and a friend would come into the bakery mornings to help out. Rachel herself would both bake and deliver products nearby. And a close friend who was dealing with cancer in her own family frequently made the more distant deliveries in the afternoons.

"It was really overwhelming for me," Rachel recalls. "I couldn't take the time out to grieve [for either my sister or my marriage] because I'd have five sets of eyes staring at me wanting tuna fish sandwiches, and the phone was always ringing off the hook" with inquiries about Madeleine's health. "So I'd have to fill everybody in with all the details about her operation and work at the same time. I was going crazy. I was actually at the brink." Rachel says she felt as though she didn't know "who was going to take over when the adrenaline ran out, because it was getting absurd." However, she figured that "if I didn't have a nervous breakdown then, I never would. That was the good news."

When Madeleine was able to come back to work, things improved, yet she couldn't handle the work load she had coped with before her illness. And, Rachel recalls, "sometimes she would just say, 'I can't take this anymore,' and break down and cry. In a way, I wished I could cry, too. But to me that was just so impractical. You've got to do what's in front of you. If later on in the day you want to sit down and cry, okay, but not now.

"I don't feel I was that compassionate because I was just so overwhelmed," Rachel confesses. "I didn't feel like I had one more piece left in me. I was there a hundred percent for my son and the business and trying to make it on a day-to-day basis here and keep it going. I thought, I'll take care of my kid and I'll keep the business together, but I can't do one more thing." Rachel has now resolved the guilt she was feeling about her lack of compassion by accepting that she couldn't "be everything to everybody. I had a lot of stuff I was going through myself and I would have liked more support, too."

Madeleine, who was unmarried, had moved into Rachel's house when the younger sister's husband had walked out. The arrangement was seen to be financially advantageous for both sisters. As it turned out, it also helped provide needed emotional support for Madeleine.

"For me, the most important relationship is with a sister," Madeleine says. "To me, that's like having a built-in friend. The parents are kind of like the enemy when you're growing up. I was alone so much [as a young child]. I remember the day my mother told me she was pregnant. I just couldn't wait until [Rachel] was old enough to play checkers. I never resented her at all. My mom and dad worked, so I took care of her."

Those roles were reversed when Madeleine got breast cancer, a reversal that taught her Rachel had grown up. "She's my baby sister," Madeleine admits, "so sometimes I treat her as though she's still six. But I got to see that she could keep things together when I'm not there [at the bakery]. She did a really good job. So I got to be able to let go. I felt I was always there for her and I got to see that she was always there for me."

Madeleine says that she doesn't know what she would have done without either her sister or her mother during her ordeal. "Especially emotionally. My mom kept saying, 'It's just a matter of time. It'll be all right.' The chemo was just a horror for me. My whole life revolved around it. It made me really mad to have to go through it and feel sick. I'd be feeling up for three weeks and then be sick again."

Madeleine also admits that the chemotherapy made her "real emotional. I'd cry over the least little thing." She felt guilty about having to rely so heavily on Rachel. "I think in her secret thoughts she was probably scared because I was so sick," she says. "Her husband had just left a year before, so it probably seemed to her like a lot of abandonment. Then all this responsibility—a lot fell on her."

Luckily, a woman Madeleine knew volunteered to help her through her chemotherapy treatments. A casual acquaintance, Madeleine says, "heard I was having a lot of trouble when I went to chemotherapy. I'm not one to reach out. I always think I can do it myself. But she said, 'I'll go with you if you want.' One of the hardest things I ever had to do was say yes. I wanted to say, 'No, I can handle it.' But I really couldn't. My mom used to go with me, but she was trying to help my sister in the store and she couldn't be in two places at the same time. That girl came with me every single time for a year. It brings tears to my eyes. There are people out there who really do care. She didn't want anything but to be of service. Now we're really close friends, so that turned out to be really nice.

"I came to see that you really aren't ever alone unless you want to be." While she was ill, Madeleine wanted someone with her all the time. Rachel recalls that Madeleine would lie on the family-room sofa after her chemotherapy treatments. "She was deathly afraid of being alone even though she was sick and out of it for the first and second day. She'd still call [the business]

and ask, 'Is Mom leaving? Is she coming over? I don't want to
be alone.' And then she'd cry."

Everybody Feels Like a Victim

Rachel admits that she resented those phone calls somewhat.
"A part of me said, 'Great! Here I am, all alone in the store
and you want Mom to come with you. I could use her help.'"
But Rachel realized that the chemotherapy had affected Madeleine emotionally and she handled things by herself as best
she could.

"Everybody feels like a victim," she explains. "Of course I
would not want to trade places. My sister's the real victim in
this case, but everybody's victimized in other ways. My mom
and I had to swallow a lot because of the emotional strain on
everybody. [Madeleine] was usually pretty short with us, so we
had to bite our tongues."

Rachel says that while Madeleine was undergoing chemotherapy treatments, she "wasn't in a place where she cared about
anybody else's problems. She was the victim and she was really
self-obsessed about it. Like she was feeling, 'I don't want to
hear about how anybody else is hurting but me.'" Rachel did
not feel that Madeleine was able to hear about her problems
at that time.

Yet Madeleine wasn't as unaware of her sister's burden as
she might have appeared to be. She told me she felt guilty for
having had to lean on Rachel. "I hated having to ask her," she
said. "One part of me realized I got to rest when I had the
chemo, but it wasn't like it was a good rest because I was sick.
Another part of me felt, 'Oh, I can't really go to work tomorrow,
I just can't help her.' She'd say, 'Don't worry about it. Just relax.
It's just a matter of time.' She had the mothering role."

Three months after Madeleine's mastectomy, the strain finally
overwhelmed Rachel. She was hospitalized with pneumonia for
eight days. "They couldn't figure out what kind of pneumonia

I had," she says. "I was so weak. I lost twenty pounds, and I'm not that big anyway."

Rachel sent her mother to help Madeleine run the business "because I knew she couldn't handle it by herself. My ex-husband went out of town on vacation, so I really had no one to turn to. I think it was my body breaking down because you handle it until you don't have to."

Rachel says she never would have gotten sick while her sister was in the hospital because "that wouldn't be practical. I'm the kind who gets sick after the last final exam. I'd never get sick during finals." So she lay in the hospital all alone, feeling weak and lonely and trying to be grateful to her sister and mother for keeping the business afloat and caring for her son. And she fretted about her little boy's having to deal with so many crises in his young life.

At the time I spoke with Madeleine and Rachel, things were beginning to look better for them. Rachel had recovered from her bout with pneumonia and Madeleine had finished her chemotherapy treatments and had just undergone breast reconstruction. "You can tell the difference in my sister's personality now, after her reconstruction," Rachel says. "She's feeling better about herself."

Madeleine agrees that her sense of humor has returned, a sign that her psyche is healing. Laughing, she told me about finding her three-year-old nephew standing over her discarded breast prosthesis, pretending it was a cake and the nipple a candle. He was singing "Happy Birthday" at the top of his lungs.

Both sisters say that Madeleine's breast cancer has given them a new perspective on each other, although Rachel says she hardly needed this kind of test to show that she could handle responsibility. "Madeleine sees me as her baby sister and I see myself as this power [source]. I see myself having a lot more responsibility than she does. I raise a child by myself and I'm practically supporting him. I have a house and a mortgage. I pay all the bills and I have a business that I have to worry about.

I don't make much money. I'm just barely making it to pay the mortgage. I already have a lot of responsibility."

Still, Rachel says, she and Madeleine are "really close. We do more things together than most sisters, so I think we experience more good and bad than most because of the intensity." Madeleine agrees. "She's my best friend. We live together, work together, play together. As much as we are together, we never fight. Sometimes we get in each other's hair, but she's got my father's disposition. She's very laid back and I'm the crazy one. Sometimes we get on each other's nerves, but then we're apart for an hour and we never have a blow-out fight."

At this time the sisters were making plans to have their widowed mother move into the house with them. "I'm sure she's going to get on my sister's nerves and my nerves at times," Rachel said. "But for the most part we're really close and we have a pretty good way of communicating. We're always together anyway and this is a financial advantage." Her mother will help with her son, too, Rachel says with relief. "There'll be somebody home when he comes home from school. He's thoroughly attached to both my sister and my mother. That's his family."

Sibling Rivalry

Not all sisters, of course, lead lives as intertwined as those of Madeleine and Rachel. Some live hundreds of miles apart while still dealing with the issues of sibling rivalry well after they've reached adulthood. When breast cancer strikes such sisters, and particularly when it seems bound to occur in every woman in the family, it can cause them to reevaluate their relationships with each other.

Bonnie was only twenty-nine and the mother of an infant daughter when her husband felt a lump in her breast. She'd had a similar lump, judged benign, removed when she was in high school, so she didn't worry too much about it. "It crossed my mind for maybe one second that it could really be cancer, because I'd been through this before," Bonnie says. "I don't think anybody expected it to be cancer until I was in surgery." She was still lying on the operating table when lab results indicating that the lump was malignant were returned. "They gave me a choice of either doing the lumpectomy right then or coming back in, so I decided to do it then," Bonnie recalls.

Eleven days later, she returned to the hospital to have her lymph nodes removed and biopsied. Unfortunately, the nodes showed signs of cancer, and Bonnie was scheduled for both chemotherapy and radiation treatments.

Bonnie, who lives in Colorado, is the eldest of three sisters. Certain that the lump would be benign, she chose not to tell her younger siblings, Pam, who lives in California, and Cindy, who lives on the East Coast, about her biopsy.

Pam, a year younger than Bonnie, recalls how she learned about her sister's illness. "My mom called on a Thursday and she sounded kind of different. I was taking a class at the time and she asked me when my final was. I told her it was the next day, and she said to call her [afterward]. When I did, she told me, 'I've got some bad news. Your sister has breast cancer.' It was the furthest thing from my mind."

But Pam wanted to help. Trained as a medical technician, Pam knew many people in the health field. She immediately began calling her doctor friends for advice on Bonnie's prognosis and treatment. Concentrating on the scientific aspects of Bonnie's breast cancer, Pam says, was her way of dealing with her fear of losing her older sister.

Pam and her mother flew in to be with Bonnie when she had her lymph nodes removed. "I don't think I was much support to her emotionally," Pam admits. Her contribution was mainly to help with Bonnie's baby, Tammy, and housekeeping chores. "We weren't real close as kids and I think that came into play here," Pam says, adding that the only occasions on which they see each other now are special family visits, with all of them on their best behavior.

Both Bonnie and Pam say that restraint in displays of emotion

is the pattern in their family, as are efforts to protect other
family members from painful truths. They also agree that they
have very different personalities. Bonnie and the youngest sister,
Cindy, "were real close growing up," Pam says. "They're both
introverted, they have the same interests, they went to the same
undergraduate college. I, on the other hand, was into sports
and real extroverted. I was always closer to my dad than my
mom." In Pam's view of the family she grew up in, she and her
father were pitted against the other three.

"My senior year in high school, Mom tried to get more involved in my life," Pam says. "I was a gymnast and I would
never tell her my schedule. I'd just say, 'I've got a meet tonight.
Can you pick me up afterward?' But that year she called my
coach and got a list of meets. She went to every one and she
got parents to provide refreshments. Mom made every effort
to come into my life, but I kept pushing her away."

Pam now regrets this rejection of her mother, partially because she's worried that she may lose her mother to breast
cancer, too. Rosemary, the mother of Bonnie, Pam and Cindy,
found a lump in her own breast while she was visiting Bonnie
to help her cope with the last of her chemotherapy treatments.
"I was supposed to stay a week and a half," Rosemary told me,
"but [Bonnie's] husband got sick and the baby got sick, so I
stayed an extra week. I felt some pain in my breast and went
to rub it and I felt a lump. I'm not sure that that lump wasn't
there three to four years prior, because I had felt what I thought
was a lump [at that time]. I'd gone to my OB and had a mammogram, but it showed nothing. As far as they were concerned,
it was nothing, so I ignored it, but I have a feeling it was the
same lump."

Rosemary told Bonnie about her lump before she left Colorado to go home to Arizona. Mother and daughter discussed
what to do about it and Rosemary decided to see her own doctors
back home rather than seek medical treatment in Colorado.
Feeling intuitively that she had breast cancer, Rosemary found
a surgeon who agreed that if her biopsy was positive, he would

perform a lumpectomy rather than the modified radical mastectomy that was the standard treatment in the area where she lived. "I was very against the mastectomy," she says.

Where she was terrified by her daughter's breast cancer, Rosemary says she felt her own was rather anticlimactic. With Bonnie, she says, "it was very, very scary. She was young, the baby was young, and at the time, my husband was very sick. He'd been sick for several months. I didn't know which way to turn. I felt I should be up there with her but also that I should be down here with him. For any of the kids, I always tried to be there for them whenever something has happened. It was very hard not to be there for her [when she had the biopsy done]. I felt very guilty."

Another of Rosemary's recurrent thoughts was "Why her? Why not me?" Within a year, both mother and daughter had the disease. Yet, Rosemary says, "that didn't really bother me. Maybe it's because with a daughter you're more upset than if something happens to you. Hers seemed so much more [important] to me than mine did." In addition, because she'd seen that her daughter could have breast cancer and survive it, the disease was no longer as frightening to Rosemary.

Although Bonnie knew about her mother's lump, Rosemary elected not to tell either Pam or Cindy until after the surgery was done. Pam had had her own health problems, having undergone many operations for a persistent knee injury, and Rosemary says she wanted to save her additional worry. "It's just that we thought if we could say, 'Mother's okay, she's fine, she's home,' that would be so much better."

Pam didn't see it quite that way, particularly when she learned that Bonnie and Rosemary had already spent considerable time discussing the operation before it happened. "My little sister and I got the feeling that Mom and [Bonnie] had strengthened their bond with what they were going through, but that we were sort of on the outside." Yet Pam didn't tell her mother how disappointed she'd felt about being closed out during this critical time until many months later. Rosemary thought she'd handled things well, but Pam told her, "If you talk to [Cindy] and you talk to me, you'll discover that we didn't like the way you did it at all."

Rosemary was stunned. She later told me that Pam "to this day has never, never forgiven us" for not telling her about the biopsy in advance. "Apparently she contacted my youngest daughter and they have decided that we don't tell them everything. I will never do that again. I know they have a right to know. We just thought it was such a minor thing. I knew I was going in [for surgery]. I was convinced it was cancer, I knew what they were going to do and that I would come home the next day."

Pam says that the thought of her mother's prognosis was far more threatening to her than her sister's. "Several times throughout the day and every night, all I would think about was my mom dying. With my sister, that was my initial feeling, but then I thought, 'Well, she'll be okay.'" Bonnie, after all, was young and otherwise healthy.

"With my mom," Pam says, "it was like a recurrent nightmare that I'd get a call saying, 'Come home, your mom is dying.' Mom had had a chest X ray taken. She's a smoker. She'd had positive findings in it before and they'd said it wasn't cancer, it was calcium. I kept thinking the radiologist was wrong and it really was cancer and it would be too late." Pam also worried about an abnormal cyst on her mother's finger. She wanted her to have it biopsied for bone cancer. "I just feel that my mom doesn't have as good a chance as my sister," Pam says, and that scares her.

Who's Next?

Pam also has valid concerns about her own health. In addition to the many operations she has had on her knee, which have discouraged and depressed her, she fears breast cancer. Since her mother's surgery, she's found two lumps in her own breasts.

When she found the first, she says, "With the family history, I thought, Now it's me."

Like many women in similar situations, Pam says, "When I first found [the lump], I kept checking it every night, thinking it wouldn't be there the next time I'd check." But it didn't disappear. Then occasionally she'd become so depressed about the prognosis for her knee injury, which had kept her from working for several extended periods, that, she said, "Sometimes I thought, Good. I won't do anything about [the lump] and that'll be it. That's one of the reasons I put off doing anything about it." Pam's despair occasionally made her feel nearly suicidal.

"My other fear," she said, "was that I was working and it was so hard to find a job after my [knee] surgery. I didn't want to lose it. I had already planned in my mind what I'd do if it was cancer. I thought I'd take a week's vacation and have a lumpectomy and radiation. I would change my hours at work. And if I had to have chemotherapy, I'd do it on Fridays." That would give her the weekend to recover.

Somehow, keeping silent about her lump "got to me," Pam said. "I told my internist, and he told me that if [the lump] was still there in a month, we'd do a biopsy. Then he went on vacation." But Pam wasn't willing to wait for a month. She went to a breast center and had a biopsy done on the lump. She was so certain she was doomed that she almost didn't believe the surgeon when he later called and told her the lump was benign.

Only six months later, however, Pam found another breast lump. "At first, I thought, No way. I don't want to go through this again. I'm tired of doctors. I decided to wait a while." But she grew more and more terrified of getting breast cancer. She read an article in a popular magazine that she interpreted as saying her chance of getting breast cancer was seven hundred times greater than normal. She began to talk about what she'd do *when* she got breast cancer, not *if* she got it.

Pam went before a tumor board at her local hospital. Such boards bring together experts in surgery, oncology and radiology to consider individual cases. "One of the surgeons asked me, 'Since you're so sure you're going to get breast cancer, have you considered a prophylactic mastectomy?' I said, 'Not on your life.' Even to save my life, I don't know if I'd do it."

The surgeon who did her biopsy supported her decision. He told Pam that while she did have lumpy breasts, she did not need a prophylactic mastectomy.

Despite her chagrin that her mother and sister had kept their biopsies secret from her, Pam seriously considered handling her own situation alone. Because of her long history of surgery on her knee, she told me, "I feel all I bring to the family is problems. So I've got to the point where I share as little as possible. I'm sick of talking about it and I'm sure they're sick of hearing about it." Not wishing to burden her family with another health crisis, she nearly didn't call to tell them that she'd found a breast lump.

However, "my friends insisted that I call and tell my parents," Pam said. "I purposely called when I knew I would get my dad. My dad's very logic oriented. He doesn't deal with emotion, so I could call and joke around about it and make light of it. I knew I would get the information out, but I wouldn't get an emotional response back."

Searching for Emotional Support

Rosemary sets a difficult example for her daughters to follow. Through her stoic behavior she conveys the message that it's not good to be too emotionally needy. Rosemary says she "didn't really want support from my daughters. What I wanted was to know they cared. I have always been very, very strong. I may be fearing something, but I don't let other people know mainly because I don't want to upset them. I've never let things get me down as far as illness goes."

After her lumpectomy, Rosemary set out to prove to herself and others that "none of this had really affected me." In her mid-fifties, she changed jobs at the department store where she worked, taking one that required strenuous physical labor. She wanted to prove, she says, "that I could do the same job as well as any young kid that they had in the store. And I did. In fact I was working with one of the young girls when I first went back and she told me, 'This is the hardest day I've had in my life, trying to keep up with you.' I needed that, to prove that I didn't change, that it didn't change me."

Bonnie tried to measure up to that norm. She went through her surgery and follow-up radiation and chemotherapy treatments with few complaints. In fact she was so stoic that most of her coworkers didn't even know she'd had cancer or was undergoing medical treatment. She managed to convince herself that her case of breast cancer was no more than an uncomfortable episode in her life, one that she could put behind her. There would be no tears, no emotional scenes from Bonnie.

But several events clustered about a year and a half after her surgery, she said, "threw me for a loop. A friend had breast cancer a year ago. She had a modified radical and six months of chemo and they found no trace of cancer in her lymph nodes. This spring they discovered cancer had spread to her lungs. They did chemo and in May she started having severe pain. She died July first. It was really hard."

A second shock was the recurrence of cancer in one of Bonnie's coworkers. "Then," she says, "they ran the Jill Ireland story in *Life* magazine. All of a sudden this belief system I had just fell apart. The last week of May, I really freaked out. I couldn't deal with it. I'd go to bed just crying. All the things I'd pent up for twenty months . . . I just fell apart.

"I found myself wondering if I was going to see my baby grow up and thinking of all these books I was going to read and wondering was I going to have a chance. I was panicked and angry."

Bonnie did not turn to her mother or sisters for emotional support, however, but to a close friend who'd had cancer herself. "Seventeen or eighteen years ago, when she was sixteen, my friend was diagnosed with a very rare form of cancer. At that time she was told she'd be lucky to live six months. She's now

thirty-four. She's in remission, but there's still something there."
After having endured more than a dozen major operations and
been the subject of medical journal articles, Bonnie's friend has
learned to live with cancer.

"She deals with her own cancer on a year-to-year basis,"
Bonnie says. "So I was able to talk to her and get some perspective on my own fear. She gave me some hints for dealing
with it. It was real helpful to have someone to talk to on that
level. I'd seen her as someone who was really brave and stoic,
but she said that every time she has an ache or pain she's not
familiar with, she gets scared.

"Her philosophy is that you deal with one day at a time and
live it to the fullest—all those nice old things. That helped."

Pam has also needed emotional support, but like Bonnie, she
hasn't sought it from her family. Pam says it helps to talk to
friends and to attend American Cancer Society events where
she can gather with other sisters and daughters of women with
breast cancer. She wishes similar organized assistance were
available for people with such debilitating injuries as her knee
problems. Occasionally Pam admits to feeling a little envious
of women who have breast cancer because there seems to be
such a vast support network available to them. "Sometimes,"
she told me, "I almost wish I could trade my knee problems in
for cancer."

When Rosemary has needed someone to talk to about her
own or her daughters' health problems, she's often turned to
her coworkers. "There's been a lot of cancer where I work,"
she says. She's helped set up a network among the women there
so they can turn to each other for help whenever they feel it's
necessary.

Although they haven't become close-knit by the standards of
some families, Rosemary and her daughters all say that the
invasion of breast cancer into the family has forced them to
reassess their bonds with each other. Bonnie says, "I think things
happen for a reason, and maybe one reason I had to deal with
[breast cancer] was so that when my mom got it it wouldn't be

such a traumatic experience [for her]." As for her relationship with Pam and Cindy, she says, "As we were growing up, I don't think we were really friends. Now I think we're closer, but I don't really feel the bond that some of my friends have with their sisters."

Pam thinks she's become closer to her mother because of her fear of losing her. "I can't undo thirty years of being closer to my dad [than to my mom]," she says, "but I think I feel comfortable now with my mom's and my relationship. We've been getting closer and closer. I've gone home several times and spent days with my mom. In fact, I've been becoming more like my mom, which has been interesting.

"I think a lot did change after the cancer," Pam says. "I went home one time because she was having trouble moving her arm after the surgery. I did some exercises with her and sent her to a therapist I knew." Getting the chance to help her mother made Pam feel closer to her. It's difficult to feel close to someone who never seems to need your help.

Individual Patterns

Each family is made up of individuals who have their own patterns of relating to one another. In some families fears, angers and regrets are discussed openly; in others, emotions are hidden. Still, all of us have these feelings when cancer strikes.

Some sisters, like Rita's, live far from one another but never fail to share important life events. Their separate lives may preclude frequent visits, but they feel bonded nonetheless. So when breast cancer claims one sister, the others mourn the loss and become more and more afraid for themselves as well as for their remaining siblings.

Sisters like Gillian and Nora share each other's lives—different though they may be—intimately. Such sisters feel safe enough with each other that they can risk the occasional demonstration of a cutting tongue. Friends and lovers, we all know, may abandon us if we dare strike out at them in a crisis-evoked rage, but a sister remains bonded for life.

Madeleine's and Rachel's lives are so intertwined that they share their work, their home, their innermost thoughts. Breast cancer reinforced their already secure knowledge that they could rely on each other through the worst of life's trying events. Both sisters feel free to be strong or to be weak. The episode of Madeleine's breast cancer taught them that they can exchange roles when necessary and that their love and respect for each other will continue to survive and grow.

Even families like Rosemary's, in which members seldom share their feelings, can't help but be changed by breast cancer's invasion. Rosemary and her daughters are taking small steps closer to each other, slowly beginning to change a lifelong pattern of hiding their emotions from one another. Without this crisis as a catalyst, progress might never have been made.

As the old Spanish proverb says, "An ounce of blood is worth more than a pound of friendship." In going through an ordeal such as breast cancer in the family, we may discover that, with a sister, we are fortunate enough to have both blood ties and a strong and lasting friendship.

CHAPTER 9

The Men in Our Lives

BECAUSE THE BREAST IS such a sexual part of a woman's body, it's impossible for it to be attacked by cancer without a woman's sense of herself as a sexual creature being altered in significant ways. Some women who've had breast cancer withdraw from sexual relationships completely, feeling they are no longer "complete." Others, in an attempt to prove that they remain unchanged by the disease, may become more highly sexed than before, sometimes seeking short-term sexual encounters with a variety of men. For others, changes may be more subtle. But a reassessment of both sexual attractiveness and sexual desires is to be expected.

The men in these women's lives are affected, too. Myth has it that many marriages end because of the wife's losing a breast to cancer. However, most experts believe that few men leave their wives for that reason alone. A man might have wanted to leave his wife in the past but wasn't able to; he may now use her cancer as the excuse for finally making that move. Another husband may try to reassure his wife of his continuing affection, may argue that his feelings haven't been changed by the disease, only to have his wife not believe him and reject him. Such women leave their husbands, either physically or emotionally or both, because they themselves feel sexually altered in some destructive way.

Still other couples, the emotionally healthiest, use the frightening situation as an opportunity to examine their relationship and grow closer to each other. Realizing how tenuous life can be, they learn to cherish each other more deeply and to appreciate the days that remain to them.

All of these are common human reactions to breast cancer, and all of them can have a profound influence on a daughter who observes them in her parents. Without realizing why, a daughter whose mother has had breast cancer may develop a negative body image, a distrust of men, or the sense that she is somehow tainted sexually because she is certain that she too will someday have the disease.

While some of the women with whom I spoke said they admired the way in which their parents handled the crisis, more elaborated on their own problems in relating to men, problems that seemed to stem from their mothers' having had breast cancer. Most of the daughters disliked their own bodies, often criticizing the size or shape of their breasts. Some of those who saw their parents' marriages crumble after breast cancer avoided becoming emotionally involved with men. One woman said she'd married and had children far too young, in an effort to use her sexuality "while I still had it."

In another case, two sisters told me that they actually blamed their father for giving their mother breast cancer. He'd been having an affair with another woman for years, they said, and they believed the stress of dealing with his infidelity had caused their mother's illness.

Taking Mom's Place

One common problem source is noted by Dr. Wendy Schain. If a mother with breast cancer becomes unavailable to her partner either emotionally or sexually (through emotional withdrawal or death), she says, "the father may switch his energies into an overzealous attention to the daughter." Such a change can leave the daughter confused about her appropriate role in life as well as her sexuality.

That happened to Cassie, who was an infant when her mother underwent a radical mastectomy. Although she has no conscious memory of her parents' relationship with each other before the breast cancer, Cassie says that after her mother's mastectomy, her parents no longer shared a bedroom. "My mother was in the master bedroom," she told me. "For a long time, I was in a crib in the back bedroom and my father slept in a double bed in the same room. My brother had a separate room" for himself.

When Cassie grew too big for the crib, she sometimes shared the double bed with her father. At other times he slept on the living room sofa. "I grew up thinking that was normal in some bizarre kind of way," she says.

As an adult, Cassie has not been able to form a lasting bond with a man. She married briefly when she was twenty, then divorced. Now in her late thirties, she says she's "attracted to a certain kind of man who is withholding. I seem to get involved with very smart men who I have to go after, and then either they leave me or I'm not interested anymore. I see it, but I don't know exactly what to do about it.

"I have a hard time seeing how much I should be there for men and how much they should be there for me," she says. "So sometimes I do the wrong thing."

Cassie's parents presented a distorted picture of male-female relationships to her when she was a child. In an inappropriate way, her father used her as a source for the emotional nurturing that he needed but couldn't get from his wife, even to the point of sleeping in the same bed with his young daughter.

Cassie says her body image is "horrible. I've always been thin. I eat like a horse. My mother is always trying to get me to gain weight. As a result, I got it into my head that I was never okay being thin.

"I've always been self-conscious about my breasts being small, too. My mother had very large breasts, about a 36C or D. I think if I could just gain weight in my breasts, I'd be okay."

Cassie feels that breasts are the most important part of a woman's body and sexuality. That's a negative legacy from her childhood. As soon as her mother lost her breast, she stopped functioning as a sexual woman; thus a woman without breasts, or even without *large* breasts, is asexual. Subconsciously Cassie feels that, like her mother, she can't function as a sexual woman. Her breasts are too small. And even if she had larger breasts, she says, she fears that she would eventually lose them to cancer, as her mother did. These long-entrenched beliefs have profoundly affected Cassie's ability to relate to men.

Sex and Body Image

Drs. Schain and David Wellisch are among the researchers who studied a group of sixty daughters of breast cancer patients and compared them with a similar group of sixty women whose mothers did not have the disease. The most significant area of difference they found between the two groups, Dr. Wellisch says, was in sexuality and body image. The daughters of breast cancer patients engaged in sex less frequently and were less sexually satisfied than the control group. In addition, they had poorer body images.

"I think if there's one area of vulnerability for the mothers, it's in the sexual realm," Dr. Wellisch continues. "I think daughters identify with that. It's their weak link in all of this." Dr. Wellisch stresses that the daughters were not "pathologically low in either sexual frequency or sexual satisfaction. They were simply lower than the controls." He theorizes that women who expect to someday be mutilated in cancer surgery may be more reluctant to develop their sexuality and to learn to take pleasure in their bodies.

Funded by grants from the American Cancer Society and the National Cancer Institute, this study was the first scientific examination of the lives of daughters of women with breast cancer. Further research remains to be done before it can be determined if the results of this study have implications for the general population, however. The one hundred and twenty women interviewed were drawn from the affluent Westside of Los Angeles. All Caucasians, they ranged in age at the time of the study from twenty-two to sixty-three. Slightly more than half were Jewish, and they tended to be highly educated and very health conscious. In addition, they were self-selected, having responded voluntarily to a notice in the *Los Angeles Times* requesting participants for the study. Dr. Wellisch notes that this group is not typical of the general population and that he hopes other studies will be undertaken to test the study's findings in various other social strata and in different geographical regions. Interviews with daughters of breast cancer patients who are less educated and with those who find it too painful to volunteer for such a study would also be most useful.

Interviews were conducted in 1987 and 1988 and, by early 1990, the final results had not yet been published. Prior to publication, however, Dr. Wellisch reported that the daughters of women with breast cancer who participated in the study generally were mentally healthy as adults. Those whose mothers had not adjusted well to having breast cancer tended to be more troubled, however, which leads him to conclude that providing mothers with psychological support at the time of crisis would also ultimately help their daughters.

Those daughters who were most severely affected by their mothers having had breast cancer were those who had been adolescents at the time the disease struck. "We had expected to find that little girls were the most severely affected," he told me, "but that wasn't the case. It was the adolescents." Those daughters who were at their most vulnerable age sexually, at the time in their lives when their thoughts were dominated by love and romance, were the most traumatized by their mothers' having surgery for breast cancer. These daughters may unconsciously have stunted their own sexual development because they feared that they would someday lose the most visible symbol of their femaleness. Assuming (wrongly, by the way) that the loss of a breast would mean the loss of any sex life, they avoided learning to enjoy their sexuality and their bodies. After all, it doesn't hurt as much to lose something you've never learned to appreciate.

Communication Between the Sexes

In healthy relationships, of course, the woman's loss of a breast to cancer does not stop the couple from having sexual relations. In fact, some couples report improved relations simply because the cancer has taught them to appreciate each other even more. But in less healthy relationships, often it's the failure to communicate openly about emotions, not the loss of the breast itself, that comes between a woman and her man.

Lorna, the daughter of a woman with breast cancer who herself had the disease before she was thirty, spoke of the effect it had on her marriage. "It pulled us together, but it also drove us apart." When they first learned that the lump in Lorna's breast was malignant, she and her husband rallied and made quick decisions about her medical care and about their young child. Lorna had a lumpectomy, followed by radiation and chemotherapy treatments that lasted about a year.

Several months after her surgery, after the surge of adrenaline during the immediate crisis had worn off, the couple began to experience problems. "We had a pretty lousy summer," Lorna admits, "not communicating, coexisting in the same house, wondering if we'd made a mistake [by marrying] and wondering if it would be better if we just split up."

Lorna now realizes that it wasn't the breast cancer itself that threatened her marriage; it was the different ways she and her husband have of dealing with a crisis. She admits she is not comfortable talking about her feelings. From her viewpoint, once her cancer treatments were finished, she says, "I felt it was history and I didn't need to talk about it. I didn't want to dwell on my mortality or the thought of recurrence or whatever because I just felt it was a time in my life that was over. It was a done deal." Lorna's way of handling her cancer was to deny that it had had any impact on her and her life, to ignore it.

Her husband's reaction was quite different, however. He too had experienced a shock, having been forced to deal with the threat of losing his young wife and being left alone with a child to rear. He wanted to talk about his feelings. Yet every time he tried to talk to Lorna, she shut him out. Frustrated, he began to develop colds and flu symptoms. His feelings came out in physical ways and he felt terrible. The couple became more and more distant with each other.

"I didn't feel I needed moral support," Lorna says, "but he did. I probably wasn't sensitive enough. I didn't want to have to deal with it. I really didn't. And he didn't really let me know that he needed to talk about it."

Luckily, Lorna says, "We came to the realization that what happened was that there was no communication. Now I think it's been worked through. We're just really different people and we have different ways of handling things. We're working on it."

While Lorna wanted her husband to forget the fact that she'd had breast cancer, women often need reassurance from their men, need their men to listen to their fears. Astrid, for instance, told me that when she had her mastectomy, she needed the support of George, her fiancé, even more than that of her three daughters. Many years divorced from her daughters' father, Astrid was a confident and independent woman, secure in her profession, when she found a lump in her breast and had to have surgery. Perhaps the most difficult part of the ordeal was worrying about what this would mean to her relationship with

George, she says. "We talked a great deal about it and he was very, very helpful to me," Astrid says. "He was probably more able to be supportive of me than the girls were because our relationship was different. I was so worried that [my mastectomy] was going to change my attitude, his attitude, our relationship."

Astrid says she was afraid that losing her breast would make her feel and be perceived as "half woman, half man." George, however, saw things differently. "He said no, that it would never be a problem," Astrid reports. "I think what it takes is a strong man with a strong image of his own ego and his own selfhood. And he has that."

Astrid had reconstructive surgery several months after her mastectomy, but she had it more to make herself feel better than to please George. The couple have now married and Astrid's daughters have all left home. George continues to be her most important source of support.

Lindsey, a decade younger than Astrid and also the mother of three daughters, was equally worried about her love life when she got breast cancer. She too had a modified radical mastectomy and was about to have reconstructive surgery when we spoke. "I was more concerned about my husband seeing my scars than about my kids seeing them," Lindsey said. "I wanted him to see [my surgery site] as soon as possible. I think I showed him in the hospital, as much as I could with all the bandages.

"He was very good. I knew he was nervous about looking and I was nervous about showing him, but he's been very good. He doesn't even want me to do the reconstruction. He's only supporting me because he knows *I* want to do it. He says he doesn't want to see me cut again. I considered having an implant on the other side to make it a bit larger, but he completely nixed that idea."

The men in Astrid's and Lindsey's lives were wise in allowing the women to voice their fears concerning how breast cancer would affect their love lives. Not all men are able to deal with emotional issues, which sometimes frustrates the women they love. Dr. Wellisch advises that husbands listen to how their wives feel about having cancer and avoid telling them how to feel. "In my work with breast cancer patients and their spouses," he says, "I often hear husbands trying to comfort their wives by saying, 'Don't be upset. I didn't marry you for your breasts.' Well, it matters immensely to a woman, and her husband's downplaying her feelings only worsens her grief."

Marlene found her well-meaning husband, Phil, doing that to her. "On the day I was going into the hospital, I took a shower," she said. "I asked my husband if he wanted to come in and take one last look at my breast while it was still there, but he said no, it wouldn't make any difference to him."

An engineer by profession, Phil has an analytical mind. He was more comfortable cross-examining Marlene's doctors about her medical care than discussing how either he or his wife felt about her brush with death. "He drove the doctors crazy" with his questions, Marlene said. For emotional support, however, she had to turn to a support group of women who'd had breast cancer. Phil "isn't the type to go to a support group himself," she says a bit wistfully.

Marlene was able to get the emotional nurturing that she needed, and that Phil couldn't give her, from her women's group and other family members. That doesn't happen in all marriages, however. Sometimes the strain of the wife's breast cancer is the final straw. And it's not always the man who calls it quits.

Four years after her mastectomy, Cara was in the process of divorcing her husband of twenty-eight years. Her marriage, she says, had been deteriorating for a long time. "I don't say that breast cancer caused my divorce, but I think my husband would tell you it did. It's just easier for him to say, '[Cara] has had breast cancer and she's having a hard time dealing with it, so she needs freedom to test herself.' I think I sort of stayed on [in the marriage] because I knew I had to deal with this fight for life. Otherwise, we would have divorced five years ago."

Cara's daughter, Marcy, was nineteen at the time of the surgery. This family crisis provided her with an opportunity to observe her parents' behavior with each other under extreme stress. She did not like what she saw, and she thinks that has made her less able to trust men. "A lot of times it was my dad and me picking my mom up from the hospital or taking her to a doctor's appointment or something," she says. "Sometimes he would get real upset with her because she'd say, 'Stop the car,' or 'Slow down,' or 'Don't go over that bump,' because she was in pain. I would get so upset at him because he wasn't handling it real well and he always sounded so angry with my mom. He always wanted to take charge and get her home."

Marcy recalls hearing her father tell her mother to hurry up; he felt she was ready to go and they had to get home right away. "My mom would say, 'I'm feeling sick. I can't get up yet.' My dad's response would be real abrupt: 'Let's get you home.' There was a lot of denial and a lot of not opening up [about their feelings]."

Today Marcy says, "I never talk to my dad about breast cancer. I don't talk with my dad real well about anything." She also never discusses the subject with her two brothers. "We're close on other subjects," she says, "but I don't think I ever talked to them about this. We've sat down and talked about plenty of other things, but never breast cancer."

Cara, however, has found her two sons to be a strong source of comfort, much more supportive than her husband. "I called my older son in Ohio and he came to be with me when I had the mastectomy," she says. "He was just devastated that I had cancer. My younger son was still in high school. He was very supportive, but very afraid. He would talk to me about whatever I wanted, but he didn't pry. . . . It was a little embarrassing for him, but now we laugh about it. Over time, we all got more comfortable about talking about Mom's breast."

Her younger son often helped lighten her mood when she was feeling sorry for herself, Cara says. She recalls one time when she left her breast prosthesis lying around the house. He placed it on top of the living room television set, then propped a sign against it. It read: THE BOOB TUBE.

Overall, Cara feels her sons handled her having breast cancer better than Marcy did. They are more open emotionally, she says, while Marcy is more like her father, keeping her feelings to herself. Perhaps more pertinent, however, is the fact that while the boys were terrified of losing their mother, they did not worry about getting breast cancer themselves. Their sister did.

Cara's marriage limped along for a time after her mastectomy and her subsequent reconstruction. Finally she decided to end it. When we spoke, she was nervously anticipating beginning to go out on dates again. "I think breast cancer is going to be an issue," she told me. "I've talked about it with my friends, both men and women. All the men say it doesn't matter, that it has nothing to do with *me*. But it does matter."

Cara is very concerned about being sexual with a new man. "I will be very cautious about who I date," she says. "There is a certain type of man I won't even consider. I'm pretty up-front about it when I meet men. The first or second time I meet them, I let them know I've had breast cancer. I have not had any of them say it would make a difference. . . . But, I don't know, maybe I will never date because of it.

"Just the initial shock of going back out there after twenty-eight years is bad enough without having a reconstructed breast."

Cara's fears about what men will think about her as a woman who's survived breast cancer are common. Yet I spoke with a number of women who had remarried after their breast cancer surgery. When they found the right men for them, their history of breast cancer didn't really matter. Love, along with open communication about their feelings, bonded these couples so firmly that the woman's breasts, or lack of them, were irrelevant.

What Women and Men Really Need

Counselor Sandra Jacoby Klein, who herself remarried after having had breast cancer surgery, agrees that communication is the key to a love relationship's surviving the disease. "Women invariably feel that they have become less attractive sexually because of breast cancer, and men almost unanimously" say it doesn't matter, Jacoby Klein reports. "The important thing to men is that the woman is okay, that she survived this. They didn't love her because she had breasts or because she didn't have breasts."

Jacoby Klein has been a co-therapist at workshops for men whose wives and lovers have had breast cancer. In these groups, she has found that "some of the men admitted that the breasts were important, or that they liked one breast more than the other, or that they enjoyed playing with the breasts. But they believed there were other things they could do [in lovemaking] to please the woman and to please themselves. The important thing to them was that she was alive."

Those sentiments are what women want to hear. The problem, Jacoby Klein says, is that "women don't believe it. They think they're letting the man down, that they're taking something away from him, that they're not sexually attractive anymore. They believe that even if the guy says it doesn't matter, he doesn't mean it." And they withdraw from the man to avoid being rejected when what they perceive to be his "true feelings" eventually emerge.

Women need to listen, to hear what men honestly value in them, Jacoby Klein says, adding that "if the man is really hung up on her breasts, then you have to question what the relationship is all about anyway."

Among the women she counsels, Jacoby Klein has found that myths about men's desires "really get in the way. Women are afraid to talk to their men about it." She counsels her clients to believe what their men tell them. "You have to start with the basic idea that you believe what your partner tells you [on any subject]. If you don't," she adds, "then you have to deal with your unwillingness to accept what he says. What is it that's going on with you? Is your self-image destroyed? Was it really important for you to wear a low-cut blouse and have men admire you? Then we can take a look at whether this is his issue or yours."

Unfortunately, the fallout from this lack of communication, this misconception so many women have that their value to men and their sexuality is dependent upon having two healthy breasts, often extends beyond the woman herself. If she is a mother of daughters, she may be passing on her negative belief system to them through her example. Or if she is with the wrong man and he leaves her after breast cancer surgery, her daughters will almost certainly be traumatized. They are likely to emerge from an episode of breast cancer in the family with a scarred sexuality, a fear of intimacy and a belief that they too will lose far more than a breast if cancer someday strikes them.

One Man's Story

Los Angeles actor Paul Linke lost his wife, Francesca, to breast cancer in 1986, when she was only thirty-seven. At her funeral, he delivered a fifteen-minute eulogy to her and their ten years of married life that soon had friends alternately laughing and crying. They urged him to expand his talk, to turn it into a one-man show honoring Francesca's memory. The result was *Time Flies When You're Alive*, which Paul performed first at Santa Monica's Powerhouse Theatre and ultimately in a videotaped version aired on Home Box Office in 1989.

What struck me most about Paul's performance was the brutal honesty with which he bared his soul in relating the nearly three-year-long ordeal of his wife's death. Francesca tried conventional surgery as well as a long list of unconventional treatments—laetrile, fasts, macrobiotic diets, colonics and "psychic surgery"—in a futile effort to live. Refusing chemotherapy treatments, she also conceived and gave birth to the couple's third child and only daughter, Rose, during the time she was fighting cancer.

I spoke to Paul following his HBO appearance and he agreed to share his experiences to help women understand what it's like for a husband and father to go through such an ordeal. He talked of raw emotions—fear, frustration, anger, self-pity and grief—but mostly of the love that grew stronger and stronger throughout this family crisis.

While the Linke family's story and Francesca's choice of treatments are highly unusual, the feelings that Paul expresses are universal. Because he is both a sensitive man and a trained actor, Paul Linke has a highly developed ability to examine and verbalize his emotions. Hearing Paul's story can help all of us understand what many men experience but have difficulty in expressing when the women they love are stricken with breast cancer.

In early 1983, when Francesca (nicknamed Chex) was nursing their second son, Ryan, she found a lump in her breast, Paul says. "Her assumption was that it was a milk cyst. She'd had one when she nursed Jasper." A firm believer in holistic medicine and natural products, she'd cured the earlier cyst by using hot compresses with camphor leaves. "So she proceeded to treat this one the same way. It did not go away."

Francesca went to see a doctor some weeks after discovering the lump. Paul says he can't recall precisely how long his wife waited before seeking medical attention, which "probably reflects my awareness as a male." This doctor attempted to do a needle biopsy, but Paul says the physician's "bedside manner was not what Francesca needed. Chex was someone for whom you really had to explain a procedure, perhaps even say in the final moments, 'Do you want to do this?' But this woman just stuck the needle in her breast, which was a shock to her body and her emotional system."

Francesca's lump was suspiciously hard, and Paul says, "There was never really a test result. I don't know if Chex even called up to find out the result. She was pissed off. So that set her back."

Because she was nursing, Francesca did not have a mammogram done. On the one hand, Paul says, she kept denying that the lump was anything more than a cyst. But on the other, he feels that "from the moment she felt the lump, she knew she was going to die."

The couple did not really talk much about their fears in those early days, however. Paul explains that the discovery of the lump came at a time in their marriage when "we wouldn't have been talking like that. I was dealing with the problem of being about thirty-five and having two kids and probably the emotions of a twenty-year-old. I was trying to figure out what ever happened to the sex life [we'd had] before we had kids. She was dealing with why she wasn't being nurtured enough [by me]."

"I just remember living a long period where she had a lump and her parents or I at times would ask, 'What are you going to do about this?' And she'd say, 'It's a milk cyst infection. I will heal it myself.'"

Ironically, it was learning that her mother had breast cancer that finally led Francesca to follow through on seeking medical help for herself. She flew from her California home to the East Coast to be with her mother during the surgery, and Francesca underwent an examination there. Later tests showed her lump was malignant. Her mother, who had discovered her cancer while it was small and dealt with it immediately, recovered fully, but Francesca was not to be so lucky.

When she returned to California, Francesca had a mastectomy. Her lymph nodes were clear of cancer cells, but, Paul says, "Francesca had a very invasive, intense kind of tumor." It was large and close to the chest wall. The surgeon and oncologist both recommended that she have chemotherapy.

Francesca, however, was the kind of woman who refused to use pesticides in her garden. So she couldn't accept the idea of putting what she considered a poison into her own body. Paul says that Francesca, a child of the sixties, believed that to regain health, one should build up and strengthen the immune system, which "is our natural defense against disease. So she couldn't justify in her head that if you do these drugs that destroy the immune system and make you susceptible to all this other stuff, how could that really be the way?

"She said, 'I know that's their way and that's the stuff that's used now, but I think it's bullshit. I don't believe in it. I think you've got to try to get at the core of it all.' That's why she did the fast, that whole notion that you don't eat and then the body feeds on the cancer, breaks it down. And the colonics to get rid of it all and the diet to not make the body have to use any extra energy in digestion. No fat, no oil, no salt, no sugar, no caffeine, no dairy."

Paul also explains that Francesca had had previous unfortunate experiences with mainstream medicine. She'd had a bad reaction to the German measles vaccine, for instance. "She developed migrating arthritis," Paul says. "What that means is that she'd wake up and her hand would be totally arthritically swollen, and within hours it would have moved and her hand would be fine but it would be in her knee. It was never like we were going to go out and sue the company [that produced the vaccine] but she always wondered what role that shot played in [the weakening of] her body's immune system."

In addition, Francesca believed she had cured herself of an ovarian cyst shortly after she and Paul were married. A gynecologist had told her she would need surgery, but she decided to delay it until after they returned from their honeymoon in Hawaii. "She got into her herbs and douches and all that kind of thing," Paul explains. "She'd sit in our backyard with this rose-colored glass plate" and let the sun shine through the plate onto her abdomen. "She went back [to the doctor] about a month later and the cyst was gone." Francesca thought she had avoided unnecessary surgery and her confidence in mainstream medical advice deteriorated further.

Paul has nothing but praise for Francesca's surgeon. "He's

great," he says, "a fantastic surgeon, a fantastic man. I think he has a great bedside manner. He took his time, he was detailed. I could not say enough about him. It just happened that he was dealing with Francesca, and the only things he could offer, she didn't want."

Paul wanted to believe that Francesca had made the right decision in refusing chemotherapy and opting for less toxic treatments. Although her tumor was large, the initial assessment was that it had not spread at the time of the mastectomy. If the entire tumor had been removed in the surgery, there was a good chance that no cancer cells remained in Francesca's body. Still, the doctors wanted to do chemotherapy to be certain.

When asked whether he felt comfortable with his wife's decision, Paul Linke replied, "There were all kinds of thoughts in there. There's the thought of 'Well, what else can one do?' I know some men get angry at me and say, 'There's no way I would let *my* wife do that. I would drag her to the doctor.' Almost like the caveman philosophy. But, you see, that was not our relationship." His other thought was "What if you make someone do this? What if you guilt them into it somehow—I don't know if this is possible—and *then* they die? I was thinking I would not want to live with that.

"And then there is, even in the darkest part of all, when you're in the deepest part of the anger and the frustration and the confusion, where you feel, Well, whatever is supposed to be, if she's supposed to get this disease, if she's supposed to die, then that's what's going to happen. Maybe that's how it has to be."

Once she knew she had cancer, Paul points out, Francesca had only about thirty days to make the critical decisions that could seal her fate. "It's not like you're going to school," he explains. "You don't go Cancer 101. All of a sudden all these friends and family [members] were giving her books to read and I didn't really want to read them. I was probably pissed off."

He remembers feeling as though everything was hitting at

once. He had just finished working on the television series *Chips,* in which he'd played the continuing role of police officer Artie Grossman, and he had opened in a play in Los Angeles. With the typical insecurity of an actor, he feared his "career was heading toward the toilet," he says. "I was trying to get something going and I'd worked very hard on this play. It had just opened a couple of days before Chex was told she had cancer. All of a sudden I was getting . . . noticed [by the drama critics], but at home this disaster was occurring.

"So I didn't know . . . Should I not do the play? How could I not do the play? What good was it going to do me not to do the play? I didn't know how to support her, I didn't want to read the books, she wanted me to read the books. It was your basic family scene."

At the same time, Paul recalls, he and his wife were doing what he calls the "basic male-female dance" in which the man resents not having sex more frequently and the woman resents not having more nurturing from her husband. Marriage, he says, forces you "to get emotionally grown up." So in the middle of the struggle that many marriages hit after children are born, Paul and Francesca were faced with cancer.

"All I remember is its being very, very stressful," Paul says. Vacillating about where his responsibility lay, about what would be best for him and his family, he asked Chex whether he should do the play, and she encouraged him to stick with it. "I said, 'If I don't do the play, what do I do, sit around the house?' There's a certain amount of life that has to continue. Now, in retrospect, the play really didn't mean that much or amount to much. It was good for me, though. It ran about four months," encompassing the period of Francesca's surgery and her trips to Mexico for alternative cancer treatments.

Paul did not read the books as Francesca had asked, although he says he would read them now if he had a second chance. "I think she wanted support," he says. "I think she wanted feedback. As I see it now, she was going to make her own decision, but I think she wanted proofreading, another set of eyes."

By the summer after her March mastectomy, Francesca was having frequent bouts of nausea. "She couldn't understand it," Paul recalls. "She had a pregnancy test at a local clinic and they said, 'No, you're not pregnant.'" A month later, when her symptoms persisted, she had a second pregnancy test. Again, the result was negative.

"She just thought she was getting really sick," Paul says, "and she went back to the clinic in Tijuana. As part of their tests, they did a third pregnancy test and said, 'Yes, you are pregnant.'"

"By that point I was just on overload," Paul says. "I really was surprised. I think I was numb."

Francesca's American doctors were not pleased about her pregnancy. She could not have chemotherapy while she was pregnant, and hormones her body produced naturally during pregnancy could accelerate the growth of any remaining cancer cells. The doctors advised her to have an immediate abortion, warning that without one, she would be dead within a year. But her pregnancy was already four and a half months along. "I felt it was pretty far along to have an abortion," Paul says. "I had never had to live through an abortion with a woman, so I didn't know how to react to that [advice]."

Francesca did, however. In her opinion, having an abortion made no sense. Paul recalls her saying, "My body is gearing up to have this pregnancy. What if I suddenly stop it? If this body that is gearing up to have this baby is also fighting cancer, how will that be something that will help me live? Metaphysically, I'm fighting for my life. How can ending a life promote that?" She decided to have the baby.

Having babies was something Francesca Linke did well. She'd given birth to her two sons at home, with the help of a midwife and without anesthetic of any kind. She would have her third baby the same way. Paul says, "We went to the childbirth center that had done our other births and said, 'We're having a baby and we want to have it at home.' They said they'd have to do some research on this."

After calling sources around the country, the clinic staff told the Linkes that their baby was not at risk from Francesca's cancer. The unknown factor, Paul recalls, was "what's going to happen to Chex after the baby's born. They said, 'We don't want her to nurse very long.' She nursed, I think, about six weeks."

The Linkes' daughter, Rose, was born in March 1985, just a year after the mastectomy and two years after Francesca discovered the lump in her breast. The child was completely healthy. "If you could look at a picture of that time and you could see Francesca," Paul says wistfully, "you'd never have thought she was dying. While she was pregnant, she was so vital looking and so healthy that if you met her on the street, there was no way you'd suspect. I think I—we—were all fooled like that. The mask of death did not happen until very late. I've got pictures of her after Rosie was born and you look at them and think, No way. She was the picture of health."

The Linkes were thrilled that their third child was a girl. "That was a big relief," Paul says. "We wanted a healthy child, and if it was another boy, that was okay. But this was a bonus."

The illusion of good health was not to last, however. Within months, new tumors began to appear on Francesca's chest along her mastectomy scar. "They were pretty constantly oozing. It was a pretty outrageous image," Paul recalls. Francesca decided to go back to see her oncologists.

At the breast clinic, Paul recalls sitting in an examining room with Francesca and baby Rose. "The first doctor took out a red pen and said, 'Well, we could cut a pie shape out like this,' and Chex said, 'How do I go back together?' He left the room, and one by one these people would come in and kind of look at her. It was almost like being in a freak show. Rosie was crying. It was a real Fellini nightmare.

"Rosie was freaking out and Francesca was getting very uneasy. Finally this very nice doctor came in and talked to us and said, 'No, I don't think we should cut and I don't really think chemotherapy is viable at this point.' He was being very good. In a difficult moment, he came into that room" and told the truth. Francesca's cancer had spread beyond the reach of conventional medical treatment.

Paul says he really did not accept the fact that his wife would not survive her cancer until about ten weeks before her death. There were moments when it seemed inevitable, however. He talks about the Christmas before Francesca died, watching her hang ornaments with their older son while he held Rosie on his lap. "I started to cry," he says. "I didn't want any of them to know . . . but there was a part of me that knew this was the last Christmas we were going to have with the five of us."

As Francesca's health declined, she and Paul became closer emotionally. They talked about their fears and doubts and about their love for each other. And they laughed. Paul says that sometimes they'd start crying and then the humor in the situation would strike them; soon they both were laughing at how hard they'd been crying a moment before.

The last few weeks, Paul says, were particularly intense, almost like the weeks before the children's births. He sometimes said to Chex, "Here we are working our asses off, and I feel like we're ready to have a kid, but really what we're going to do is lose you."

On March 27, 1986, Francesca Linke died at home, in the same bed in which she'd given birth to her babies. It was one day after her daughter Rose's first birthday.

Paul Linke says that his marriage was tested far more strongly than most and it survived. Referring to the traditional tug-of-war men and women have over fear of abandonment versus fear of commitment, he says that in the end, "I didn't leave her. I was committed." When they married, he says, they had no idea what real commitment in a marriage meant. Both had come from privileged backgrounds—wealthy families, private schools, good health.

At the time the cancer hit, he says, "What we really were was children of the sixties who'd made these promises in the seventies, who'd come of age and become adults and parents in the eighties. Both of us were dealing with our own issues.

"Fortunately, for us, rather than the pressure and reality of the [cancer] experience exploding our reality . . . it strengthened it. It really became a matter of, in the darkest times of our lives, its suddenly becoming the best of times. There's an odd kind of perfection in the whole thing."

Paul's therapist once asked him, "If she hadn't had cancer and died, would you still be together right now?"

"That's a fascinating question," he says. "Would we have been forced as people to take those steps toward one another? We all tend not to walk toward one another. We all tend to want to stay separate, in fear. . . .

"I don't want to say that I credit the cancer. I think that was who Chex and I were. We really did love each other and really were committed to one another and had a special relationship. I think it took this kind of test to discover that."

Rose is now a sunny, flaxen-haired little girl, the picture of health. But her father cannot help but be concerned about her risk of getting breast cancer someday. Both her mother and grandmother had it. "Her odds are either fantastic, because they can't *all* have it, or they're terrible, because they both had it," Paul says. He's careful about his daughter's diet and expects that she'll be watched more carefully than many women once she reaches adulthood.

The idea of Rose's someday contracting breast cancer is so painful that Paul says, "I don't really allow myself to think about it. But since you brought it up, I saw myself in my sixties and my daughter having breast cancer and what that would be like. That would be very fearful. There's no question that's the worst," to have something happen to a child.

"One thing I learned about loss," he says, "is that there's a pecking order to it. Loss is loss, but for all those people who said to me, 'I know just what you're feeling because I lost my mother' or 'I lost my father,' I would always say, 'Thank you.' But there would be a part of me that would think, Having lost your father, how can you think that isn't different from losing a person you spend every day of your life with? That would be like my saying to someone who had lost a child, 'I know what you're feeling. I lost my wife.'

"You don't know. It seems to me the worst thing that could possibly happen is someone losing a child. Second worst, mate. Third worst, brother or sister. Fourth, a parent. With parents, it's more natural."

Although Francesca did not survive, Paul says, "I think it's important that people know that breast cancer is not the end of the world. Until I had this experience, I thought that cancer was a death sentence. Even though in this case that's what happened, it isn't always nor does it have to be."

Mastectomy is not the end of the world, either. Paul recalls seeing Francesca's mastectomy scar for the first time: "Chex had small breasts and it was very clinical [looking], very flat. We talked about whether she would ever have reconstructive surgery, and I don't know that she would have. I don't know that it would have been necessary. It depends on how much surgery you want in your life, how much anesthesia. I would kid her about it, saying, 'Maybe you could have the other one made bigger too, get designer breasts.' "

But, he stresses, "as a husband, I discovered a woman's sexuality is not in her breast. It's in her being." That's a message Paul Linke intends to pass on to all of his children, particularly to his daughter, Rose.

Reexamining Femininity

A woman learns how to be feminine, how to relate to men, in a number of different ways. The most important is through her childhood relationship with her parents. Her mother shows her through her example what women are, what they do, how they act with men. And in relating to her father she learns firsthand what it's like to relate to a man.

If her mother emphasizes physical appearance as the most important thing about herself, then undoubtedly she will learn to consider beauty essential to femininity and, through extension, to female sexuality. If her mother falls apart emotionally or ceases to function as a sexual being when she loses a breast to cancer, she will learn that she, like her mother, could never function completely as a woman without both of her breasts.

If when she was a child, her father praised her mainly for her looks, she may come to the conclusion that a woman without traditionally defined physical beauty, a woman whose breasts are marred by surgical scars, is not a "real woman."

Yet those negative ideas can be overcome through a reexamination of femininity and sexuality. As Paul Linke says, a woman's sexuality is not in her breast, it's in "her being." Put another way, the most important sex organ in the body truly is the mind.

Sexual and body-image problems are common among daughters of women who've had breast cancer. Yet they need not be. Through analysis of what we really want in a relationship with a man, we can come to the realization that the *right* man will love us whether we have one breast or six. In addition to our body, he will love our mind, our thoughts, our sense of humor, and especially, the fact that we love and care for him. He will love the essence of us, not simply our body. That's mature love, mature sexuality.

Unlikely as it might seem, breast cancer in the family can have a positive impact on our sexuality and our relationships with men, if we allow it to. It can serve as a catalyst for a reexamination of our values and our desires.

For example, Sybil, whose mother died of breast cancer, told me she had spent her first fifty years with the wrong kind of man. "My pattern was to choose men who were not quite my equal and to be their momma," she says. "I always thought I was choosing them because they were strong, but they really were emotional and they did a lot of acting out. They were *not* strong. I tended to choose men who were drinkers, too. I've only lived with two men in my life and both of them were drinkers and let me earn the living. I can see now that I did that in order to gain control."

This insight came to Sybil when she, like her mother, was struck by breast cancer. Her mastectomy and brush with death, she says, spurred her to reexamine her entire life, to cast out the things she no longer needed and to learn what was really important to her. "There was a time when I just needed to fulfill my sexual needs," she says. "I don't have those same feelings any longer. I almost wish it [the cancer] had happened earlier, because those feelings got me in trouble with men."

Now, Sybil says, she no longer looks for the same qualities in men and she no longer feels that she must choose men who are so needy that they won't leave her. She says she's no longer "a walking time bomb. I've ended up feeling that very few things are important enough to allow myself to get stressed out over. I tend to be able to handle situations [with men] now, to put them into perspective."

Several daughters of women with breast cancer told me they hoped that if they ever got breast cancer, they would be with men like their fathers. Charlotte, for instance, watched her father help nurse her grandmother and later nurse her mother until both women died of breast cancer. "He really was a terrific person," she says. "I can't say enough about how he cared for [both women]. It was an example that I must admit I think very few women have the chance to experience in a man. He was such a caring man and he was still able to support a family. He ran his own business and he was a caretaker at the same time."

Marnie recalls how after her mother's breast cancer was discovered, her father accompanied her mother on visits to several different doctors to help her decide on the appropriate treatment. "He was just very supportive," Marnie says. "If anything, it's deepened their love for each other. They have a real strong marriage and they love each other. That's really apparent."

Marnie says that her mother worries about the risk of breast cancer in "both my sister and me. She's concerned that neither one of us is married. If we did get diagnosed with breast cancer, she's worried that there'd be no spouse there to take care of us, that there wouldn't be someone for us to love."

All of us want someone to love who will love us in return. Yet, ironically, allowing the threat of breast cancer to color our attitudes toward men and toward our own sexuality can prevent us from having that desire fulfilled. It's not the breast cancer itself, but our fear of it that can stand in our way. If we continue to believe that the disease forever diminishes the sex appeal and sexual activity of a woman, that it makes her unlovable, we will have sabotaged ourselves far more than breast cancer ever could.

We need not settle for the impaired body image and sexuality that is common among daughters of women with breast cancer. If we acknowledge the source of these problems, analyze our beliefs carefully and restructure our values, we actually can end up far happier, far more likely to have a lasting love relationship with a man. By allowing breast cancer in the family to motivate us to change in such positive ways, we can actually turn a family tragedy to our own and our man's ultimate benefit.

Part III

Summing Up

CHAPTER 10

What Mothers Want from Daughters

WHEN BREAST CANCER STRIKES a woman, it's likely to be one of the most devastating events of her life. Any woman's reactions and coping mechanisms will vary according to her age, personality and current life situation, but it's the rare person who doesn't want and need both emotional and physical support from those closest to her. Often the female closest to her is her daughter.

The women who told me their stories had had a variety of experiences with breast cancer, some of them recent and others dating as far back as twenty-five years. The types of surgery they had undergone ranged from lumpectomies to Halsted radical mastectomies. Some had had no chemotherapy or radiation treatment. Others had had both. Some of these women had suffered recurrences of their cancer, although all considered themselves to be in good health when they spoke to me.

At the time their cancers were diagnosed, the ages of these women varied from their late twenties to their late sixties. The ages of their daughters ranged from infancy to middle age. Some of these mothers were themselves the daughters, granddaughters or nieces of women who'd had breast cancer.

Clearly, each woman's story, as well as her needs and desires, was unique. And of course, what less fortunate women who did not survive their breast cancer may have desired from their daughters, particularly during their final days, might have been quite different from what the healthier mothers wanted.

Still, among the life stories I heard, I found common threads that can help other daughters understand how to help their mothers through the family crisis of breast cancer.

Emotional Support

The need these women mentioned most frequently was for the emotional support of their daughters. A typical mother summed up her feelings: "I just wanted to know my daughters cared. I didn't want them waiting on me hand and foot; I'm not that kind of person. But I did need to feel they cared."

For some women, reassurance of a daughter's concern may entail having her constant attention. Other mothers asked no more than daily long-distance phone calls during their initial medical treatment. Both the personalities of the mothers and the ages and life situations of their daughters were the determining factors.

Helen was thirty-nine and the mother of three very young daughters when she underwent a mastectomy. For her, the girls' efforts to be well behaved while she had her surgery and chemotherapy treatments were sufficient. One particularly warm memory she shared involved her youngest daughter, who was not yet attending school. When Helen had her chemotherapy treatments, she often spent the following day in bed. "My little one was only four at the time," she said, "and she would climb into bed with me and turn on the TV. She'd just watch TV lying next to me. She knew I didn't feel good and she didn't make any demands on me. She was just very good." Something as uncomplicated as her little girl's physical presence beside her made Helen feel loved during a very difficult time.

Some mothers may need very specific psychological reassurance, particularly about their feelings of being physically altered. "I needed my daughter to look at me and not gasp," one mother said about her mastectomy scar. "If she had reacted with horror, I think it would have been devastating." Luckily this daughter, like many others, sensed her mother's need and was able to fulfill it.

Teenage daughters seem to have the most difficulty in providing their mothers with emotional support. Adolescence, as we know, is a time when daughters normally are trying to break away from their mothers' control. So if they do nothing more than act like typical teenagers, their mothers may feel rejected.

The teen years are also a time of tremendous self-absorption. Child psychiatrist Dr. Margaret Stuber recalls one mother who was shocked and saddened by her teenage daughter's unthinking remark. The mother had suffered a recurrence of her breast cancer, and when she told her daughter about it, the girl's immediate response was "So you mean we're not going to have Christmas again this year?"

The mother understandably felt terribly hurt and rejected by her daughter. Still, Dr. Stuber says that the girl's remark, however cruel it may seem, probably was merely her way of protecting herself from the truth. "Rather than thinking, This means my mother is going to die, she thought, This means my life is going to be ruined again." The latter concept was less threatening to the daughter.

Los Angeles clinical psychologist Dr. Robin S. Cohen, Ph.D., who works with breast cancer patients while they are undergoing medical treatment, often hears the complaints of those who have teenage daughters. "They talk a lot about how the daughter's not around," Dr. Cohen says. "That's the time when teens are separating, pulling away from the family. They want to be out on a date, they're shopping with friends, doing all the cool things they do when they're teenagers. Their peer group is very important to them. I don't think that teens don't care about their mothers, but I think they're very anxious themselves and they're very wrapped up in their own lives."

The mothers of teenagers, Dr. Cohen says, "kind of understand" their daughters' failure to demonstrate sympathetic, caring behavior, but often that isn't enough. "They understand, but also they're upset, they feel disappointed, they're let down. At the same time, they can realize [the behavior] doesn't really have anything to do with them. It doesn't have anything to do with their being bad mothers or with their daughters not caring or loving them. They realize that this is just what a teenage daughter does. The mothers were teenagers, too, so I guess that's what's good about being the same sex."

Dr. Cohen recommends that mothers and daughters talk with each other about their feelings, with the help of a neutral therapist, if necessary. "I encourage them to open up the communication. One of the problems is that when there's no communication, people make assumptions about how other people feel and then they get very uncomfortable." They begin to act and react based on these assumptions, and sometimes family ties are permanently broken.

Indeed, many mothers who spoke to me eventually acquired insight into their daughters' seemingly callous actions and believed that their relationships ultimately were strengthened. Tina, for example, told me that, when her breast cancer was discovered, her fourteen-year-old daughter "seemed to be angry, she seemed to draw away from me. She would make offhand, almost sarcastic comments like, 'Well, I hope you're not gonna *die!*' "

In retrospect, however, Tina says she understands that her daughter was frightened and this was her way, however inept, of dealing with her fear. Tina now also takes part of the responsibility for her daughter's withdrawal. "At that time I took my cancer stoically," she explains. "I didn't break down at all, so she didn't see that side of me. I was very clinical and reassuring, saying things like 'This is just the way it is.' Or 'It's nothing to worry about; everything's going to be fine.' "

Today Tina feels her stoic attitude may have prompted her daughter's cool reaction. "It's hard to get close to a strong person who doesn't seem to need you," she says. About a year after her surgery, Tina's own emotions finally caught up with her. She'd finished her chemotherapy treatments and, she says, "suddenly I didn't know how to handle things. I felt I was waiting for something to happen, but I didn't know what it was. Maybe for the cancer to come back or for me to die."

Tina's delayed reaction was not unlike the letdown a woman experiences after her husband's funeral. The widow manages to get through arrangements for the funeral and the event itself, possibly on sheer adrenaline. Then after all the emergencies have been handled and the relatives have gone home, leaving her alone, harsh reality hits. When she no longer has to deal with people or handle details, the widow begins to realize her loss and her emotions take over.

After Tina became seriously depressed, she entered counseling, which she believes helped her sort out her feelings of loss and grief. It also helped her understand her daughter's reactions and eventually helped them feel closer to each other emotionally. Ironically, as Tina learned, sometimes it is the daughters who actually care the most, but who simply are unable to deal with their fears, who appear to be the most rejecting of their mothers when breast cancer strikes.

It's important to note, too, that few daughters (or even husbands) can provide *all* of the emotional support women may need to help them deal with breast cancer treatment and the normal psychological reactions to cancer's assault. Some women said they found that kind of support in psychotherapy. Many more told me they found it in attending meetings of organized support groups for women who've had breast cancer. "The support groups can be wonderful," one woman told me. "I really think there's something different about talking to someone who's been through it." Another said, "You can't know how it feels not having a breast until you've been there. There isn't one woman in my group who, if I called her tomorrow and said, 'I've had a recurrence,' would not be there for me."

Few daughters can fully understand what their mothers with

breast cancer have gone through. To expect them to have that insight, particularly at a young age, is unrealistic and may actually make the daughters feel inadequate and overburdened.

Physical Assistance

Most of the women with whom I spoke said they depended on their daughters for help with the practical aspects of everyday life while they underwent their breast cancer treatment. Some women expected only simple assistance from their children: for example, the youngest could set the dinner table or the oldest do an occasional load of laundry. Other women wanted a more major contribution from their children, expecting their daughters, for example, to run the entire household, at least on a temporary basis. In situations in which women had no husbands to help them, the amount of assistance expected of their daughters was far greater. For example, Beatrice, a divorcee, says she needed assistance from her two younger daughters, who were still living at home. "I wanted them to drive me back and forth when I couldn't drive, to reach up and get things down off a shelf, to do anything physical that I couldn't do."

Wisely, Beatrice says she "learned long ago that if you want something, you have to ask for it. People are willing to do anything that you want them to do, particularly if you are physically impaired in any way. But you have to say, 'This is what I need. This is what I would like you to do for me.'" By asking her daughters for specific kinds of assistance, Beatrice avoided the trap into which many women admitted they fell.

In most cases, children are willing and able to help their mothers when help is requested. The problem is that many mothers fail to ask. They expect their daughters to volunteer assistance or somehow to know intuitively what they need and to provide it. These women are almost always disappointed, not because their daughters are unsympathetic or callous, but because the children don't want to make their mothers feel like invalids by taking over the traditional role of the mother. Many daughters told me that they waited for their mothers to ask for their help, but that no such request ever came. As a result, they felt unneeded and their mothers felt resentful of their daughters' perceived selfishness.

Dr. Robin Cohen says that some patients actually find it easier to talk about dying than to ask for favors from others, even from their own daughters. Yet not asking, she says, "becomes a self-fulfilling prophecy. [The mother] feels trapped—in a sense by herself—because she doesn't try to get what she needs. She doesn't feel she has a right to."

Psychologists have long argued about whether there is an identifiable personality common to breast cancer patients; some experts theorize that many such patients are women who have taken care of others throughout their lives. These women tend to put others' needs before their own and are often passive people, hesitant to make demands on others. When such women become ill with breast cancer, they are likely to feel great anxiety about asking for assistance. To do so—in fact, even to admit they need help—threatens the caretaker identity these women have established for themselves.

Dr. Shirley Devol VanLieu says the breast cancer patients who attended her Mastectomy Assistance Program workshops fit that profile. They tended overwhelmingly "to be really, really nice women who took responsibility for things that weren't really their responsibility." All women in our culture are socialized to do this to some extent, she says. "I think that women are conditioned from birth that what we're supposed to do is give service, keep other people happy, be sensitive to others' needs and know what those other people need almost before they know themselves." Another important part of that conditioning, she says, is "to repress our own needs, [to exhibit] selflessness. It used to be a real compliment to say about a woman, 'Oh, she's so selfless.' [But] it's actually to a woman's detriment" to be selfless. If a woman is truly selfless, she may well find it too difficult to ask even her own daughters for what she needs. Often, in fact, such women are so accustomed to ignoring their own needs that they may not even recognize them.

On the other hand, a diagnosis of breast cancer frequently serves as a catalyst for patients to reexamine their lives and make changes. Many women told me that they decided to live their lives for themselves instead of for others after breast cancer forced them to come to grips with their own mortality. Some began or changed careers. Some divorced husbands they hadn't loved for years. Many decided they would no longer devote their lives to their families' needs. If a woman undergoes such a change in priorities, her daughters are often forced to take on new responsibilities permanently.

How the family reacts to a wife and mother's change in priorities depends in part on how she presents her desire to change, says Dr. Devol VanLieu. "I think that it tends to either make the family system weaker to the point of breaking it up or it tends to make it stronger. Many women will decide that their priorities are going to be different and they're going to be less a servant and facilitator than they used to be. When they stop providing the services that they used to, some of the family members may have quite a reaction to that.

"It depends on how she does it," Dr. Devol VanLieu says. "If she does it with anger—'Look at how [badly] all of you have been treating me all these years!'—it will be greeted one way. On the other hand, if she presents it as, 'Oh, boy, I didn't realize how much I was giving away pieces of myself and not allowing all of you to develop your own [sense of] responsibility,' then it will be received" far more favorably.

The women who reassessed their lives and decided to change said they had become far happier women than they'd ever been before the disease struck them. In addition, they became more positive role models for their daughters. Instead of being living proof that women must subjugate their lives to others, they now showed their daughters that women could become complete, equal human beings. Although the family may have been in turmoil while the change was taking place, eventually both mother and daughter benefited from it.

The key to avoiding misunderstandings and unfulfilled expectations, as well as the predictable resentments between mother and daughter that can result from change, is open communication. Dr. Robin Cohen says it makes no difference whether the mother or the daughter begins a discussion about who is to do chores and how much of her own previous responsibility a mother wishes to turn over to her family. The important thing is that somebody makes the first move. Dr. Cohen suggests that "the mother might say [to the daughter], 'I know you're really busy with your own life, but I wonder if there are times when you'd like to help me. Is it okay if I ask you for things?'

"Or the daughter might say [to the mother], 'I don't know what you need,' or 'Is there anything I can do to help? How would you like me to deal with this?' Then they can start a dialogue or at least be open" about their own needs. Both mother and daughter must be completely honest about their own desires to avoid later resentment.

Even adult daughters who live too far away to be with their mothers on a daily basis can be helpful. They can arrange either paid or volunteer assistance for their mothers during the time of their surgery and follow-up treatment. And afterward, these women can support any desire to change priorities that their mothers might express.

Daughters' Breast Care

Finally, these women wanted their daughters to take into account the family history of breast cancer and to show extreme vigilance about their own health. These mothers wanted their daughters to follow the basic breast health guidelines: to do monthly breast self-examinations; to see their doctors for an exam at least annually; and to have regular mammograms as soon as they reached the appropriate age.

This sensible desire might be expressed by any mother of daughters, of course, but for mothers who've had breast cancer themselves, the issue was likely to be vitally important. First, these mothers did not want their daughters to suffer as they had. And, second, prodding their daughters to be careful, to catch any cancer that might develop at the earliest possible moment, seemed to help the mothers feel better about possibly having passed on what one woman termed "bad genes" to their offspring.

That daughters at risk would follow the basic breast care guidelines proposed by the major cancer organizations would seem only logical. Yet many failed to do this, which often caused their mothers great anguish. Unfortunately, the mothers frequently reacted by pushing their daughters even harder, which made them feel and sound like nags. One mother told me, "I'm so worried about my younger daughter. She's thirty-two and single. She's never had children. And she's at very great risk for breast cancer. But she won't even talk to me about it. I know she doesn't examine herself or even see her doctor as often as she should." This woman said she clipped every newspaper or magazine article she could find about breast cancer and mailed them all to her daughter. Unfortunately, the issue had turned into a power struggle between them, with the daughter demonstrating her independence at the possible cost of her own life.

Sadly, some women are so severely threatened by the idea that someday they could have breast cancer like their mothers that they play ostrich; they think that ignoring the threat of cancer will somehow make it go away.

Breast cancer can definitely be an emotionally volatile issue between mothers and daughters. Helen, the mother who during her chemotherapy treatments felt comforted when her four-year-old climbed into bed with her to watch TV, has experienced it from both ends. When Helen was fourteen, her own mother had a radical mastectomy, followed a week later by removal of her ovaries, a common treatment for breast cancer in the early sixties. "I remember it vividly," Helen says. "My mother was very open and honest with us. She told us she was going in for a breast biopsy and that they would decide while she was under anesthetic whether to remove her breast or not. I remember visiting her in the hospital."

After her two major operations, Helen's mother began experiencing abdominal pain. "After one misdiagnosis, she was rushed to emergency surgery for internal bleeding. So my mother was in the hospital for about a month in all." During that time and afterward, Helen and her two sisters helped with the household chores and kept their mother company.

Luckily Helen took her mother's warnings seriously and learned to do breast self-exams. Twenty-five years later, when she had three daughters of her own, Helen found a lump in her breast and had it biopsied. As she was waking up from the anesthesia, Helen's husband and doctor told her the bad news: the lump was malignant.

"I started crying," she says. "I asked my husband, 'How am I going to tell my mother?' This is the first thing I worried about—not that I had cancer, but how my mother was going to react to this. I was really worried about her. I was very, very nervous about telling her." At the time, Helen's mother was battling a rare metastasis of her breast cancer; nearly a quarter of a century after her cancer was first diagnosed, it had come back in her hip.

Ironically, Helen got her biopsy results just before her mother was scheduled to fly in for a visit. "I said to my husband, 'You'll have to tell her. I don't think I can do it without breaking down.' I was there when he told her I had breast cancer. She took in a quick breath, but she didn't start crying. She was very logical and matter-of-fact." Helen's mother got involved in the practical details of treating her daughter's illness and provided care for her granddaughters.

As the date for Helen's mastectomy approached, however,

her mother, who had been very strong at first, began to break down. Helen recalls, "She broke down crying and said, 'I'm sorry this happened to you. I wish I hadn't had it so you wouldn't have gotten it.' I sensed she felt responsible because I think I would feel that way if my daughters got breast cancer."

Although her girls are still very young, Helen worries about their risk of someday getting the disease. "I've said to my husband many times, 'Gosh, I have three daughters. Look at the terrible legacy I've left them!'" Helen has concentrated her hopes for her daughters' good health in two areas. One is that by the time her girls reach adulthood, there may be more effective preventive measures available. The other is to convince them to be meticulously careful about their own health so that if they ever do get breast cancer, they, like Helen herself, will catch it in its earliest stage.

One of the most important gifts any daughter can give her mother is simply to take good care of herself. When a mother has had breast cancer and is worried about her daughter's getting it too, that gift becomes far more significant. Such mothers may indeed nag their daughters about breast examinations. But their sometimes irritating reminders are generally nothing more than the mothers' way of trying to relieve their own anxiety about the inheritance they fear they've left their daughters.

Logically, giving our mothers this simple gift is easy. In the long run, too, making what may seem a minor sacrifice of our time may well benefit us far more than it does our mothers.

CHAPTER 11

What Daughters Want from Mothers

WOMEN STRUCK BY BREAST CANCER often become preoccupied with their own physical and emotional survival. They're facing the imminent threat of their own death. Yet despite their necessary self-absorption, these women must not ignore or underestimate the lasting impact this family crisis is certain to have on their daughters.

Just as all mothers react to the diagnosis of breast cancer in their own ways, according to their own psychological and physical resources, so do their daughters. Yet despite individual differences, most daughters say they want and need certain things from their mothers at this critical time and in the following years. Identifying and examining these issues can help mothers and daughters become closer so they can better assist and comfort each other during the struggle.

Although some of these women's needs and desires have been touched upon in earlier chapters, it seems useful to collect and address them briefly here as well.

Efforts at Survival

Predictably, virtually all of the women to whom I spoke said their primary wish was that their mothers would survive breast cancer and regain their health as quickly as possible. Sadly, granting this simple wish was not always within the mothers' power. Many of the daughters saw their mothers succumb to the disease, either rapidly or over a period of years. The loss was softened somewhat, however, if the daughters felt that their mothers had done everything they possibly could do to survive. Every daughter wanted to feel her own mother had made a valiant effort not to leave her, even if the mother eventually died of breast cancer.

The mother of one of the most disturbed daughters I spoke with had committed suicide after undergoing a radical mastectomy. If her mother had died of breast cancer, this daughter says, she believes she could have handled it. What she has been unable to cope with—even after a quarter of a century of tears and rage—is her belief that her mother didn't love her enough to fight for survival. That her mother left her *voluntarily* has affected every aspect of this daughter's life in a negative way.

While this is an unusual story, a number of the women told me that they felt a somewhat lesser version of this young woman's anguish. Their own mothers did not choose to die by their own hands, but they failed to follow basic good health practices, which ultimately resulted in the cancer returning and often in their death. These women also felt that their mothers had not loved them enough to make the effort necessary to live. Some of the most negatively affected daughters spoke of finding out their mothers had ignored breast lumps for months, sometimes for more than a year, before seeking medical care. If as a result of this negligence the mother died, her daughter was likely to feel not only unlucky but actually betrayed.

Even in cases where women received early medical treatment for their breast cancer, they sometimes frustrated their daughters by failing to change destructive health practices. "Here my mother has had breast cancer and she still smokes two packs a day," one angry thirty-year-old told me. "I can't believe how stupid she's being!"

Others railed against their mothers' failure to change poor

eating habits or behavior patterns that the daughters believed were health-threatening. "My mother wouldn't recognize her real feelings if they crawled up and bit her," one daughter said in disgust. "She's been pretending she hasn't even got any for nearly sixty years. She's totally threatened by the idea of therapy, too. There's no way she'll even consider it. I tell you, if repressing your feelings really gives you cancer, my mother hasn't got a chance."

It's hard enough for a daughter when her mother dies of breast cancer after having made a valiant effort to survive. When a woman believes that her mother didn't make that effort, she's likely to have a much more difficult time adjusting to the loss of her parent.

Open Communication

Virtually all the daughters I spoke to told me that they wanted to feel they were playing an important role in their mothers' fight against breast cancer. They wanted to be privy to information about their mothers' medical treatment and prognosis as well as about her feelings during this crucial time. Those daughters who felt shut out by their mothers' silence were often severely troubled.

Many mothers believe they are protecting their daughters by keeping silent about their disease. But Dr. David Wellisch reminds us that what they're really doing is protecting themselves from having to deal with their daughters' emotions. When women are not comfortable expressing their own emotions, they often fear other people's. Yet a failure to express appropriate emotions always keeps others, including daughters, at arm's length.

Practically speaking, how much a mother can reveal about her breast cancer and her fear of pain, mutilation and death depends at least in part on the age of her daughter. One obviously does not burden a four-year-old with information beyond her ability to comprehend or with facts that may terrify her.

Still, one mistake frequently made by mothers whose daughters were very young when breast cancer hit is to consider the subject to be finished business, forever closed. As that four-year-old grows older, reaches puberty and begins to develop breasts of her own, she very well may need to know all about her mother's cancer, to ask questions she may have harbored for years. Even better is an open atmosphere in which a daughter feels free to ask such questions as they occur to her, to gather information at her own pace. For this gradual fact-gathering effort to work well, her mother must be willing to provide information freely and honestly.

Ideally, a mother will give a child as much information as she can absorb at the time of diagnosis and will answer the child's questions as honestly as possible at that time and at any time thereafter. Dr. Margaret Stuber warns that a lack of frankness from parents leaves children at the mercy of their own imaginations, which generally create stories that are far more terrifying than the truth. Children can accept reality much better than adults realize. But lies and evasions leave them not knowing who or what can be trusted, including their own senses.

Older daughters can be given the entire truth and be encouraged to participate as much as they are able in their mothers' treatment. Open communication makes them feel that they are important to their mothers, that they are loved. Information withheld, on the other hand, makes them feel there's something wrong with them, some way in which their mothers find them essentially untrustworthy. Although few mothers intend to burden their daughters with self-doubt, it's a common result of secrecy. Many daughters of women with breast cancer told me they'd lived their lives feeling "like a bad person" because their mothers hadn't entrusted them with the truth. Many years later, they were still haunted by having been closed out of this vitally important event in their mothers' lives.

Open communication remains important even years after the initial diagnosis of breast cancer. This is particularly true if either the mother or the daughter has any regrets about the way she handled the original crisis. For instance, as long as both are still alive, it's not too late for a mother to tell her daughter that she's sorry she was secretive and she now wishes to become more open. Likewise, a daughter who feels bad about her behavior while her mother was fighting cancer may find relief in confessing those feelings. As we have seen, daughters who were teenagers when their mothers became ill are particularly likely to feel guilty about their actions.

Opening the lines of communication, no matter how long after the initial event, can help mothers and daughters to understand each other and create a warmer, more loving relationship between them.

Reasonable Expectations

While the daughters told me they wanted to participate with their mothers in their fight against cancer, they also said they needed their mothers not to expect too much of them. This was particularly true of daughters who were forced literally to switch roles with their mothers. Except when the daughters were adults and their mothers were elderly, the daughters generally resented having to play the part of their mothers' caretakers, their mothers' mothers.

There is a fine line in this area between the daughters feeling left out and feeling overburdened. In many ways, it seems unfair to expect women to be able to figure out where their daughters' limits are, particularly when they're engaged in a fight for their lives. Yet communication can make this easier to do. If mothers and daughters will simply *talk* about what each wants of the other, chances are greatly increased that a common ground acceptable to both can be found.

A Positive Role Model

The daughters also spoke of seeing their mothers' behavior during the battle with breast cancer as a model for their own lives. In many cases, they greatly admired how their mothers acted and reacted in this crisis. "I only hope I can handle it as well as my mother did if I ever get breast cancer," one thirty-five-year-old said. "She read everything she could find about it, asked questions, made her own decisions and didn't let the doctors bully her into anything she didn't want to do. And she kept her sense of humor, too."

Another woman who herself had breast cancer at age thirty-nine found it easier to get through her own ordeal because of her mother's positive example. "My mother was forty-two when she got it," the daughter said. "Her surgery was much worse than mine, but she went through it without complaining. And she always made a point of letting us know what was happening, even though my sisters and I were just kids. My mom was a real inspiration to me."

The mothers most admired by their daughters were those who didn't collapse either emotionally or physically. These women did their best to become informed about breast cancer and to make rational medical decisions with the assistance of their doctors. They communicated with their families about both the physical aspects of breast cancer and what they were thinking.

Ironically, many women felt that keeping a stiff upper lip was the key to helping their daughters cope, but the daughters disagreed. More than one daughter of a stoic mother complained that she didn't feel that she herself had been given permission to grieve: if her mother didn't cry, how could she? The daughters generally felt alienated from mothers who kept their fears and anxieties completely hidden.

On the other hand, daughters did not want to find their world spinning out of control. Mothers who became hysterical prompted equally terrified reactions in their daughters. If the mother collapsed emotionally, the daughter, particularly if she was young, was unlikely to feel she could do any better herself.

This doesn't mean that women have only one chance to get it right, that if in the midst of the most difficult ordeal of their lives, they flub one little thing, they've scarred their daughters for life. What it does mean is that if a mother is having trouble either identifying her feelings or dealing with the stress caused by her cancer, she may wish to seek professional counseling, at least temporarily. It can be important not only for herself but for her daughter as well, and there's certainly no shame in seeking help in handling such a life-and-death issue as breast cancer.

Sometimes it can be critical. For instance, Dr. Shirley Devol VanLieu tells of a family she counseled. The mother, who had had breast cancer when her children were quite small, withdrew emotionally into herself until she became unavailable to any of her children.

"As the children grew up, that pattern in response to stress could be seen to some extent in all three of them," she adds. "When their stress level went up, they withdrew into themselves and became emotionally disconnected from the rest of the family. Finally the family got into therapy because one of the children was having very serious problems."

In another case Dr. Devol VanLieu recalls, the mother illogically believed that having breast cancer marked her as a bad person, a morally defective woman. This woman had grown up in a home where humiliation was used to punish her, and subconsciously she saw breast cancer as the ultimate humiliation. Unfortunately she projected her feelings of low self-esteem onto her children, so "when her kids did something that kids do, like spill a glass of milk, she felt that further reflected her 'badness,'" Dr. Devol VanLieu says. This mother "got to the point where she was becoming physically abusive to her children."

Our ability to handle stress is similar to a rubber band, Dr. Devol VanLieu explains. When it's stretched beyond its tolerance, it snaps and cannot be repaired easily. This mother's "rubber band" snapped when she got breast cancer and had to have her breast removed. After that point, she became completely intolerant of her own or other people's mistakes. She would fly into a rage at the smallest provocation. Finally, Dr.

Devol VanLieu says, "the husband packed up himself and the two kids and moved to a motel to get this woman's attention. She was headed in such a dangerous direction that something had to change."

The mother agreed to enter therapy, which has helped the entire family learn to cope with breast cancer and with stress. Dr. Devol VanLieu says that the mother is still not as tolerant of stress as might be desired, but she now realizes her problem and why it exists. "There are times when in order not to act in a cruel way to her children, she actually has to walk out of the house. But she's now able to do that. She stays out until her husband comes home or a neighbor comes over. It's a very tough, uphill battle for her."

Had this mother not entered counseling, she might well have physically and psychologically damaged her children permanently. At best, she would have set an extremely negative example for her children, particularly her daughter. The pattern of abuse, of the inability to cope with stress, would have been passed on to future generations.

Girls watch the ways in which their mothers handle various difficult life events; this helps them develop their own style of coping. Most mothers are not required to fight breast cancer. Those who have to do battle with the disease bear an extra burden, particularly if their daughters are still young and living at home. Not only is it important for the mothers themselves to find a mechanism for coping with the disease's stresses, it's vital for their daughters as well. At least some of these daughters will eventually face the ordeal of cancer in their own breasts. Even if daughters don't get cancer, they likely will emulate the emotional coping skills they observe in their mothers as they face future stressful events in their own lives.

All mothers have a tremendous impact on their daughters' lives. Indeed, the mother-daughter bond can be so strong that some daughters, particularly young ones, are psychologically unable to distinguish their own minds and bodies from their mothers'. They believe that whatever happens to their mothers actually happens to them as well.

Even in the case of older daughters who have achieved a healthy psychological separation, the impact of a mother's breast cancer is likely to be dramatic. This illness evokes primal emotions—fear, anger, grief, loneliness—in daughters. They may well be unable to handle these feelings without help.

So whenever a mother's breast cancer is diagnosed, her daughters' needs must be addressed as well as her own. Although a woman may find it hard to think past her own physical and emotional problems when she's literally fighting for her life, her daughters' future welfare may require her to make that effort.

Breast cancer in a mother of daughters is never her ordeal alone; it forces her daughters to experience their own kind of trauma. In order for all family members to emerge healthy from this crisis, they must recognize and satisfy one another's needs for emotional and physical support.

CHAPTER 12

Sisterly Love

SISTERS OFTEN NEED each other's support when one of them contracts breast cancer. In fact, during a serious illness such as breast cancer, one sibling may well become a "mother" to the other. When we're seriously ill, we all want to be mothered to some degree, and sometimes a sister is the only one available to perform that function for us.

Generally, how much and what kind of support and assistance sisters require from each other depends upon several variables, including their ages; whether they live near each other; whether they feel close to each other; whether their mother is still alive and able to help; and whether one or both have family responsibilities of their own.

Several women who've had breast cancer told me they leaned heavily on their sisters during their time of crisis. "I don't know if I would have made it without my sister," said one, a single, childless woman in her forties. "I really didn't have anybody else and the medical treatment I had was a pretty horrible experience." This woman's younger sister tried to give her the emotional and physical assistance that other breast cancer patients got from their husbands and daughters. It put a strain on their relationship. Now, the younger sister says, "I've learned that I can't be all things to anybody." She recommends having "lots of friends" in addition to family so that the heavy demands of caring for a person with cancer can be shared.

While these sisters both felt overwhelmed for nearly a year, until the surgery and chemotherapy were completed, they now say their relationship has emerged stronger than ever.

Even some breast cancer patients with husbands and children found that a sister could provide them with something vital and unique. "My younger sister was there when I had my surgery," said a woman whose breast cancer was diagnosed when she was in her late thirties. "That was very important to me. [My sister] also has a daughter the same age as my little one. She took care of my kids whenever I needed her. It really took a lot off my mind to have somebody I could trust be with them." This woman said that both of her sisters "freaked out" when they learned she had breast cancer. They immediately saw their doctors for tests. Luckily, both were found to be cancer-free.

Some of the sisters of the women who told me their stories eventually did develop cancers of their own. One breast cancer patient said that her sister was diagnosed with cervical cancer four years after she herself had completed cancer treatment. "One good thing that came out of this is that I was able to help my sister through her own problems," she said. "I'd pretty much been there myself, even though I had a different kind of cancer. I don't think my sister was as scared as I was."

Another said the fact that she had survived her bout with breast cancer had given her sister hope when she got the same disease. "If I could get through it, Meg figured she could, too. I think the unknown is the scariest thing for anybody to face. Since she'd been with me when I had my treatment, Meg knew what to expect and it was easier for her to handle."

Stresses and Strains

There were of course predictable points of friction between sisters. Sometimes the cancer patient expects more than her sister can give, particularly if that sister has her own family obligations and a job as well. Many modern women feel their circuits are already close to overload. When a sister has cancer, the added responsibility can cause an explosion. The overburdened sisters told me they felt guilty because they believed they should do more for their sibling who was fighting cancer. Yet at the same time they confess to resenting their sisters for forcing them into this difficult position by becoming ill.

Ironically, an equally common complaint I heard was nearly the opposite: that some healthy women feel shut out of their ill sisters' lives. Sometimes, particularly if sisters live far apart, the one with breast cancer doesn't tell her siblings about it until after she has already begun medical treatment. When confronted, she generally rationalizes that she hadn't wanted people to worry about her. As a result of this secrecy, however, the healthy sisters feel excluded and angry, as if they were not important enough to be informed about this life-and-death situation.

Talking It Out

Communication is the solution for both of these common problems. If each woman is to recognize her sister's needs, she must know what they are, and none of us is a mind reader. Most of us have never been down this path before, either, so we don't know what twists and turns to expect along the way.

We must find the courage to tell each other what we feel, what we need, even though such discussion can sometimes be painful. Many sisters told me that for them, such conversations involved reopening childhood wounds, airing petty resentments that had been harbored for years. Yet in the end they felt the experience had added something positive to their relationships with their siblings and to their own lives. "There's a lot more depth to our relationship now," one woman told me after she'd helped her younger sister get through her breast cancer treatment. "We used to talk all the time before, but I can't say it was with the depth there is now. We're still very different people, but now we can cut through that and really talk."

Another woman who lost two sisters to breast cancer says she's grateful she made the effort to be close to them during their fatal illnesses. "I'm real comfortable with it because I remember going to see them sometimes for a week at a time when it wasn't convenient for me," she told me. "But we had a really good relationship. I think it's a great source of comfort to me that we did what we did and were close as a family."

Understandably, all the healthy sisters feared their own vulnerability to breast cancer. If the disease could attack their sisters, it could strike them as well. They had to learn to handle a new fear in their own lives.

It was uniformly painful for them to watch their ill sisters' physical and emotional trials, too. Yet having to support a sister while she fights for her life was not entirely a negative experience. These sisters learned that they could depend on each other, and on themselves, when it really counted. They gained confidence that they could survive and prosper in the face of any hardship life could hand them.

From this family ordeal, they learned firsthand what the poet Christina Rossetti said more than a century ago:

> *For there is no friend like a sister*
> *In calm or stormy weather.*

CHAPTER 13

The Second Gift of Life

HAVING A FAMILY HISTORY of breast cancer impacts on us in many unfortunate ways. This dreaded disease can steal our mothers, sisters and grandmothers from us, and it can threaten our own survival as well. The powerful legacy we've inherited affects our self-esteem, our sexuality, our career choices, our relationships with our husbands and children—virtually every aspect of our lives.

The knowledge that we're at risk for breast cancer provokes in us strong emotions—fear, anger, guilt, grief, a sense of isolation. These feelings are both normal and very common. Virtually all of the daughters and sisters with whom I spoke acknowledged having experienced great inner turmoil about breast cancer.

Yet while none of us would choose to have the specter of breast cancer hovering above us or our loved ones, I found that being forced into this position did not have to be entirely without positive results. If we choose to, we can learn to see our family history of breast cancer as a challenge, as an opportunity for personal growth and self-enhancement.

Living Healthy

Before my mother's breast cancer was diagnosed, I seldom thought about breast self-examination. Cancer was something that happened to other people, not to my family or to me. If I thought about what I ate, it was less for health reasons than to control my weight. If I didn't have the time to see my doctor annually, I simply didn't. I wasn't feeling sick, I told myself, so why worry?

But in 1983, after my mother's mastectomy, all that changed. I was forced to recognize that cancer didn't happen just to other people. It happened in my family too, and this was a particular kind of cancer that could well be hereditary. Suddenly, eating a sensible diet, exercising regularly, reducing my stress level, doing monthly breast self-exams, and having annual medical checkups and mammograms all became important parts of my life; I now knew I was at risk for breast cancer.

While my previous state of ignorance had its element of bliss, it might have ended badly. I could have had a tumor growing in one of my breasts that I wouldn't have found until it had metastasized. Luckily I did not. But perhaps equally important is the fact that my cavalier attitude about caring for my body might have caused me to suffer any of a dozen other future illnesses . . . even if I *never* get breast cancer.

Being forced to examine and change my health habits has had only positive results for me. I feel healthier now, and I am confident that if someday I do have breast cancer, I will find it early enough for a cure. I'm encouraged by the statistics that show this disease does not have to be fatal if it's caught in its earliest stages.

In addition, I believe I will live a longer, healthier life because I'm taking good care of myself. As former Surgeon General C. Everett Koop tells us, we can prevent many of the diseases that cause premature death simply by following sensible health practices. I take him seriously these days. All of us who have a family history of breast cancer can heed Dr. Koop's sound advice.

The fact is that we, the daughters and sisters of women with breast cancer, have been forewarned. In a sense, we have an advantage over the eighty percent of women with breast cancer who have no family history of the disease. Because our mothers or sisters had it, we're motivated to be on the lookout for any changes in our own breasts. As a result, we're more likely to find a tumor early, when treatment is more likely to be a hundred percent successful. If we ever do get breast cancer, we have an excellent chance of surviving it.

And if the disease never strikes us, our improved health practices can give us a far better quality and quantity of life than we might otherwise have had.

Emotional Inventory

As we well know, having a family history of breast cancer causes psychological turmoil. Yet if we choose to, we can turn this emotional ordeal into a chance for self-knowledge and individual growth.

Many women told me that realizing they could lose their family members to cancer forced them to recognize what was truly important to them and to mend fences while they still had the chance. This process greatly improved the quality of their lives in many ways. They learned to live each day to the fullest. They began to appreciate their loved ones while they still could and to *tell* them how much they cared. And they found that by gaining perspective, by prioritizing the many elements of their lives, they became happier, more productive women.

Even those women who lost their relatives to breast cancer were presented with an opportunity to improve their lives, if they chose to take it. Sometimes these women had spent years feeling overwhelmed by guilt and loss, but once they realized that their actions (or lack of action) were neither unique nor unforgivable, they had the chance to achieve self-acceptance and learn from their losses. Adversity, after all, builds strength.

When we make a personal inventory of our lives—whether

alone, with the help of a trusted friend or relative, in a self-help group or in professional therapy—we begin the process of self-knowledge. Although knowing who we are and what is truly important to us is essential if we're to live happy and fruitful lives, many people never achieve that insight. Some never even try. Again, we have an advantage. We've been handed the gift of knowing that we don't have forever, that life is indeed terminal . . . for everyone.

We daughters and sisters have been given the motivation to do whatever it takes to make our lives better—beginning today.

Our mothers once gave us life. And our sisters shared our lives with us. If we choose to, we can see their ordeals with breast cancer as a kind of gift to us, a second gift of life. Because they suffered this disease, we've been given the opportunity and the motivation to live a longer and better life ourselves.

The second gift of life has been offered to each of us. It's up to us to accept it and use it to the fullest.

Appendix

Breast Cancer Risk Analysis Services

CALIFORNIA

* Children's Hospital of San Francisco
  Patricia T. Kelly, Ph.D., Medical Geneticist
  3700 California Street
  San Francisco, California 94118
  (415) 387-8700

* Memorial Breast Center
  Long Beach Memorial Medical Center
  2801 Atlantic Avenue
  P.O. Box 1428
  Long Beach, California 90801-1428
  1-800-334-5444

DISTRICT OF COLUMBIA

Comprehensive Breast Center
Vincent P. Lombardi Cancer Research Center
Georgetown University Medical Center
Dr. Sandra Swain, Director
Dr. Karen Johnson, Preventive Medicine
3800 Reservoir Road N.W.
Washington, D.C. 20007
(202) 687-2113

* These centers offer the type of risk analysis, designed by Dr. Patricia Kelly, that is described in Chapter 2. Some of the others incorporate medical care into their programs. Some may not include psychological support. Contact individual organizations for a full description of their programs.

225

MARYLAND

Breast Surveillance Service
Johns Hopkins Oncology Center
Michael E. Stephanek, Ph.D.
Patti Wilcox, R.N., A.N.P.
Suite 1003
550 North Broadway
Baltimore, Maryland 21205
(301) 955-4850

NEBRASKA

The Hereditary Cancer Institute
Henry T. Lynch, M.D.
Creighton University
P.O. Box 3266
Omaha, Nebraska 68103-9990
1-800-648-8133

NEW YORK

High Risk Surveillance Clinic
Michael Osborne, M.D.
Memorial Sloan-Kettering Cancer Center
1275 York Avenue
New York, New York 10021
(212) 639-2000

Breast Protection Program
Genetic Counseling Program
Preventive Medicine Institute/Strang Clinic
55 East 34th Street
New York, New York 10016
(212) 684-6969
Note: The Breast Protection Program offers risk analysis in conjunction with medical services. The Genetic Counseling Program offers risk analysis only.

TEXAS

° Susan G. Komen Breast Centers
Komen Alliance Clinical Breast Center
Barbara Blumberg, Sc.M., Director of Education
Sammons Cancer Center, Third Floor
3500 Gaston Avenue
Dallas, Texas 75246
(214) 820-2430

WISCONSIN

Cancer Prevention Clinic
Richard R. Love, M.D.
University of Wisconsin
7C, 1300 University Avenue
Madison, Wisconsin 53706
(608) 263-2118

Breast Cancer Information Sources

AMERICAN CANCER SOCIETY

Founded in 1913 by a small group of physicians and lay people, the American Cancer Society was organized to explore the causes of cancer and to alleviate the suffering of cancer patients. Today, with the assistance of its 2.5 million volunteers, the ACS's mission is to control cancer and minimize its burden through funding research directed at cancer prevention, detection and cure; sponsoring, supporting or directly operating educational and advocacy programs to prevent, detect, treat and cure cancer; and providing cancer patients and their families with services and rehabilitation programs at no cost.

For the location of your local ACS chapter or Reach to Recovery contact, call the national hotline: 1-800-ACS-2345
or write:

American Cancer Society National Office
1599 Clifton Road, N.E.
Atlanta, Georgia 30329

ENCORE

ENCORE is the YWCA's discussion and exercise program for women who have had breast cancer surgery. It is designed to help restore physical strength and emotional well-being. A local branch of the YWCA, listed in the phone book, can provide more information. Or contact the national headquarters:

YWCA of the USA, National Board
726 Broadway
New York, New York 10003
(212) 614-2827

THE HEREDITARY CANCER INSTITUTE

A nonprofit institution, The Hereditary Cancer Institute at Creighton University is dedicated to research about hereditary cancers. It also disseminates information on cancer genetics and research and evaluates families to identify hereditary cancer.

The Hereditary Cancer Institute
Creighton University
P.O. Box 3266
Omaha, Nebraska 68103-9990
1-800-648-8133

NATIONAL ALLIANCE OF BREAST CANCER ORGANIZATIONS

NABCO is a not-for-profit central resource that provides individuals and health organizations with accurate, up-to-date information on all aspects of breast cancer, and promotes affordable detection and treatment. NABCO is also active in efforts to influence public and private health policy on issues that pertain directly to breast cancer, such as insurance reimbursement, health care and funding priorities. The late Rose Kushner was among the founders of the organization.

NABCO does not have the staff to handle phone calls, but further information can be obtained by writing:

NABCO
Second Floor, 1180 Avenue of the Americas
New York, New York 10036

NATIONAL CANCER INSTITUTE

The National Cancer Institute is part of the National Institutes of Health and is funded by the U.S. government. It funds research into the causes and treatment of cancer and offers a variety of informational services.

To ask questions, request NCI publications, or obtain information on certified radiologists, call the Cancer Information Service hotline:
1-800-4-CANCER
In Alaska, call 1-800-638-6070
In Hawaii on Oahu, call 524-1234 (on neighbor islands, call collect)
or write:
National Cancer Institute
Bethesda, Maryland 20205

NATIONAL COALITION FOR CANCER SURVIVORSHIP

The Coalition for Cancer Survivorship is a network of independent groups and individuals offering support to cancer survivors and their loved ones. It provides information and resources on support and life after a cancer diagnosis.
For more information, contact:
National Coalition for Cancer Survivorship
323 Eighth Street, S.W.
Albuquerque, New Mexico, 87102

REACH TO RECOVERY

See the entry for the American Cancer Society.

Y-ME NATIONAL ORGANIZATION FOR BREAST CANCER INFORMATION AND SUPPORT

Founded in 1978, Y-Me is a not-for-profit organization that provides information, hotline counseling, educational programs and self-help meetings for breast cancer patients, their families and friends.
National Office:
18220 Harwood Avenue
Homewood, Illinois 60430
(708) 799-8338
Hotlines:
1-800-221-2141 (9:00–5:00, weekdays)
(708) 799-8228 (24 hours)

Recommended Reading

BREAST CARE, BENIGN BREAST DISEASES AND BREAST CANCER

BOOKS

The Breast Cancer Digest: A Guide to Medical Care, Emotional Support, Educational Programs, and Resources, U.S. Department of Health and Human Services, National Cancer Institute, Bethesda, MD, 1984.

Greenberg, Mimi, Ph.D. *Invisible Scars: A Guide to Coping with the Impact of Breast Cancer*. Walker & Co., New York, 1988.

Kushner, Rose. *Alternatives—New Developments in the War on Breast Cancer*. The Kensington Press, Cambridge, MA, 1984.

Love, Susan M., M.D., with Karen Lindsey. *Dr. Susan Love's Breast Book*. Addison-Wesley, Reading, MA, 1990.

Lynch, Henry T., M.D. *Genetics and Breast Cancer*. Van Nostrand Reinhold, New York, 1981.

McGinn, Kerry A., R.N. *Keeping Abreast: breast changes that are not cancer*. Bull Publishing Co., Palo Alto, CA, 1987.

Seltzer, Vicki, M.D. *Every Woman's Guide to Breast Cancer*. Penguin Books, New York, 1988.

Strax, Philip, M.D. *Make Sure You Do Not Have Breast Cancer*. St. Martin's Press, New York, 1989.

PAMPHLETS

Free copies of the following National Cancer Institute publications may be obtained by calling the Cancer Information Service at 1-800-4-CANCER or by writing the Office of Cancer Communications, National Cancer Institute, Building 31, Room 10A24, Bethesda, MD 20892.

Breast Exams: What You Should Know
Questions and Answers About Breast Lumps
Breast Biopsy: What You Should Know
Breast Cancer: Understanding Treatment Options
Mastectomy: A Treatment for Breast Cancer
Radiation Therapy: A Treatment for Early Stage Breast Cancer

Adjuvant Therapy: Facts for Women with Breast Cancer
Breast Reconstruction: A Matter of Choice
After Breast Cancer: A Guide to Followup Care
When Cancer Recurs: Meeting the Challenge Again
Advanced Cancer: Living Each Day

THE MIND-BODY CONNECTION

BOOKS

Borysenko, Joan. *Minding the Body, Mending the Mind*. Addison-Wesley, Reading, MA, 1987.
Cousins, Norman. *Anatomy of an Illness as Perceived by the Patient*. Norton, New York, 1979; Bantam, New York, 1981.
———. *Head First: The Biology of Hope*. E. P. Dutton, New York, 1989; Penguin, New York, 1990.
Siegel, Bernie S., M.D. *Love, Medicine & Miracles*. Harper & Row, New York, 1986.

INDIVIDUAL EXPERIENCES WITH BREAST CANCER

BOOKS

Ford, Betty, and Chris Chase. *The Times of My Life*. Harper & Row, New York, 1978.
Ireland, Jill. *Life Wish*. Little, Brown & Co., Boston, 1987.
Murcia, Andy, and Bob Stewart. *Man to Man*. St. Martin's Press, New York, 1989. (This book offers the perspective of men whose wives have breast cancer.)
Rollin, Betty. *First You Cry*. J. B. Lippincott Co., New York, 1976.

Notes

CHAPTER 1:
Mothers, Daughters, Sisters
and Breast Cancer

PAGE

11 *"insecurity and shame"*:
Brownmiller, 1984, p. 40.

CHAPTER 2:
Personal Risks

20 *descendants of Eastern European Jews: Breast Cancer Digest*, 1984, p. 20.
22 *"in both breasts"*: Love and
Lindsey, 1989, p. 17.
22 *no increased risk of breast
cancer: Breast Cancer Digest*,
1984, p. 20.
22 *"what your risk is"*: Love and
Lindsey, 1989, p. 17.
25 *"a disease of aging"*: *Breast
Cancer Digest*, 1984, p. 26.
26 *developing invasive breast
cancer:* ibid.
26 *"spread beyond the breast"*:
McGinn, 1987, p. 139.
26 *no increased risk of breast
cancer: Breast Cancer Digest*,
1984, p. 27.
26 *"the clinical symptoms"*: Love
and Lindsey, 1989, p. 17.
27 *their own doctors' advice:
Breast Cancer Digest*, 1984, p.
11.

27 *younger than twelve do:* ibid.,
p. 27.
27 *less than fifty at menopause
are:* ibid.
27 *"ovulation does not occur"*:
ibid.
28 *never given birth at all:* ibid.
28 *the X-ray treatment: Los Angeles Times*, October 13, 1989,
p. B3.
28 *time of the bombings: Breast
Cancer Digest*, 1984, p. 21.
28 *from these exams: Los Angeles
Times*, October 13, 1989, p.
B3.
29 *more common among thin
women: Breast Cancer Digest*,
1984, p. 28.
29 *waist-to-hip ratios:* Doheny,
February 6, 1990, p. E6.
29 *very pear-shaped:* ibid.
30 *thighs and buttocks, he said:*
ibid.
30 *rose thirty percent:* Mayer and
Goldberg, July 13, 1989, p. 38.
31 *considered statistically significant:* Foreman, August 15,
1989, p. 3.
33 *refute these findings:* Kolata,
January 17, 1989, p. B5.
34 *her developing breast cancer:*
Cimons, June 7, 1989, p. 4.
34 *take estrogen supplements:*
Scott, August 2, 1989, p. A1.

34 *importance for American women:* ibid.

34 *someday may be reevaluated:* ibid.

37 *medical breast exams annually:* Gail et al., December 20, 1989, p. 1879.

37 *negative breast biopsies she has had:* ibid.

37 *average for American women:* Squires, January 15, 1990, p. B3.

37 *high as the average woman's:* ibid.

38 *it can be removed immediately:* ibid.

43 *because of genetic factors:* Children's Hospital of San Francisco.

CHAPTER 3:
Necessary Precautions

46 *this far advanced: Breast Cancer Digest,* 1984, p. 54.

47 *collarbone as well:* ibid., p. 55

48 *"persistent in her efforts": Los Angeles Times,* January 13, 1990, p. A32.

48 *arm swelling and shoulder stiffness: Breast Cancer Digest,* 1984, p. 55.

48 *nodes are left intact:* ibid.

48 *a supplement for this surgery:* ibid.

49 *conjunction with this surgery:* ibid.

49 *therapy after surgery:* ibid., p. 56.

57 *damage has been done:* Dean, November 19, 1989, p. E1.

57 *an appropriate diet:* ibid.

58 *reduce cancer risks as well:* Lemonick, November 13, 1989, p. 90.

59 *medium fitness group:* ibid.

59 *succumb to the disease annually:* ibid.

CHAPTER 5:
Why Me?

104 *"your conscious awareness":* Forward, 1989, p. 227.

CHAPTER 6:
Lasting Regrets

122 *American Psychiatric Association in San Francisco:* Scott, May 11, 1989, p. A1.

CHAPTER 8:
Peas in a Pod

139 *"the strongest relationship":* Fishel, 1979, p. 213.

139 *"you feel absolutely discomfited":* ibid.

140 *suffer the way her sister did:* Beyette, May 2, 1989, p. V1.

CHAPTER 12:
Sisterly Love

220 *"calm or stormy weather":* Rossetti, 1862.

Bibliography

Beyette, Beverly. "A Family Crusade." *Los Angeles Times*, May 2, 1989, p. V1.

Brownmiller, Susan. *Femininity*. New York: Linden Press/Simon & Schuster, 1984.

Children's Hospital of San Francisco. *Cancer Risk Analysis and DNA Banking* (pamphlet).

Cimons, Marlene. "No Added Breast Cancer Risk Found in Pill Study." *Los Angeles Times*, June 7, 1989, p. 4.

Dean, Paul. "Citizen Koop: Former Surgeon General's New Shingle Could Read: 'America's Family Doctor.'" *Los Angeles Times*, November 19, 1989, p. E1.

Doheny, Kathleen. "Physique May Relate to Breast Cancer." *Los Angeles Times*, February 6, 1990, p. E6.

Fishel, Elizabeth. *Sisters: Love and Rivalry Inside the Family and Beyond* New York: William Morrow & Co., 1979.

Foreman, Judy. "Medical Notebook: New Weight Lent to Diet as Breast Cancer Factor." *The Boston Globe*, August 15, 1989, p. 3.

Forward, Dr. Susan, with Craig Buck. *Toxic Parents*. New York: Bantam Books, 1989.

Gail, Mitchell H., Louise A. Brinton, David P. Byar, Donald K. Corle, Sylvan B. Green, Catherine Schairer, John J. Mulvihill. "Projecting Individualized Probabilities of Developing Breast Cancer for White Females Who Are Being Examined Annually." *Journal of the National Cancer Institute*, Vol. 81, No. 24, December 20, 1989.

Kolata, Gina. "Cancer Fears Throw Spotlight on Estrogen." *New York Times*, January 17, 1989, p. B5.

Lemonick, Michael D. "Take a Walk—and Live." *Time*, November 13, 1989, p. 90.

Love, Susan, M.D., and Karen Lindsey. "Breast Cancer: Who's at Risk?" *Sojourner: The Women's Forum*, September 1989.

Mayer, Dr. Jean, and Jeanne Goldberg. "Low-Fat Diet Can Help Cut Risk of Breast Cancer." *Los Angeles Times*, July 13, 1989, p. 38.

McGinn, Kerry A. *Keeping Abreast: breast changes that are not cancer.* Palo Alto, CA: Bull Publishing Company, 1987.

"Rose Kushner, 60; Medical Writer, Advocate." *Los Angeles Times,* January 13, 1990, p. A32.

Rossetti, Christina. "Goblin Market." 1862.

Scott, Janny. "Hormones May Increase Cancer Risk, Study Says." *Los Angeles Times,* August 2, 1989, p. A1.

————. "Study Says Cancer Survival Rises with Group Therapy." *Los Angeles Times,* May 11, 1989, p. A1.

Spiegel, D., et al. "Effect of Psychosocial Treatment on Survival of Patients with Metastatic Breast Cancer." *Lancet,* October 14, 1989, p. 888.

Squires, Sally. "Study Refigures Odds of Getting Breast Cancer." *Los Angeles Times,* January 15, 1990.

"Two Studies on Breast Cancer." *Los Angeles Times,* October 13, 1989, p. B3.

U.S. Department of Health and Human Services. *The Breast Cancer Digest.* Bethesda, Maryland: National Cancer Institute, 1984.

————. *Questions and Answers About Breast Lumps.* Bethesda, Maryland: National Institutes of Health, Publication No. 88-2401, November 1987.